THE RULES OF ORDER

THE RULES OF ORDER

A Novel

CARMACK

Franklin Alexander Carmack, III

AUTHOR'S NOTE

This is a work of fiction. While a true event was the inspiration for this novel, this is in no way a true story. The characters are not real people and any similarities are accidental or incidental. The timeline, conversations, backstabbing, lies, corruption, extramarital affairs, and weather patterns were all made up by the author.

CHAPTER 1

Tuesday, November 4, 2008 – Election Night

The music from the party in conference room carried into Gregory's office. The mix of whiskey, markers, and burnt black coffee filled the dark room. One of the few sources of light was the TV in the corner broadcasting the local news, which, like most of the country, was celebrating the election of Senator Barack Obama to President of the United States. One hundred and fifteen votes, out of twelve thousand two hundred and six in what was supposed to be a safe Democratic district, had elected Gregory Anderson to his fifth term in the Tennessee House of Representatives. He was going back to the "People's House," and until tonight he had felt confident he would be elected by his peers back to the leader of his party in the House. Jubilant voices celebrating the election of the country's first black president leant the party on the other side of the wall an excitement that all in attendance would never forget. Tears of joy, hugs and handshakes; a milestone for the United States. Yet the mood in the office on the twenty-sixth floor of the Nashville skyscraper was neither relief nor elation, but lament.

"Look, Leader Anderson, you got your next term. Two more years. You're going to be elected Democratic Leader in the House again. Just take some time to enjoy this," said Charlie, twisting the green marker in his hand with his head resting against the whiteboard.

"I'm going from majority leader to minority leader," said Gregory, spinning the ice in his tumbler trying to water down his whiskey.

"We don't know that yet." Charlie was trying his best to be reassuring.

"Shit, Charlie," said Gregory, "you've been around long enough to know better." He raised a finger to the whiteboard behind Charlie. "The writing is literally on the wall, there's more red than blue."

"There's still five seats up in the air," said Charlie defensively. The room fell quiet except for the falsetto of Frankie Valli drifting in from the room next door.

Gregory covered his eyes with his palms and tried to rub his eyeballs into his brain. "Tom," he groaned, "give me an update on the remaining five."

From the computer screen behind Gregory, in his unsure baritone Tom read out the up to the minute results from the Secretary of State's website. "Handley down fifteen percent, sixteen of twenty-five precincts in. Majors down less than ten percent, twenty five of thirty precincts reporting. Let's see. Um. Ryan Allen down eight percent, roughly, with twenty-eight of thirty-three precincts reporting; they're probably going to call that one soon. Richardson's down eighteen percent--"

"Shit," whispered Charlie.

"--all thirty-three precincts reporting, so that one's over."

"Goddammit!" Gregory and Charlie exclaimed at the same moment.

"Shit birds!" Charlie stood up, grabbed the red marker, and wrote 'SLATER' next to the number eighty-eight. Gregory held his breath and rubbed his forehead with his hand.

Tom continued, "And finally, Blair is down five percent with eighteen of twenty-three precincts reporting."

"We're going to hold that seat!" exclaimed Charlie. "That one seat is all we need to keep the House. Between that and the Governor getting reelected tonight we're sitting pretty."

Gregory, knowing better than to get his hopes up, simply asked: "Which precincts haven't reported in that one?"

"I don't know, the site doesn't tell you that sort of thing," said Tom.

"Ok," said Gregory. "Get on the phone and find out."

"Yes sir," said Tom as he pulled his phone out of his pocket and began to cycle through his contacts.

"One hundred and thirty-four years, Charlie . . . Charlie . . . Charlie!" Gregory threw a blue stress ball across the office hitting Charlie in the back to get his attention away from the TV. Charlie turned around to face Gregory. "One hundred and thirty-four years, our party has been in control of the Tennessee House of Representatives. I was the last majority leader for our party in the House. Do you get that?"

Charlie could only nod in agreement.

"Sir," said Tom. "Blair just conceded. The remaining precincts have never gone his way."

The room fell quiet again; even the music had stopped. "Well," said Charlie, "on the bright side, you're going to be the first Democratic Minority Leader in Tennessee in over a century. That means your name will go down in history."

"Like Rudolph," Tom interjected with a smile.

"Shut up," said Gregory. Letting the room fall quiet again as a new song started to make its way into the room. *You ain't nothin a but hound dog,* sang Elvis from the conference room party. "Our Governor is a Democrat with an approval rating over seventy. Our Democratic US Senate candidate got a respectable forty percent of the vote, our country just elected a Democrat to be President. How in the hell could we lose the state House of Representatives? We got shellacked!"

"Well," began Charlie, "we lost the State Senate two years ago, our US Senate candidate only got thirty percent of the vote, not forty, and the standard bearer for our party is a black liberal from Chicago, and we're in Tennessee. Native state to the KKK. No offense Tom."

"You are allowed to call us black, Charlie. You don't have to say 'no offense' when you do, as long as you aren't being a dick about it," said Tom clicking the mouse and not looking away from the computer screen.

"What's the Speaker's phone number? I should probably call him." Gregory began to move papers on his desk looking for his phone. As Charlie began to go through his contacts, Gregory's phone began to vibrate on the desk beside him under a stack of files left by his paralegal last week that Gregory hadn't yet gone through. "Never mind," he said, "he's calling me."

CHAPTER 2

Monday, November 10, 2008

The walls of the Speaker Caputo's office were lined with pictures marking milestones in his long career. Him with each president during his tenure, him with war heroes, sports heroes, music icons, and old black and white family photos. There was a picture on the credenza behind his desk of his father's sandwich shop from his small hometown in west Tennessee. From that one shop Speaker Bob Caputo, with help from his brother Ron, built fifteen sandwich shops across rural west Tennessee, bringing them both an income far above what they could have ever dreamt of as children of an Italian migrant who fled his home country during the rise of fascism. His story read as the polished autobiography of a Presidential candidate from central casting, but Bob's dreams had stalled when he became Speaker of the Tennessee House of Representatives twenty-two years ago. He got use to the power of the Speaker's chair, and never wanted to give it up for the term limits as Governor or the long flights to D.C. A young man by most standards when he was elected Speaker by his peers at the age of forty-six, he had turned old.

The hair on top of his head was gone, leaving only a ring of salt and pepper running temple to temple along the rim of his head.

"How in the hell did this happen Greg?" the Speaker said slamming his fist against the desk. "Goddammit! Last week, while everybody else in our party, across the goddam country, got to celebrate winning the fucking White House and getting a supermajority in Congress; my tall Italian ass was sitting in Brownsville worrying about losing my fucking job! For shit's sake, the Governor won every fucking county! First time ever! And here we are with our necks on the fucking chopping block!" His fist hit the desk again.

"Hello, Mr. Speaker," said Charlie as he and Gregory unbuttoned their suit jackets and sat down in the chairs across from the Speaker.

"Yeah, 'Mr. Speaker,' for now, you better have a plan for me to keep that name, goddam it!" said the Speaker. "You can go now, Carroll. Thank you, shut the door," he said in a much softer tone, noticing his assistant standing in the doorway.

"Look, Mr. Speaker," said Gregory, "we've known for a long while that this state was trending Republican. I mean, eight years ago this state voted for a Republican to be president over a Democrat from right here. It didn't help to have a black man on the top of the ticket running this far south."

"A black man?" said the Speaker, wincing with concern.

"It's ok," said Charlie, "Tom said we can call black people, black."

The Speaker rolled his eyes. "Great. I'm glad you saw this coming. Now how the hell am I going to stay Speaker?"

Charlie cleared his throat, "Mr. Speaker, it's not that bad."

"Not. That. Bad?" The Speaker was growing more agitated. "Not that bad? I've been Speaker of the House longer than most people keep any job. Longer than anyone else in this state. One more year and I'll be the fourth-longest serving Speaker this country has ever goddam seen! And you, a fat white kid who was still pissing the bed when I first got this job, is going to tell me it's not that bad?"

"What Charlie meant, Mr. Speaker," Gregory intervened, "is that they only have fifty of the ninety-nine seats. They tried to tie every single one of our members to some national liberal brand where our women don't shave their armpits and all the men are afraid of loud noises. They also tried to tie each one of our members to the Tennessee Stud bribery scandal, and they only picked up twenty-one seats."

"Only twenty-one seats? Like twenty-one seats aren't a big fucking deal," mumbled the Speaker.

"I'm not minimizing them," said Gregory. "What I am trying to say is, the Republicans gave us their best shot and only got a one seat majority. Now, you've been awfully kind to a lot of the incumbent Republicans; I think we can find one of them to vote for you."

The Speaker leaned back in his chair and put his fingers together tip to tip, with his index fingers touching his nose. "You find me that one vote, and while you're at it you find me at least one more for insurance. You and your staff do this, leave my staff out of it, I don't want them bogged down in politics, I want it to look like this office is operating business as usual, doing the people's work and not getting in the mud. Even if we're all shitting our pants in here, y'all will find me those two damn votes. Understand?"

"Yes sir," said Gregory.

"Yes, Mr. Speaker," said Charlie.

"I'll walk you out, and when I open that door we all better have the best shit-eating grins on our faces. Understand? There could be anywhere between two and forty reporters out there just waiting on us and I don't want our frowning ass faces on the front page. Got it?" The two nodded in agreement as the stood up and walked out of the office. As they opened the door their smiles fell away as they were met with the rattle of a tape measure retracting back into its case. Two men were standing across the left wall, while a third was standing in the middle of the room with his arms crossed and his black hair lazily parted on the left side of his head.

The man turned around, "Hello, Mr. Speaker. Leader Anderson." He extended his right hand and shook the hands of the men he had addressed, ignoring Charlie.

"Hello, Leader Humphrey," said the Speaker, his politician's smile returning to his face. "What can I do you for?"

"Oh, nothing," said Leader Humphrey. "Just measuring the office here, trying to figure out if the couch I've had my eye on will fit. I think it will, although it won't match this carpet. I think I'm gonna take up the drab gray stuff you got here and lay down some nice red throughout this suite." Leader Humphrey spread his hands out palms down showing the vastness of the Speaker's office suite.

"Let's not crack the eggs till the stove is hot, huh?" said Charlie. All the men laughed, three of them smugly.

"I appreciate your optimism, Charlie. Always have, probably always will. Maybe when I, excuse me, the next Speaker makes the staff approvals he'll find a spot for you. I'll put in a good word," said Leader Humphrey. "And don't worry, the Minority Leader's office has plenty of room, just not as much as you're probably used to." He stared at the three Democrats in suits, with a small grin on his face. "Y'all take care, we're done here." With that, Leader Humphrey and the two other men walked out of the office.

"Fuck that guy," said Carroll, who had been standing behind her desk.

"At least we got to use our shit-eating grins," said Charlie.

"Gregory," said the Speaker, "you find me those two damn votes."

Joe Humphrey walked down the hall from the Speaker's office, or his office as he had already started to call it, past the entrance to Legislative Plaza where he said goodbye to his two staffers who had helped him rub just a little salt into the wound of Speaker Caputo. He walked just a little further down the hall into his current office. A small suite, with a large welcoming area, three offices, and a small conference room. He couldn't wait to leave this beige prison for the Speaker's office where he could pick and choose the color of the walls, the carpet, and blow his office budget on new furniture. Then it occurred to him, as Speaker of the House he had authority over all the decor of Legislative Plaza. He could rip up all the carpet and lay down hardwoods, he could paint every wall gray, he could hang crown molding in the hallway, he could have murals painted in every committee room and put chandeliers in each one. It was all up to him.

"Marcy," he nodded at as his assistant sitting behind her small cubicle desk as he walked toward his office door.

"Joe, you just missed a phone call from Anthony Lawrence with the RNC," she said with wide eyes peering over her reading glasses.

"What did he want?" asked Joe, his pulse quickening.

"Don't know," she said.

"Well, what did he say?" he asked, exhausted by his assistant's lack of urgency.

"He asked if you wanted to run for President," she said with a disapproving look.

"Dammit, Marcy."

"I don't know, Joe. He asked if you were here, I said no. I asked if he wanted to leave a message. He said no. He asked when you'd be back, I said any minute. I asked––"

"Did he leave a number or not, Marcy?" he interrupted, agitated.

"I was getting there," said Marcy as if talking to one of her five grandchildren. "I asked if he wanted to leave his number, he said yes. Here you go," she said, handing him a messenger paper. Joe thanked her and went back to the office. He read the name Anthony Lawrence RNC written in Marcy's impeccable script. He dialed the number. He heard the phone ring twice.

"Hello," said a man with a hint of a Boston accent.

"Chairman Lawrence?" said Joe in confusion.

"Yes?" asked the voice on the other end.

"This is Joe Humphrey from Tennessee," he said with a laugh. "I'm sorry I didn't expect you to answer, I thought it would be an assistant."

Anthony laughed on the other end. "Well, I gave your assistant my direct line. She's a hoot by the way. Seems like a real southern belle."

Joe laughed. "Well, she's something for sure."

"Joe, I just wanted to call and congratulate you on taking the Tennessee House. We thought we'd hold on to the State Senate down there, but the House we weren't so sure about. You all should be very proud. It was one of the few bright spots our party had last week."

"We are very proud, Mr. Chairman. We are very proud. First GOP majority in this state since Reconstruction," said Joe blushing.

"Yes, well, next we need to take the governor's office there in four years, but we can worry about that later. How are you feeling about being Speaker?"

"I haven't, officially, announced yet, but I've got the votes. Every Republican in this chamber is here because of me, and they all know I'm running for it. I've got a few Dems in my pocket for insurance."

"What promises did you make to those Dems?"

"Well," said Joe anxiously, "I promised some of their bills would get fair hearings, I promised we wouldn't go after abortion, but, just so you know, I'm not going to keep that promise, and I offered vice chair to a few others."

"Sounds like you've got it covered then," said Anthony. Joe could hear him shuffling papers through the phone, losing interest and preparing to move on with his day. Clearly the phone call had been obligatory, a polite call just to acknowledge that the national party had noticed the victory. "If there is anything we can do to help you all down there, let me know."

"There is one thing," said Joe. He wasn't ready for this call to end.

"What's that?" asked Anthony. The sound of moving paper stopped.

"In Tennessee, everyone who works for the legislative branch is technically a state employee," Joe began.

"I see, it's like that in a lot of states," said Anthony, wanting to hear more.

"On the House side, they all answer to the Speaker."

"Ok . . ."

"That means all ninety-nine assistants, fourteen leadership staffers, eighteen committee staffers, twenty people in the Clerk's office, and twenty lawyers that work drafting legislation, all work for the Speaker and not the members they are assigned to."

"Where are you going with this?" asked Anthony, sounding curious and confused.

"Well, traditionally, each member gets to pick their assistant. Each committee chairman gets to pick their committee staffers, the Chief Clerk gets to pick his people, and the legal staff is selected by the head of the legal department, and Speaker Caputo has been a rubber stamp for all these hires. Approving each one with no questions asked. I'm going to change that," Joe said with a faint smile.

"Joe, where does the RNC come in?" asked Anthony, still not getting it.

"I want a list of every valuable intern, every field director, every promising college Republican, and every Law School Republican the RNC has. I want them all working here, fully employed. They work here during the week, and have political workshops on the weekends. I want the Tennessee House of Representatives to be a training ground for young Republican operatives. A place where they can get their feet wet and make some money doing it. Then in two years they'll leave, go across the country to other states and help us win offices there, and we'll get a new crop the next year. I want Tennessee to be the launching point for our young Republican campaign machine."

Anthony laughed. "We would be able to retain a lot of young people that way. We could keep them all involved between elections. Damn it to hell, that's brilliant, Joe."

"Thank you, Mr. Chairman," Joe said with a chuckle.

"But," said Anthony with concern, "that does mean you are going to fire a lot of people; that won't look good."

"Mr. Chairman," Joe said, "we won on a message of small government and fiscal responsibility. We'll say the current employees wanted more money and less work and the new employees want more work for less money. Current employees want a union, the new ones just want to work. We'll pay the new ones less, but not much less, save the taxpayers some money."

"Joe, are you sure you've got it in you to fire all those people?"

"Mr. Chairman," said Joe solemnly, "this is what I was born to do."

CHAPTER 3

Thursday, November 20, 2008

Charlie sat with his legs crossed in the Adirondack chair, his hands crammed into his bomber jacket. He hated having to meet members in their district, especially districts that were five hours away from his downtown apartment. Yet there he was, somewhere between Sevierville and North Carolina, trying to bargain with one of the old guard Republicans, his ass freezing and lips numb. In the two weeks since they had started this mission no Republican had gotten on board with saving Speaker Caputo.

Larry Pickard emerged through the sliding glass door on to his back deck carrying two steaming hot toddies. He closed the door with his foot and handed a mug to Charlie as he took his seat.

"Dammit, Charlie. It's not that cold. It's above forty. The real cold won't start till after Thanksgiving," he said. The steam from the drink fogged the State Representative's glasses. Charlie thought hard, but he could not ever remember seeing the man without contacts. Larry looked as if he was in his mid-thirties and had never needed to shave. In fact he was only a year over fifty, still young by politician standards, but not nearly as young as his smooth face and soft smile suggested.

"I know Rep. I just can't quit the shivers." Charlie took a long slow sip of the hot toddy. "By God, this will help." Larry laughed. "Listen, Rep. Pickard, I know this is gonna seem strange--"

"Charlie, out here at my house you can call me Larry. You don't got to be that formal this far from the Capitol. We go back a good ways, so just come out with whatever it is that brought you here."

"Thanks for that, I guess," Charlie took another sip of the hot toddy and sighed. "Look, Larry, Speaker Caputo has an offer."

"Uh-huh."

"Pick your committee, it's yours. Pick two more committees and pick their chairs. Pick the members of those committees, pick the chairs of those sub committees, pick the--" he was cut off by Larry's right hand wafting those ideas out of the air like bad smoke.

"And then what? Pick a new party after mine throws me the fuck out?" He looked at Charlie. "No. No. No. I can't, I just can't," Larry said with a shrug as he rolled up the sleeves of his red flannel shirt.

"You could though, you could and you would be a hero to half this state," Charlie pleaded.

"Do you really think half the people in this state know who the Speaker of the House is? I'd be a hero to small group of extreme liberals, and Judas to the people that voted for me. Charlie," Larry leaned close and put his elbows on his knees while he rubbed his temples, "I don't think you know what you're asking me to do. I won't do it, I'm sorry. It's time y'all get use to not being in power anymore. Let's change the subject. Found a steady girl yet?"

"Go fuck yourself."

"I know. Charlie, you probably shouldn't tell anyone you came out here to ask me this."

"Fuck you," Charlie took a sip of his drink. "By the way, that's what all the others said."

"How many others?"

"I'm not telling you that."

"Charlie, look, we all like you on our side. We aren't going to let you be unemployed. We'll find something decent for you to do. You'll be fine, I promise."

"Goddammit, Larry, I'm not going to be fine! We lost the House for the first time in a century and I am partly to blame. No other campaign is ever going to hire me, I know I'll have a job up there as some lower-middle class desk jockey but everyone knows that's not what I want. At least, it wasn't what I wanted but now it's all that's left."

Charlie drank his drink and looked out over the frosted hills. He was afraid to look back at Larry; he could feel tears coming up in his eyes.

The drive back to Nashville was long and cold. Charlie drove through the Smokey Mountains for over an hour before getting to a major highway; it would be half an hour to the interstate, and then four hours to Nashville. Normally, this part of the country was beautiful, especially in the early fall when the leaves change colors and the mountains are painted yellow and red, with sudden brilliant bursts of orange and maroon. Yet this time of year, a week before Thanksgiving, it was harsh and dead. No life existed in the trees, and the mountains create a cold prison of a valley. Charlie thought about how fitting it was that the mountains, so full of life and beauty just a few weeks before, now appeared so desolate and foreboding. This state was his home, always had been, and he hoped it always would be, but he was starting to feel unwelcome in it. It knew him when he was the only child to a single teenage mother, and it was as if the state no longer took his professional persona seriously. This state knew him when he was a nobody, and now it was never going to let him become a somebody.

Charlie arrived at his apartment, a little studio that sat on the hill behind the State Capitol, shortly after 10 PM. He found his leather portfolio on his desk, he opened it, took out his blue pen and started to draw a line through the name 'Larry Pickard.'He crossed it out once, then again with more force, then again, and again with more force each time. Finally the tip of the pen broke. Blue ink slowly oozed across the yellow legal pad, covering the other three names he had been assigned. He watched as the liquid slowly covered his own indecipherable handwriting. He needed a drink.

He sat down on the couch at the foot of his bed and sipped some whiskey. He ran through the list again in his mind. Nine names, nine Republicans, the "Caputo Circle" as they were known. Nine GOP State Representatives who had been in office almost as long as the Speaker. The Speaker was closer to them than most of the members of his own caucus. He had put them on their choice of committees, he had made them vice chairmen, given then chairmanships of special committees, allowed their legislation to pass uninhibited by his own party. Yet none of them were willing to repay his years of loyal friendship with a vote for him to retain the gavel.

It was over. At least Charlie knew it was over. Caputo was done as Speaker. Maybe Tom would come up with some brilliant plan to save the old man; if anyone could it was Tom. Yet Charlie knew, deep down in his gut, that it was over.

He began to think about where he was going to go for Thanksgiving. He was thirty with no wife, no kids, his mother lived on the other side of the continent, his grandparents were all gone except for one whose mind had left him around the time Charlie had graduated from college. He was alone. A month ago he was on pace to be a deputy commissioner for some department with the state. The Governor was, after, all still a Democrat, but now that was doubtful. A shame too. Had he gotten that appointment maybe he could have gone to some lobbying firm in four years when the next Governor took office.

Dear god, thought Charlie. It suddenly dawned on him that the next Governor would be a Republican. So would the next. And the one after that. Slowly each chamber would become more and more Republican, they would probably get a super majority and hang on to it for at least two decades. There would be no demand for a Democratic lobbyist in Tennessee, perhaps for the rest of his life.

Getting a job on a major campaign was out too. No candidate for Governor, US Senate, or President was going to hire him to run the show in Tennessee while the stench of a loss this heavy laid on him. His reputation was shot. He was finished. Maybe he would get a legislative assistant position with a no-name freshman representative keeping a schedule and answering phones, but that was it. There was still the Nashville mayor's office, he could work in city hall; or Clarksville's mayor, that city was still controlled by his party, there was also the congressional seat for Nashville, it was held by a Democrat, as was Memphis. The other Democrats in the state's congressional delegation were probably going to lose in two years, Charlie was smart enough to see that coming. He could leave Tennessee, but he didn't want to; he didn't want to leave Nashville either, this city had become his home.

He finished his whiskey and put on some sweatpants. His body, pudgy now from years wasted with the best alcohol and fried food in the city, ached from the drive. He wanted to sleep for two days. Three days, or maybe even two months. Then he could wake up and someone could just tell him how this all played out. He crawled into bed. He turned out the lamp on his desk as he put his head on his pillow. He contemplated praying before falling asleep, but he fell into a slumber while still debating his personal stance on theology because he was unsure if God actually answered prayers about something as simple as politics.

Tom was in the office early the next morning. Like Charlie, his attempts at trying to convince one of the Speaker's old Republican friends had been fruitless. A part of Tom admired Leader Humphrey; the man wasn't the easiest person to like but he certainly ran a tight ship on his side of the aisle. Every Republican seemed too scared to cross Humphrey, even if it meant a personal gain for themselves for two years. The plan wasn't working.

He unlocked the door to the Majority Leader's suite, a bunker with a much lower ceiling than the Speaker's office in the hallway behind the committee rooms. He walked past the reception area and into the conference room. He always hated the fact that the door to his office was in the conference room; it made it difficult to get in and out when there were meetings. It was also difficult to think when people were arguing at the conference table. The one positive that would come from Humphrey becoming Speaker of the House was there was no way he would let them keep this suite, and that meant that maybe Tom would get an actual office. He wasn't worried about his job; Senior Policy Advisor was a non-political position. Even if the Democrats voted for a new House Leader, he would retain his position for at least one more year. Although his job would now be to stop bills from becoming law rather than the other way around.

He opened his door and turned on the light. As he walked in, he reached up and tapped the small orange tin sign shaped like the state, pressed with the words "I will give my all to Tennessee Today" that hung above his door. He put his leather messenger bag on his desk and sat down. He leaned back in his chair and surveyed his office. Campaign signs from former candidates he worked for lined the wall in front of him. To his left hung his diplomas, the framed bachelor's degree from University of Tennessee in Knoxville, and below it a law degree from Samford in Alabama. He turned his head to the right and saw the framed poster of Lyndon Johnson. He wondered what a savvy politician like that would do in this situation. He sighed and rubbed his eyes. He needed coffee if he was going to think their way out of this one.

He went to the small break room behind the reception desk and got an aluminum pouch out of a drawer, ripped it open and poured it into the industrial coffee maker and turned it on. Watching as the black liquid began to drip into the carafe slowly drop by drop, and then into a steady stream, he put his hands on the countertop, lowered his head and closed his eyes. He stayed that way until he heard the beeping of the coffee maker and poured some into his mug. He took a sip and went back to his office while checking his watch. Two hours before his meeting with Charlie and Leader Anderson. He loosened his tie, signed onto his computer, glancing one more time at LBJ, and then got to work.

Down the hall and up an escalator three women were sitting in another, bigger, breakroom. They were enjoying their morning coffee and watching the news. Delores was also enjoying her morning cigarette which was prohibited indoors but nobody was brave enough to tell her to stop.

"Twenty-three years," said Shannon tracing the rim of her mug with her index finger. "I've been here twenty-three years, and now some hot shot prick is going to give my job to some no-body, some damn-know-nothing from another damn state." She emphasized each word with a head nod. Her cold blue eyes looked at Delores through the thin white smoke. Shannon waved a hand to clear the cloud between them, her bracelets jingling as her arm moved. Delores took another puff and blew it in a different direction.

"I don't know what you're so damn worried about," said Brittany, the youngest of the three by fifteen years. "You should know better than to take the rumor mill so seriously."

"Oh, hush," said Delores, pointing her ash at the young blonde. "Baby doll, you haven't been here long enough to know when something is serious and when something ain't." She moved the cigarette back to her mouth for a quick hit. "Now look, Shannon and I, and you if you're being honest, have all heard the same thing. Humphrey is going to bus in younger Republicans looking for a job, and as soon as he takes the oath, that's all she wrote of us."

"Not us," said Shannon. "Just you and me. Brittany, darling, you're going to be ok. You're too young to be gotten rid of."

"That's not what I hear," said Delores putting her cigarette out in her coffee which had gone cold in the small white Styrofoam cup.

"What did you hear?" Brittany's voice was dripping with concern.

"I heard we're all gone, all of us," Delores waved her arm in a circle to present the grand scale of the layoffs before running her fingers through her short and thinning brown hair.

"Nope, that's not right," said Shannon.

"What do you know?" responded Delores, agitated at her friend's disbelief.

Shannon sat up, adopting a more aggressive posture, "Now look. Tony, y'all know Tony works for Chester, Tony--"

"Yeah, worked for Chester," said Brittany.

"May he rest in peace," said Delores.

"He's not dead," said Brittany.

"Well he sure as hell ain't coming back here after that buttwhoopin he took," said Delores.

"Y'all hush and look," said Shannon tapping the table to get them back on track. "Tony, who works for, or worked for, or whatever the hell you want to say, for Rep. Chester. Tony has been . . . let's say he's been spending quality time with Becca. Now, Becca is Rachel Garrison's assistant."

"Wait, wait!" Brittany threw her hands up; she was having trouble keeping up with the names. "Who's Rachel Garrison?" The other two women groaned and rolled their eyes in near unison.

"Who's Rachel?" said Delores in her raspy smoker's voice. "You know Rachel. Works across the street, does the hiring and firing and checks our timecards and all that."

"Oh, yeah," said Brittany, slightly embarrassed by her question.

"Now, hush, I want to hear this," said Delores motioning Shannon to continue.

"So, Becca told Tony the other night that she has been getting resumes and assigning pay levels to all these young out of state Republicans. Some fresh out college, some fresh out of law school, and grad school. But – now this is the important part – all of them are fresh off of some small, local level, Republican campaign from somewhere else." Shannon took a break to take a drink of coffee.

"Well, how many resumes?" asked Delores with some urgency.

Shannon shifted the coffee to one cheek and said, barely opening her lips, "How the hell should I know?"

"You're telling the story," said Delores.

"Well I didn't live it, I'm just telling it," said Shannon. "Here's what I do know. I know that Tony said it was enough to kick every single one of us out. Assistants, researchers, clerks, janitors, mailroomers, all of us. And I'm telling you, that's what Humphrey is going to do."

"Even you?" asked Brittany.

"Hell yeah even me," said Shannon mockingly.

"But you work for a Republican," said Brittany.

"Don't matter none," said Shannon, taking another sip of coffee. "I don't work for the GOP, I work for the state, so I'm a goner too."

"Why don't you talk to your member then, let him know what's going on?" said Delores.

"You think I haven't!" said Shannon letting her frustration crack the surface. "He said there's nothing to it, but he's so low level on the totem pole Humphrey wouldn't let him in on any secrets like this."

"All I'm saying," said Brittany leaning her elbows on the table, "is until my replacement marches in here and tells me to clear out, I'm not going to believe a thing."

Delores got up and threw her cup away before getting a clean one and pouring herself another cup. She leaned against the counter and faced the TV. Weatherman Gerald Kinder was on, standing in front of a map of the city. Delores spoke up, "I'd crawl all over that man's mustache if he'd let me." Brittany laughed.

"You ain't lying," said Shannon, "me too." Brittany offered an uncomfortable laugh.

Leader Anderson walked in his usual ten minutes late. Tom and Charlie were already in their seats at the conference table. They had been in the middle of a conversation regarding dress code. Tom, dressed in a fine business suit, thought Charlie, who had chosen to wear a simple red sweater and khakis, was in violation of the dress code. Charlie pointed out that he was within the dress code since the General Assembly was out of session for the year. Tom was quick to point out that since their member was in the office and they were meeting with him, they should be observing the session dress code of a collared shirt and tie. Charlie then declared that he did not "give half a fuck about that; next week is Thanksgiving. Hardly anybody's here!" The arrival of the Leader, who like Tom was also dressed in a suit, ended the conversation.

Gregory was clearly in no mood to wade into the waters of an administrative debate. He made no eye contact with his subordinates as he took his seat the head of the table, tossing a file folder onto the table. He took his glasses off and scratched his head. "How fucked are we boys?" he asked in his groggy morning voice.

"Like the quarterback on prom night," said Charlie. The phrase made Tom grimace but Gregory laughed.

"We don't have a single vote," said Tom. "Unless one of your guys came through."

"Shit," said Greg with a hint of a laugh. "No, none of my guys want to crossover." They all laughed awkwardly, gallows humor keeping them focused. "What are we going to do?" he asked, looking at his trusty staffers.

"Beg for mercy," said Charlie quickly.

"No, no," said Tom. "I mean, sort of." He leaned forward and clicked his pen against the table. The door opened behind Gregory suddenly, and the group froze and looked at Alice, their assistant. She walked in dressed in a blue dress that was uncomfortably short for a woman quickly approaching 80. She carried a tray with a pot of coffee, three mugs, cream, and sugar. The group stayed quiet and kept their eyes on her as she sat the tray down on the table between them. She started walking out, and then stopped and turned around as she opened the door.

"Good morning to you too, assholes," she said and walked out. The three men laughed out loud together as the door closed.

"Thank you, Alice," Charlie yelled from his seat.

"Anyway," said Tom looking down at his notes to calibrate his thoughts. "Next year there will be no Speaker Caputo, unless we divide the Republican vote." He stopped and looked at his compatriots to gauge their feelings. He saw nothing in their faces. "So we get a Republican to run against Humphrey. We have three nominees for Speaker, two Republicans and Caputo. All of our people vote for Caputo, most Republicans will vote for Humphrey, some Republicans will vote for the other nominee. With any luck the disarray in their caucus will cause some of their old guard to want to keep the status quo and vote for Caputo. Hopefully we'll get at least one of theirs to vote for Caputo giving him the fifty-vote majority and the win."

Gregory pondered the suggestion for a moment and said, "There are a few problems. First, if none of these guys are brave enough to vote against Humphrey, what makes you think they've got the stones to run against him?" Tom started to speak but Gregory held up his hand. "Next, what happens when Caputo gets forty-nine votes, Humphrey gets we'll say thirty-eight, and the third person gets twenty-two? It still goes to a runoff between Caputo and Humphrey, third place goes away. Fifty votes win, a majority not a plurality of the votes. Then we're back to where we started."

"No we aren't," offered Charlie. "Whether it's twenty-two votes or three votes from Republicans for the third person, there is no way they'd vote for Humphrey in a runoff. If they don't vote for Humphrey the first time they'd be screwed. Even if they voted for him in the runoff, they'd have to vote for Caputo to save their asses." Charlie slapped the table.

"Ok, hold on," said Gregory. "We still need someone to step up and run against him. Any suggestions?"

Tom looked at his notes. "No," he said. "At least not yet." The shared anxiety among the three of them came back. "Just give me a little more time."

Tom looked at Gregory, who looked at Charlie, who looked at Tom. Finally Gregory spoke up.

"The week after Thanksgiving, the House Republicans are having their caucus retreat. Where they kill puppies and dance around bonfires slapping each other's ding dongs or whatever the hell they do there. I want to have the name by then, but there's no need to ask until after their retreat. It's bad enough that so many of them already know we are trying to flip some of their votes, we don't need them talking about this. Are we clear?"

"Yes sir," said Tom and Charlie and unison.

"Ok, the Governor's inauguration wants someone from our office to help with the planning, Charlie get to work on that, it shouldn't take up too much of your time," said Gregory standing up. "Charlie, come to my office, so I can go over some of the inauguration bullshit." Charlie nodded, and followed Gregory out of the conference room and across reception, he winked at Alice, and into Gregory's legislative office.

Charlie tried to hide his dread as he walked into his boss's cavernous office. He was about to get one more thing thrown on to his plate. The walls lined with gavels mounted on plaques from past committee chairmanships, pictures of Gregory with the big names from the National Democratic Party, a picture of FDR delivering a fireside chat, and bookcases containing the Tennessee Code Annotated and pictures of Gregory's kids from his first marriage. Charlie set his coffee mug on the table in front of the red leather couch.

"Charlie, don't worry, all you have to do is hand out the inauguration passes whenever we have our caucus retreat," said Gregory.

"Oh, thank God," said Charlie. He turned the leather chair around to face Gregory. "So what am I doing in here?"

"Tom is the brains, no offense."

"None taken."

"But he's a Boy Scout. I need you to do something."

"What's that?" asked a slightly confused Charlie.

"Charlie, when was the last time a Democrat held Humphrey's seat?"

Charlie scratched his head and thought about it. "Not since before the Civil War."

"Really?"

"Really. His part of the state was pro-Union during the Civil War and has stayed pro-Republican ever since. They had a Democratic Congressman back in the early 1960s, cause, you know, we were the racists' party back then, but after the party switch they switched back to Republicans. On the state level the northeast has never had a Democrat, at least not from district two. We've had a few from district four and six but they were all one-termers."

"When was the last time we had a competitive race in district two?" asked Gregory.

"Never," said Charlie.

"Never?" repeated Gregory in amazement.

"Nope. We ran a guy against Humphrey the first time he ran. Humphrey walked away with eighty percent of the vote so we stopped wasting money up there. Now, before that I don't know, but I would assume not."

"So we don't have any opposition research on Humphrey?"

Charlie laughed, "Hell no."

"Well I want you to get some," said Gregory.

"Easy enough."

"But I want you to get something that the oppo won't find."

"Ok, and what's that?"

"Whatever you can find," said Gregory. Charlie squinted his eyes in confusion. "We need to cover this guy in his own shit till he chokes on it. There's got to be some girl he's fucking behind his wife's back, or some guy. Maybe he's battling a coke habit or is paying off cops so he can speed through his little town. I don't fucking know, but if Tom's plan is going to work we need something more. Now I need both of you for this to work. I need him doing his thing, and I need you to do your thing." Charlie took a moment to collect his thoughts. This was nothing Charlie hadn't done before though.

"Ok, I have a buddy that can help with that," said Charlie. "But I'm going to need some cash."

Gregory opened his briefcase and pulled out a packing envelope and tossed it to Charlie. "That's ten thousand in cash, I want receipts and don't rent a car or a hotel room unless you absolutely have too. I expect to get some, if not most, of that back. Understand? Your Thanksgiving break starts now."

Charlie opened the envelope and sniffed the familiar smell of cash. "Ok, I'll see you in December."

CHAPTER 4

Monday, December 1, 2008

As she walked to the stage she ran her hands down the front of her blouse, trying to press out the wrinkles left by her seatbelt on the drive to Montgomery Bell State Park. She finally gave up on it and buttoned her white cardigan over the blouse as she climbed the stairs. She waved a hand and smiled as the applause continued.

"Thank you," she said into the microphone, laughing and motioning the crowd to return to their seats. "Thank you, truly, I thank you." She said again smiling as the applause died down. She looked out over the faces in the conference room. The early morning sunlight was still coming in through the windows along the east wall, giving a warm glow to the white walls and green carpets and drapes. Seated at the round tables throughout the room she took stock of all the people there; diversity clearly wasn't their strength, but she was going to work to change that.

"Friends and colleagues, I thank you for that warm reception. I also want to thank Brett Kyle for that fantastic introduction. We're lucky to have staffers like him at the Plaza," she began.

"Again, for those of you who don't know, and if you don't then you probably shouldn't be here, I am Mary Ellen Guess. I am not only Chairman – yes chairman not chairwoman – of our state Republican Party, but I am also your colleague in the Tennessee House of Representatives. Proudly serving the residents of Nashville and Davidson County that make up the 53rd district.

"As I lookout over this crowd I realize two things. Two things we should all be very proud of. First, we all survived Black Friday 2008 unscathed." She paused for laughter. "And second," she paused again as the laughter was dying down and the sound of forks against plates began to subside. "And second, just how remarkably historic election night 2008 really was.

"We woke up on November 7th with only twenty-nine members of our caucus – that's a super minority. We were too small to stop any piece of legislation on our own. The liberal progressives, with whom we shared the chamber, had tried to push through a radical agenda. They tried and failed to force an income tax on our state, they tried and failed to make Tennessee an abortion destination state, they tried and failed to strengthen labor unions that kill jobs and productivity, they were scaring away employers, they were sinking our economy, and they were failing our schools. And a huge group of them were caught taking bribes in exchange for their votes, proving how rampant corruption within our state government really was under liberal leadership. Our fellow Tennesseans said 'no more' and went to the polls. We held every single one of our twenty-nine seats, and gained an historic twenty-one more. On November 7th, we went to sleep with a Republican majority in the Tennessee House of Representatives." The crowd erupted from their seats in cheers. Their wails were deafening, and the thunder from the applause drowned out all other noise. She took a step back from the lectern, smiled and joined in the applause.

She stepped back up to the microphone. "I think it's safe to say," she said as the cheers lessened, "that our state needed to correct its course. And Tennesseans decided the only way to do that was," she paused and looked over the room, "to take a hard! right! turn!" The crowd, again, erupted in cheers.

She held her hands up to quiet the crowd. "I just wanted to take a moment and introduce myself and tell you how honored I am to be here with you and be part of this historic caucus. You all, hopefully, already know this but should you need anything as member of the House or as a member of our Grand Ole Party do not hesitate to come to me directly. Now it is my distinct pleasure to introduce our minority leader, although I assume he will be getting a promotion shortly," she paused for laughter, "from Colonial Heights in upper east Tennessee, Joe Humphrey!"

Joe walked over to the lectern and removed the microphone from the stand. He pulled at the waistband of his khakis trying to give himself some more room. He had gotten the pants at Belk last Christmas when they were on sale, but a summer and fall of tough campaigning around the state had given him some extra padding he hadn't even realized he gained. He noticed the buttons on his blue oxford shirt were also a bit stretched when he put it on that morning. He waved at his audience. "Thank you," he said over the applause. "No, really thank you. Take your seats," he said with a smile.

"JOE! JOE! JOE!" Someone in the back started chanting, in a matter of seconds the chant had spread across the room. Joe laughed and spread his arms in a shrug, trying to display some humility.

He raised a hand and held the microphone to his mouth. The crowd began to quiet, but before they sat back down, in a very low and forceful voice he said, "U! S! A! U! S! A!" The crowd got the picture and began chanting with him, increasing their speed until it was too fast, and then they broke into applause.

"Ok, Ok," he said with a grin. "Sit back down. Thank you all for your kind welcome. I was only going to go over the agenda for the next two days with you but Chairman Guess – y'all, aren't we blessed to have such a great woman captaining our party? Let's give her another round of applause!" He tucked the microphone under his arm and clapped facing Mary Ellen. She stood up and gave a quick wave to the crowd, she put her hands together and gave a quick bow to Joe, who returned her thank you with a nod of his head.

"Ladies and gentlemen, we were elected for a specific purpose. And let's not mince words here. Let's not get carried away with over-the-top political fluff and rhetoric. The truth is we were elected because Tennesseans were tired of the same old same old. Democrats had been in control too long and got used to it and took it for granted. So let me challenge all of us: let's not take it for granted," he paused for applause. "Let's not wake up in three years and be used to being in power. In fact go ahead and toss that term out of our vocabulary. We are not 'in power', the people are in power, not us!"

"Amen!"

"Yes!"

"That's right!"

Joe held up one finger, "and let's never forget that." The applause grew louder, so he spoke over it. "Never, ever." He held the microphone down by his waist and let the applause die down on its own.

"Ok," said Joe. "Here's the deal. In this room, in fifteen minutes, the greenhorn caucus, which is most of you, is going to meet in here to learn the basics of Mason's Rules of Order. Now look, this is important, we do not – I repeat do not – use Robert's Rules of Order in Tennessee. That's important. Don't worry about the difference, just know that it is different.

"All y'all that aren't starting your first term, we are going to hike down to the Farragut Conference Room down the hall and to the right. We are going to have a Q&A session about what to expect now that we are the majority. Those sessions are going to last three hours and then we come back in here for lunch at noon.

"During lunch, we are going to have a few guest speakers. Two long time lobbyists have agreed to come here and fill us in on their, and their clients', agenda. They're also going to talk about how to interact with a lobbyist, that should be fun. After that, we are going to take a break till three o'clock.

"At three, we will be in here for leadership nominations. So if you want to run for Whip, Treasurer, Secretary, Assistant Leader, Leader, Caucus Chair, or be our nominee for Speaker Pro Term, Deputy Speaker, or Speaker of the House then someone has to nominate you and you must accept. You must be in the room to nominate or accept a nomination. That is going to happen in here at three, so be here for that.

"Then we will take another break. At six o'clock, our friends at Winston, Harper, and Roe are providing dinner and drinks. There won't be any speaking or anything like that; that time is strictly for socializing and getting to know each other. That will be in the golf clubhouse over yonder.

"And that's it, y'all. That will wrap up our day today. I will mention quickly that tomorrow morning at breakfast we will have a Q&A with all the nominees for leadership positions, after that we will go over our agenda for tomorrow. But that's your schedule for today. Y'all got about fifteen, eh maybe twenty, we'll say twenty minutes. If you're starting your first term, be back in here in twenty minutes. The rest of you, I'll see you down the hall and to the right. Ok thank you," Joe finished and looked for the sound guy to hand back the microphone.

Larry Picard walked into the hallway heading to the Farragut Conference Room when Dick Weber grabbed him by the elbow.

"Larry you gunslinger! How are ya?" said Dick in the voice of a former police officer, who had cut down to four packs of cigarettes a day.

"Hellfire, Dick, I thought you were gonna get ousted for sure! But boy I'm glad to see you!" said Larry as the men shook hands. "How are things in Alamo?"

"Slow and steady, you know that old song," said Dick as the two men approached the conference room doorway. Dick grabbed Larry's elbow again and pulled him past the door to the conference room down the hall five feet away from the crowd. "Larry, I got to bend your ear a bit."

Larry looked down at his shorter and fatter friend. Dick's signature mustache was more yellow than normal. Larry said, "you know Dick, from this angle, it looks like you've lost more hair on your dome this summer."

"Fuck you. You know it only grows on the sides," said Dick. The two men laughed.

"Damn, I missed you buddy," said Larry.

"I know, but hey I really gotta talk to you about this," said Dick lowering his voice. He began rubbing a skin tag behind his ear. "I stopped by my legislative office Friday. Shannon said the boys and girls are still talking about that mess."

"What mess?" asked Larry twisting his face in a confused manner.

"You know what mess," said Dick folding his arms. "She said everyone up there is still convinced that they're all getting axed when Humphrey takes over." Dick looked up at Larry, and then around the hall to see who was near. He waved and smiled to someone passing behind Larry. Larry turned and saw Dale Reiff. Larry gave him a quick smile and wave. Dale stopped just short of walking into the conference room.

"Good to see y'all boys," he said.

"You too," hollered Dick.

"Go on in and save us some seats," said Larry.

"You got it," said Dale giving his friends a thumbs up before disappearing into the room.

"Look," said Larry continuing in a low whisper, "my girl mentioned something about it but I can't believe Joe would do that."

"You can't?" asked Dick with surprise. Larry shook his head no. "Joe is one of the biggest egotistical, ambitious, slimy moth-erfuckers at the Plaza. Everyone knows it, party be damned."

"Yeah, but this is something beyond all of that. I mean, firing every single assistant? There's no way that's going to happen."

"Larry, that's what everyone there is saying is going to happen."

"Think about this real hard for just a minute, Dick, just think. Do you think Mary Ellen Guess, or Mark Cullen, or any other big-name Republican like you and me, are going to let Joe Humphrey rip their assistants away from them?"

"Yeah, maybe, but––"

"And there's at least four men in that conference room right there that are either trying to or are rubbing naughty bits with their assistants."

"Ok," said Dick, considering his friend's words. "Maybe I just bought too much into the fishbowl up there," he held up his hands, "but I still want to ask him about it."

"Well," said Larry, "I think that's what this next meeting is for." He patted Dick's shoulder and turned to walk away.

"One more thing," Dick grabbed Larry's arm to keep him from leaving. "If it turns out to be true, then we are going to have to come up with a plan to stop it."

"Ok," said Larry motioning to Dick to get in the room.

"Promise me," said Dick.

"Dammit, I promise. Ok? Now let's get in there."

The Farragut Conference room, named for the Tennessee native who was admiral of the United States Navy during the civil war and a staunch Unionist from the south, was arranged with three rows of seven brown metal folding chairs. There were no windows in the room which, coupled with the nine-foot ceilings, made the room feel much smaller than its one hundred twenty-person capacity would suggest. Larry and Dick walked in, each man looking across the room to familiarize themselves with their new setting. They saw Dale already seated, looking through pages in a red folder. They went over and sat on either side of him.

Mike Hayes stood up and approached the microphone at the front of the room. The audience of reelected incumbents gave him a polite applause. As Chairman of the GOP House Caucus it had technically been his job to make sure all incumbents had the money and resources to run successful campaigns. Though his caucus had just gone through the most successful election cycle in their history, no one credited Hayes for their victory. Yes, he had raised ample amounts of money, and the majority of that money had ended up in their campaign coffers, or had been used to run TV and AM radio ads supporting their campaigns, or at the very least attacking their opponents, but there was still a hefty sum that was spent on Mike's own campaign. A campaign in which he was unopposed. Regardless, he was still the Caucus Chair, and as Joe Humphrey's right hand he would surely be elected to the same position again by his GOP peers.

There was something different about him now, Larry noticed, but he could not place what exactly. He seemed rested. Well, good for you, you son of a bitch, thought Larry to himself. Larry and Mike had a long running rivalry within the caucus. Larry, at one point in his career, had been a well-respected and effective Caucus Whip. During his two terms as Whip, he had kept the entire GOP caucus together on votes. Every single vote for four consecutive years. Not a single Republican in any committee, on any amendment, on any procedural vote, or on any final vote had ever voted with the Democrats while he was the Whip. Of course, there had been only seventeen members of the House Republican Caucus at that time, but still it was a very extreme seventeen. Their districts had been so gerrymandered that only the whacks got through the primary, with the exception of himself and others who had become close with Speaker Caputo, who took it easy on them. Then when Larry decided to run for his third turn as Whip, after a cycle where their caucus had picked up two seats, Mike Hayes decided he wanted to run for Whip too. Mike was young back then, just starting his second term. He still had those piercing blue eyes, slim frame, and that slick shiny dark hair.

Two years after losing his race for Whip, Larry stepped up and ran for Caucus Chairman. It was a bitter and brutal race within the caucus, leading to a schism that still hadn't quite healed. The result was another loss to Mike Hayes. Fast forward another two years and Mike was poised to either be reelected Caucus Chair, or take over as the first Republican Majority Leader. Both options made Larry's skin crawl while he was wasting away on the Republican backbench. Larry's once-promising political career now stalled like an airplane that flew too high; he felt gravity slowly pulling him down to Earth with no way back up.

"Ok folks," said Mike. "The fine people here gave us a couple of microphones for this session, but y'all know how loud I can talk, so I don't think I'm going to use one. If that's ok? I think y'all can hear me can't you?" A few voices in the crowd responded to let Mike know that his voice was coming through just fine.

"Ok, then," Mike continued. "This part of the retreat is just for us incumbents. It's for us to have an open and honest conversation about what to expect now that we are the majority. To be clear, these are uncharted waters for all of us. We've never had a Republican majority in this state since Reconstruction and . . ." There was spontaneous applause at the mention of the Republican majority; Mike raised his hands to try to calm the crowd. "And we are trying to get our act together before we start in January.

"Now, there are a few things I know you all want to hear about so I'm going to cover those now. When I'm done Joe, Mary Ellen, and maybe a few others are going to join me up here and y'all can ask us questions at that point. Sound good?" Mike smiled and clapped his hands. "Ok, let's jump right in.

"First, I need to address a rumor I've been asked about. No, we as a caucus are not broke. Not by a long stretch. We did spend a lot more money this time than ever before, but we still have one hundred and fifty some grand in the bank. Ok? I'm not sure how these rumors about me spending all our money got started but it's not true.

"Second point. A lot of you have asked about committee chairs. Yes, now that we are the majority we will have Republican committee chairs. And these will be real committees, Ok? Not ad hoc or special committees, but actual standing, formal committees. Now, who the chairs will be is up to the new Speaker. Whoever that maybe," Mike winked at Joe who was sitting in the front row, drawing laughter from the room. "But he, or she," again there was laughter, "will get to make those choices. And whoever they chose will be going to a conference over in Charlotte, North Carolina, for three days on intense parliamentary training. Those expenses will be paid by the caucus and not the state. That training will take place during the two-week break in January between our first floor session, the Organizational Session, where we formally elect our leaders, and the first day of regular business.

"Third, and final, office assignments. Again, we are in the majority so we will all be getting new offices." The announcement of new offices and moving out of the windowless guts of Legislative Plaza was cause for celebration. Mike laughed and raised his hands again. "Ok. The move will happen during that two-week break. If you are going to be a committee chair make sure you are clear with how you want your new office arranged so it will be done before you return. My office is handling this, ok? All incumbents should know where they are moving to before that first day of regular session, not the organization session. Ok?" Mike looked around the room with his eyebrows raised, looking for questions.

"Well," he said. "In that case. Joe? Mary Ellen? Why don't you two come on up and we'll get rolling."

Tom had made the trip across the street to Crumbs, a little coffee house bistro across Union Street from the Tennessee Performing Arts Center and State Museum. It was a quick downhill walk for employees at the plaza who could no longer stomach the state-issued coffee; the state-issued coffee wasn't kind to the stomach. Tom needed his caffeine fix for the day. He had been an hour late that morning, and while most employees of most members were more than comfortable treating the 8 AM to 4:30 PM hours as recommendations, Tom did not. A brief stint in the Air Force Reserves had drilled in his 'ten minutes early is ten minutes late' demeanor. Yet last night's events at Five Points in east Nashville made his 5 AM alarm seem pointless.

Crumbs was surprisingly empty. He had expected the spot to be full of people finishing their nine o'clock Monday morning break. He checked his watch: 10:30. Ah, Christ, he thought. He ordered a large peppermint cappuccino to go. He heard Charlie's voice mocking him in his head. He didn't care; he was hoping the peppermint might help his stomach or his head or with a little luck maybe both. He got his phone out; he needed to check for voicemails or texts, or at the very least look busy.

The door opened; Tom looked up as the cold air hit his face. It was refreshing. Callie Procter walked in. A lobbyist who got that position after working as the legislative assistant for Representative Afton Kramer, a Republican starting his sixth term, while she studied for the bar exam. After passing the bar, however, the money that The Waltrip Firm offered her to be their Junior Legislative Liaison was double the best offer she had received from any law firm, so she picked a life as a lobbyist over becoming a practicing attorney and never looked back. Well respected by most incumbents in both the House and Senate, she was also well liked by all staffers because she did not ride coattails to get her position. With very close ties to all the Republicans, Callie's stock had gone skyrocketing since election night. Tom saw an opportunity to get out while he still could. He smiled and waved, Callie recognized him and smiled as she walked over.

"Hey Tom! I figured you'd be playing hooky with the rest of the Plaza this morning," she said as she gave Tom a hug.

"Now Callie, you know that's not my style."

"Oh, of course not, you're one of the good ones," she laughed and readjusted the purse on her shoulder. "Can I buy you a cup? We'll keep it off the books, of course."

"Not that I'm afraid of violating ethic laws, but I already got mine," he said holding his cup up.

"Well, don't say I didn't offer. One dark roast, regular, with cream please," she said to the woman behind the counter. "So how are things?"

"Not all bad, considering we aren't the majority anymore."

"Yeah, I'm gonna be real sad to see Caputo give up the gavel. He's turned into an ok guy in his golden years."

"Between you and me, Callie, we've got a plan to save him," Tom said with a smirk.

"Huh, yeah. Trying to convince old guard Republicans to vote for Caputo. Listen, I don't think that's going to work."

"How do you know about that?" Tom asked with authentic surprise.

"Afton told me about his conversation with Leader Anderson," she responded in a tone that matched Tom's surprise. "You all didn't really think the word wasn't going to get out, did you?" Tom could only stare blankly. "Oh dear, I'm sorry, I think a lot of people know. You know secrets don't last longer than a day or two in our world."

"Ok, fine, but we still only need one vote," he said defiantly.

"No, you're going to need at least five," she said, her expression now serious.

"What do you mean?"

"I mean Leader Humphrey went to Memphis the week before Thanksgiving. You know, his wife's family is from that area.

While he was there he met up with some members of the Black Caucus. He reminded them that Caputo has never once made one of their members a committee chair or pushed for them to have higher office, all that stuff. Long story short, every black rep from Memphis is going to vote for Humphrey as insurance votes, and in return they'll get some committee chairs out of it."

"Christ. You're serious?"

"Yes, dead serious. At least, that's what I've heard."

"How many?"

"Well all the ones from Memphis, apparent––"

"No. How many committee chairs?"

"Two chairs, two vice chairs is my understanding."

"That's it? You're kidding."

"Here's your coffee ma'am," said the girl behind the counter. Callie handed her a five-dollar bill and told her to keep the change.

Callie took her coffee and turned back to Tom. "Look," she said, "I'm not telling you how to do your job, but you need to sure up your own caucus before trying to pull from theirs. Also, do your business away from the Plaza to stop leaks. Rookie mistake, Tom." Tom's mouth was open and he turned his head to face the window. "Just smooth things over at your retreat. When are y'all having a retreat? We'd love to pay for the food."

"I'm not sure," said Tom trying to focus on the question. "Bob Atley was our caucus Secretary, he was supposed to organize it. But, well, he got beat in his race, so I guess we're supposed to throw something together now. Shit."

"I'm sorry Tom. I didn't mean to upset you."

"It's fine," he said with a smile. "I'm more upset that I have to organize the retreat now than I am about losing votes for Caputo." Callie laughed. "Hey, listen, I've got to go now but let's get lunch. I'd love to talk about my future with someone that got out of the Plaza."

"Well, I'm half out, as you know, but yeah let's do it after session gets rolling, once the dust has settled." They shook hands and said goodbye outside. Callie walked down Union Street towards her building, Tom ran uphill the half block back to Legislative Plaza.

The question and answer session in the Farragut Conference Room was almost over, but the intensity in the room was still building. It started when Keith Zachary from Elizabethton in northeast Tennessee, who was about to start his third term, announced he was interested in being chairman of a committee. He wanted to know if there was a set criteria or litmus test to be considered for a chairmanship. There would not be, Joe assured him, instead the next Speaker would be encouraged to look at the ranking members of the committee and Caucus members who had mastered Mason's Rules of Order, who could speak clearly, were decisive in their decision making, and could help push the Speaker's and party's agenda over the Governor's agenda. Keith possessed none of these things, and sat down visibility dejected along with half the room.

This led to a question by Paul Moseby regarding the rumors about laying off staff once Humphrey became Speaker. Paul, a more senior member of the caucus, had always rebuked leadership positions but as a former County Commissioner and County Mayor he was interested in being chairman of the Local

Government Committee. If Joe was honest, Paul was his top choice for that committee. In a Dillon Rule State like Tennessee, where local governments only have the specific powers laid out by the state and must ask the state permission to do anything outside those specific authorities, the Chairman of the Local Government Committee could be a powerful politician should they wish. Which means Joe could potentially be appointing a future rival for higher office if he made the wrong choice for that committee chair. Every small town and big city mayor, any commissioner or city council member worth their salt, would be in frequent contact with the Chairman of Local Government. Whether they want a new sidewalk, change the colors of their public parking lines, increase hotel taxes, or allow a band to play in a public square past 8 PM; a local elected official would have to speak with the Local Government Chairman. Lots of deals could be made that way. Paul would provide Joe a safe choice, the committee's ranking GOP member, a former local elected official, but most importantly a person with no ambition for higher office. The issue, however, was that Paul wanted to keep the committee's staff in place despite the fact the staff was selected by Democrats. Paul only wanted to know who would have the authority to make those staffing choices. Would it be up to the Chairman or the next Speaker? If it were not up to the chairman of a committee, Paul would not be interested. Mike Hayes actually answered the question; all staffing decisions are ultimately the Speaker's decision.

This led to the inevitable questions from other members about the rumors surrounding a complete turnover of staff by Joe in favor of a younger and more conservative staff across the board. Joe pointed out that he wasn't guaranteed to be Speaker and such rumors were just that, rumors. This did not satisfy the crowd, who wanted a more concrete answer. Some people pointed out the longevity and seniority their assistants had accumulated. Others suggested that Democrats not be allowed to make their own staffing decisions, but Republicans should have that right as members of the majority. Joe pointed out that staff with enough time vested with the state would automatically be reassigned; if Republicans got to make their own decisions and Democrats did not there would be a lawsuit brought by the Tennessee Association for Public Employees (TAPE for short). After withstanding the barrage for forty-five minutes Joe had finally had enough.

"Look it!" he said forcefully in the microphone. "Let me remind y'all what is at stake here, because it seems we've taken our eye off the ball. We have a real chance of passing bills that will truly protect the life of the unborn. We could be the number one pro-life state. We could also be the state that leads the way in protecting traditional marriage. We could put a prohibition on an income tax in our state constitution. We could end estate tax, death tax, and lower the business and grocery taxes. We have a real shot at being the best state for business and having the lowest unemployment rate in the nation. We could end the stranglehold unions have on our workers, unions that force even nonmembers to pay their dues. We have a chance to bust this mythological recession everyone is convinced we are going through.

"Also, let's not forget who is going to be president. Tennessee could lead the way in resisting Obama, in fighting against the far-left liberal agenda. Don't forget, because I haven't mentioned it yet, we still have a liberal Democrat as Governor, we are going to have to fight his agenda these next two years. This state has a weak Governor veto. If he vetoes one of our conservative bills, it only takes fifty of us to overturn his veto, that's it, just a simple majority will undo his veto and turn that bill into law. Finally, there's redistricting, the Governor has to sign off on those. Do we want liberal staffers actively working to draw our districts?

"Let me ask you, how do you expect to do this with people who are union members? Huh? Nearly every single person that works in the Plaza this instant is a member of TAPE. How can we be pro-life when so many of our staffers are pro-choice? They're also pro-gay. They are also pro-tax, pro-union, anti-business. Many, if not most of them, voted for Obama. And don't forget our Governor was the Mayor of Nashville. When he ran for re-election as mayor he got seventy percent of the vote; both times he ran for governor he carried Nashville and Davidson County by ninety percent or more. Where do you think our staff lives? They live in Nashville. They are loyal to the Governor, not to us. What's going to stop them from sabotaging our agenda? The answer is nothing." He paused and surveyed the room. Every eye laid on him, captivated, no one spoke.

"Now, listen. I don't want to get rid of any of them. When the margin is this thin, we have to have people we know support us, and our agenda. This isn't about me, or you, or even the Republican Party. It's about God and His will, and His judgement. We need our people in those positions to make sure His agenda gets through." Joe stopped speaking. There was a rapt silence across the room. Everyone understood the point he was making. Many of them now agreed with him; the mission was too big to not have everyone working at Legislative Plaza be bought in one hundred percent. Yet there were still those who could not believe what Joe had just said. They understood his reasoning, but they could not buy in to it. Despite his candor, they recognized he was going too far.

As the session dismissed, Creed Edmunds hustled across the room as quick as his seventy-year-old legs would allow. He grabbed Dick's elbow and got his attention. Dick turned slowly as he grabbed Larry by the arm to keep his friend from leaving without him.

"Creed, where's your walking stick?" asked Dale who was standing just ahead of Larry and Dick.

"Ah shit boys I left it over yonder," said Creed slightly winded. "Listen, y'all need to help me get back up to my room. I'm old and shit my pants during that little verbal vomit Joe and Mike were doing."

Larry looked at Dale with concern. "Ok," said Larry looking around. He was concerned and wanted to save his friend from embarrassment. "Ok, Dale. Take him up to his room and help him. I'll go grab his cane."

"No, no, fuck my cane," said Creed. "Larry stay close behind me and I'll hold on to Dick here. There's Darren over there, run over and tell him to bring my cane up to me when he goes to his room. He's staying next door." Larry waved to get Darren's attention, then he pointed at Creed, then he pointed up, and then at the cane. Darren gave Larry a thumbs up to let him know he received the message.

Darren grabbed the cane and started walking towards his room ten minutes after the others had left. His long legs carried his thin frame gracefully across the room and down the hall. He had played power forward for the Memphis Tigers in college, in the years before there was a three-point line in college basketball. He briefly held the school record for points in a game, but it had since been broken multiple times. It didn't matter much to his colleagues in the House; he hadn't played for the Vols so it wasn't anything to brag about.

He was worried about his friend and mentor. Creed was a decade and a half older, but Darren had never seen him need assistance just to walk out of a room. Larry and Dick had looked ill too. Whatever happened, surely to God they would tell him if they were going to take Creed to the hospital. He kept hoping he had misread Larry's lips. Surely Creed hadn't shit himself. As he approached the door to Creed's room he could hear laughing. He knocked on the door with the cane. Dick, with a drink in his hand, let him in. There were the three men already in the room, Larry in the chair in the corner, Dick sitting on one of the two beds, and Creed, looking as healthy now as he did five years ago, was sitting with his legs crossed at the desk with a whiskey and ice in his hand.

"Representative Hope," said Creed to Darren in a mockingly serious chairman's voice. "I'm glad to see you have brought my walking stick! Furthermore, I am most pleased to see the stick is not lodged in your ass." The room broke out in laughter, except for Darren.

"Goddammit, what in the name of hell is wrong with y'all?" said Darren, throwing the cane on the empty bed.

"No wonder, your walking stick wasn't up his ass," said Dick. "He's already got one up in there!" The room broke into laughter again.

"Damn it all," said Darren. "Somebody better tell me what the hell is happening, cause I'm lost as all strays." There was a knock at the door before anyone answered the question. Darren, being the closest, opened it. Travis Flagler walked it, one of the few other men who could look Darren in the eye without looking up. He smiled at Darren and looked past his shoulder at Dale and Creed.

"You ok, Creed?" Travis asked with a snort, trying his best to hide his laughter. Darren rolled his eyes as Travis walked in followed by the much shorter Kenneth Arnold, who Darren hadn't noticed.

Kenneth patted Darren on the shoulder. "I told them not to, Hopie. I swear I told them not to do it."

"Do what, goddammit?" Darren slammed the door closed so hard it rattled the fixtures on the wall.

"Calm down there, beast," said Larry raising a palm toward Darren. "Creed got me and Dick to believe he had shit his pants, but he didn't, it was just a joke." He took a sip of his drink.

"You boys help yourself to my personal bar," said Creed pointing to the desk. "As my way of apologizing, help yourself."

"Dammit, Creed!" yelled Darren running his hands through his hair. "I thought you were dying."

"Well, I'm not," said Creed. "My wrinkled ass will be at your funeral. I'm sorry about the little prank. Make yourself a drink, Darren. Really, I'm sorry but I needed to get you all up here."

Darren took a breath and then walked to the desk, he poured some coke in a glass with some ice and whiskey. He sighed; the rest of the room was still laughing. Then it hit him. "Wait, why did you want us all up here?" he asked just before taking a sip.

The room went quiet as the six men looked around. Then Creed spoke up, "The fuck you think I wanted to get us all together?" They all knew but no one wanted to say it. "Lord bless you boys," Creed continued. "Every single one of us was talked to by either Greg or one of his boys about voting for Caputo. And after what we just heard we need to figure out which one of us it's going to be."

The room stayed quiet. Larry looked into his cup and said, "I can't do it, I love Speaker Bob, we all do, but I can't be the guy that does this to our party."

Kenneth groaned and leaned against the wall, "I don't want Joe Humphrey to be Speaker but if Bob Caputo wants me to be his surprise vote then he should be talking to me instead of sending Tom."

"Look it," said Creed. "Gregory came to me directly. Bob wants to appear to be out of this backroom dealing stuff for the sake of running the House."

"What the hell does that even mean?" said Darren. "Why don't you vote for him!" Darren pointed at Creed.

"Me?" asked a shocked Creed.

"Yeah you," countered Darren. "You've been round the longest and have the least to lose." Darren sat his drink down and took off his sport coat. "I'm running for Shelby County mayor next year. Ain't told nobody, y'all are the first to know. But if I'm gonna win that, I need the party and they won't get near me if I vote for Bob. Kenneth is probably running for state senate; hell-fire Travis thinks about running for Congress every two years! You almost retired before this last go-round, Creed. It should be you."

"No sir," said Creed. "I'm the second-longest serving Republican in the state at any level. I've never, not once, voted for a Democrat and I won't let my last vote in office be for a Democrat. Bob knows that."

"I still don't get why Bob won't ask us directly? I don't think I could tell him no to his face," said Travis as he sat down on the bed next to Dick.

It was Dale who responded. "Because, you know how disastrous the Senate has been the past two years. Because the Lieutenant Governor got Cathy Wright to vote for him. He, himself, convinced a Democrat to vote for him, a Republican. It was slick and dirty, and it ousted Doug Kittrell, the longest-serving Lieutenant Governor in our state's history. They shouldn't have done that to Doug. I'm glad we got a Republican Lieutenant Governor two years before we should've, but the Senate now can't get jack shit done unless the actual governor tells them to. Bob don't want that; he wants peace and order, and good ol' fashioned status quo."

"Yeah. But . . ." said Travis pausing to collect his thoughts. "If Bob wants our vote he should ask us himself. He knows how much we could lose if we break lines and vote for him. The party would kick us out."

Larry suddenly saw a way to pull himself back into the atmosphere. "The party would only kick us out if we vote for a Democrat. What if we voted for a different Republican? What if we nominated someone else? A sneak attack on the floor of the House?"

"Same deal, just a different name," said Kenneth. "All support from the party would be gone, no money, no volunteers, and we'd be kicked out of the caucus."

"No, no," said Creed pointing at Kenneth. "The agreement for our party is to only vote for a Republican. We don't have to vote for our caucus nominee." Creed laughed. "That could work, Larry. By God, it could work."

"Now hold on," interjected Darren. "What happens when none of the three get fifty votes?" He looked around the room. "The top two get to move on and we revote. Back to this shit, Bob and Joe."

"Yes," said Creed. "But what if Caputo comes in third? Then we have two Republicans to pick from and no way the Dems vote for Humphrey. We just need half of their caucus to not vote for Caputo."

"Never going to happen," said Travis. "No way they vote for a Republican and there's no way they vote for someone else if Caputo is an option."

"Then I vote for Caputo in round two," said Larry. Everyone stared at him silently.

"You would do that?" asked Darren.

"To save our caucus from being split, yes," Larry said.

"You would lose all support from the party," said Travis.

"That's Mary Ellen's call to make," said Larry with a smile. The affair between him and Mary Ellen was an unspoken fact within the party.

"Leveraging y'all's . . . situation," said Dick, "is a mistake. She'd call your bluff."

"Let's find out," Larry said reaching into his pocket. He pulled out his phone and sent a text to Mary Ellen asking her to slip away and come to Creed's room. The men sat quietly and waited. There was no response to his text.

"Maybe try calling her?" said Creed after several awkward silent minutes, but there was a quiet knock on the door before anyone could respond. Dick got up and let Mary Ellen in.

She looked around the room without saying anything, then finally "What's this about?"

Kenneth responded as the others shifted uncomfortably. "Let's say, hypothetically, someone ran against Joe for Speaker. Another Republican. Hypothetically he gets nominated on the floor and then beats Joe. Would they lose support of the party?"

Mary Ellen considered the question. She crossed her arms and leaned against the wall by the bathroom. "Hypothetically, they'd be an idiot. And realistically, and honestly, they would lose. But no, the party would not abandon them."

"What if, hypothetically," said Darren, "someone from our caucus would then break rank and vote for Bob Caputo in the next round of balloting, and he stayed Speaker?"

"You're serious," she said looking at Darren who nodded back. "You're fucking serious. Jesus. If someone did that, I'd kick them out of the party personally on the spot and worry about the bureaucratic bullshit later. You're fucking serious? What the hell is wrong with y'all?" She looked around the room.

"He can't be Speaker," said Creed. "You heard what he wants to do, Mary Ellen. We can't let Joe become Speaker."

"What if it was me that votes for Bob?" asked Larry, leaning two fingers against his temple. Mary Ellen looked shocked. She started to say something and then stopped.

Then she said, "Not only would I kick you out of the party personally, but I would also be most disappointed."

"Then what can we do?" asked Dick.

"We are going to have a Republican Speaker, and if you don't want it to be Joe then you have to nominate someone else this afternoon. That's the only way," she said, looking around the room. "The only way."

"Fine," said Creed. "Then I'm going to nominate you, Chairman." He said looking at Mary Ellen.

"No," she said flatly.

"It should be you," responded Creed. "You got us the majority. You turned our party into a serious machine. You've run our caucus before. You know what you're doing. You're already our leader, it should be you. Plus you'd be the first woman Speaker our state has ever had. I'm nominating you. It should be you, not Joe."

"It's not my turn," she said.

"What do you mean?" asked Darren.

"I'm going to run for Speaker in four years. Nominate me then, vote for me then. It's only four years, I'll fix whatever damage Joe has done."

"Why in four years?" asked a very surprised Larry. Mary Ellen didn't respond.

"Christ," said Darren. "No, no, no. Don't tell me."

Creed took in a deep breath. "That son of a bitch is running for Governor!" The men cursed and groaned.

"Guys, politics is about making deals and I've made mine," she said. "Y'all can go to hell but this is happening."

"No it's not," said Larry. "Goddammit, I'm gonna run for Speaker." The noise stopped.

"I'll nominate you," said Darren in a meekish voice. "I've got your back on this."

"Mary Ellen," said Dick. "If we nominate Larry, and he runs within our caucus?"

"Then it is a matter to be determined within the caucus and not the party's business," she said staring directly at Larry. "I've got to go. Good luck, gentlemen."

She left the room.

"Ok," said Larry. "Nominations are at three today, and then the caucus votes for our nominee the week before session starts. I need all of you on board to make this work."

"You got it," said Travis.

"Yeah," said Dick. "Fuck Joe."

"Amen," said Creed.

"I'll order us some food. I think we're going to have to skip lunch," said Darren.

Joe had planned on spending his break before dinner calling donors, making one last big push on fundraising before the start of session when lawmakers are prohibited from accepting donations. His plans were derailed during the three o'clock nomination meeting. He had expected there to be multiple people running for lower leadership posts like Caucus Secretary, Assistant Leader, and Whip. He had even expected there to be multiple members who wanted to run for his position as Leader of the Republican Caucus. He had given an excellent address when he announced he wasn't going to run for re-election as Leader. He highlighted the accomplishments they had achieved while he had held that position, he thanked all the right people, kissed all the right asses. Then Justin Tanner nominated him for Speaker, Justin had knocked the nomination out of the park, the applause when he had finished had filled the entire park.

Then Mike fucked up. He was supposed to move to close nominations after Joe accepted. But Mike was too busy applauding and Darren Hope was recognized by Tucker Pyle, the current Caucus Secretary. Darren nominated Larry Pickard, stressing the need for bipartisanship to keep the House running smoothly. Larry accepted, promising to let everyone pick and choose their own assistants, thereby maintaining order in House. Larry had framed the entire race as a contest for who best could keep the House running as normal before handing the gavel off to the next generation, casting the role of Speaker as some sort of stewardship rather than a political office. Joe had offered a distinct vision to fundamentally change the House and the state.

Joe walked into his room and tried to slam the door. Mike and Tucker were close behind; Mike caught the door before it hit him in the face.

"That son of a bitch," said Joe. "I can't believe he would do this to me. That goddamm son of a bitch!" He paced the room. "And you," he pointed at Mike, "what in the fuck were you doing?"

"Joe," began Mike, taking a deep breath trying to calm the room, "I tried but Darren got up before I ever had the chance to be recognized."

"Ah bullshit," said Joe. "You were too busy smiling your shit-eating grin and clapping like an asshole to realize what was going on. Tucker, the fuck were you thinking recognizing Darren before Mike. Did you forget the goddam plan?"

"I'm sorry," said Tucker. "I thought he was going to close the nominations. I thought maybe the plans had changed––"

"I would have told you if the plans had changed, you dumb shit! You're done. Done. You're not going to be in leadership anymore." Joe dug at his scalp.

"Don't worry, Joe. Larry can't beat you, you've got this wrapped up," said Tucker trying to be reassuring.

"No, you don't get it," said Joe turning to face Tucker. "Right now, at this moment, he probably has at least ten votes. At the very least. A couple of well-placed promises to some freshman, and he could get fifteen votes. He could use those to get another five. Once people realize he's close to twenty votes they'll start jumping ship. From me, to him."

"No they won't, just calm down," said Mike.

"How many people in our caucus have fucked their assistant, or some other assistant, or clerk, or committee researcher? Huh?" Joe shrugged. "Once those pervs see a chance to keep their secrets and slam pieces in the Plaza, they're all going to vote for Larry.

"One dent, just one dent in my armor and this shit could be over." Joe sat on the bed, exhausted. "I've worked too hard to lose it now. If I don't get Speaker I've got nothing. I'm out of leadership, and probably out of office in two years. This has to work." He put his head in his hands. Mike looked at Tucker, without speaking they agreed that their friend was losing his mind.

"Then," Mike spoke up, "we need to bury him." Joe looked up at Mike with concern. Tucker shook his head no. "I mean figuratively speaking."

"Oh, right," said Joe.

"Obviously," said Tucker.

"The majority of this caucus is here because of you," continued Mike. "Do you really, honestly, believe these freshmen are really going to abandon you just because Larry Pickard might offer them a vice chairmanship? Come on."

Joe stood up and went across the room to the desk where his suitcases lay opened. He dug around his belongings until he found a bottle of vodka. He opened it and put the bottle to his lips and took a long swig. He closed his eyes and lowered his head and started to breath heavy.

"You know, you could probably get Larry to drop out of the race if you agreed to not fire any staff," suggested Tucker.

"No," said Joe with a touch of annoyance. "Here's what you aren't getting about this situation. Larry isn't running to protect the staff. He isn't running because he wants to unite the parties. He isn't running to try to keep order and peace in the House. He's not doing this because he wants to be Governor, or our next US Senator, or Vice fucking President." Joe slammed his fist down on the desk and turned towards the other two men. "He's doing this to fuck me over! That's it, that's the only fucking newsflash here. He hates me, and you, and you, and the party I've been building. He might as well be a fucking Democrat, and he fucking hates the fact –fucking HATES – that I've gotten so many actual damn conservatives elected. So, no. Me letting people pick their own goddam staff wouldn't solve shit. He's just doing this to spite me." Joe put the lid back on his vodka bottle and tossed it onto the bed, and turned to look out the window.

After a few moments passed Tucker said, "You're just going to have to beat him like a drum, and you have to start tonight at dinner at the reception. You have to, excuse me, *we* have to sure up the votes."

Mike picked up the vodka bottle. "You got any ginger ale?"

"Top drawer on the right," said Joe finally turning away from the window. "Make me one too. I'm going to need a buzz to get through this night; easy on the ice and soda."

The golf clubhouse at Montgomery Bell State Park sits, for the most part, unused from December until Valentine's Day. For those seventy-four days the fifteen hundred square feet of the pro shop, snack bar, gathering area, the three upstairs conference rooms, and wrap around porch of the colonial-inspired building can be rented out completely, for the bargain price of four hundred dollars a day. If you are a state employee, you can get a discount of twenty percent during those seventy-four days. At one point, a state legislator was able to get a hundred percent discount, but thanks to a crackdown on ethics laws they could now only get an eighty percent discount.

The event planning company hired by Winston, Harper, and Roe had arrived at three o'clock that afternoon. The crew of six spent the majority of that time cleaning the seasonally abandoned space, until half the crew had gone back to headquarters to get the food and drinks for the party that night. By 5:30 they were ready for the guests to arrive. Joe, Mike, and Tucker arrived appropriately late at 6:30.

"What are you going to say to him?" asked Tucker as the trio walked on to the clubhouse front porch and checked in.

"To who? Larry?" responded Joe. Tucker nodded as he put the sticker featuring his name over the front breast pocket of his tan sports coat. "Hell, I don't know and I don't care. Whatever comes out of me comes. Fuck that guy," whispered Joe as he crumpled his name tag into a ball and threw it in the trash can by the door. Everyone in the clubhouse knew who he was; he didn't feel he needed a nametag.

Most of the fifty-member caucus had already arrived by the time Joe walked in. The room, in Joe's mind, went quiet as Mike closed the door behind them. Joe put on his best political grin and looked around the room; he shook a couple of hands before being pointed towards the bar. He wasn't in the mood for deep conversations, he realized after ordering a vodka tonic from the bartender. He felt a sudden rush of dread and could feel the sweat beginning to seep out of his forehead; his blazer suddenly felt twenty pounds heavier. He hadn't planned on having to campaign for Speaker, it wasn't supposed to happen like this at all. This was supposed to be easy; he was just supposed to be going through the motions. Now, thanks to Larry Pickard, he actually had to try. Campaigning was something Joe Humphrey loathed.

When he had been elected to the State House he had done only the bare minimum to get the job done. He spoke to a couple of women's groups, had gone to a few local Republican events, and a few community outings. He won the primary by twenty-five votes; less than two hundred people had voted. Then he was essentially unopposed in the general election – some high school teacher with no name recognition and no foothold in the community had tried to run against him that year. Joe slaughtered him. He had actually never had a real opponent in a general election, he wasn't even sure if the Democrats had any organized chapter in the Tri Cities. He had also never had a primary opponent since his first election. Larry Pickard was his first real opponent in years.

His long-term plan was slowly unraveling. He had coasted into office and into leadership. He was going to coast into the Speaker's office. He knew he had caught a lucky break when Obama got elected; the President-elect wasn't popular in Tennessee. Not by a long shot. This wasn't a place where one could sell hope and change. Change wasn't a Southern thing. A student of history, Joe didn't need tea leaves to know that in two years, during the midterm elections, his party was going to be in a super majority in this state. The Democrats had no real prospects for statewide candidates heading into 2012, and they weren't stupid either; they were going to save what little money they had for the seats they know they can hold. In four years the Republican Primary was going to determine the next Governor of Tennessee. As Speaker of the House his resume would be easy to pitch to voters; he would also be the only person in the race with an actual conservative record to run on. Any bill that passed or died in the House he, as Speaker, could take credit for. In a crowded field, and in 2012 a crowded field for Governor was guaranteed, being Speaker and having his conservative record and bonafides would be enough.

He spied Larry walking into the room towards the bar. He watched as the man so easily pulled off the politician persona. People just gravitated to Larry who, in return, offered firm handshakes and reassuring smiles. He could carry on conversations for just seconds and make whoever he talked to feel heard and understood. Larry wasn't exactly handsome but he was suave, something Joe was not. The only advantage he had on Larry was age, when Larry was graduating from college Joe was still four years. Yet in the Republican Party youth wasn't always an asset. Joe watched the man make his way towards the bar; he thought to himself how pathetic it was that Larry's highest aspirations to this point was State Representative. Joe could be President, he thought, if he was half the politician Larry was.

Joe felt his stomach turn as the bartender handed his drink over at the same moment Larry arrived at the bar, wearing a long sleeve polo and v-neck sweater, with not an ounce of sweat on his brow. Larry stood up straight as he walked up beside Joe, who was bent over with his elbows on the bar. Larry patted Joe on the back as a form of greeting.

"I'll just have a ginger ale with lime in it, please and thank you," Larry said to the bartender.

Joe stood upright. He flipped a switch somewhere in his brain and began to play a role on a stage. "None of the good stuff for you tonight?"

"No, no," replied Larry. "I never drink as a candidate at a campaign event." The words cracked over Joe like a whip. Larry sighed. "You know, Joe. I owe you an apology."

Confused, Joe could only reply, "For what?"

"Well, I'm from a generation in politics where, when you intend on running against someone, you tell them to their face first," said Larry. "You don't blindside your own party. And that's what I've done to you, and for that I'm sorry. I would have told you sooner but I made up my mind minutes before I walked into the room for nominating. Otherwise, I would've sought you out."

"Look here," said Joe, "I don't hold it against you, not one iota. I honestly believe that competitive races only make the ultimate nominee and office holder better. You can hang on to your apology, it's not needed. Good luck Larry." Joe held out his hand and Larry took it; the two exchanged a slow shake. "How's your campaign going?"

"Hell," began Larry. "I've had so many people come up to me and ask for things that I'm not sure what I've promised to who or when. The only thing I know for sure is that I promised Keith I'd think about making him a chairman of some committee."

"Ah, Christ," said Joe laughing as he took a sip of his drink. Larry joined in on the chuckle. "You aren't actually going to give him a gavel, are you?"

"Hell no," said Larry laughing harder. "I'm as big a fan of train wrecks as the next guy, but I'm not going to put anyone through a committee ran by that bumpkin." The two stood there for a few beats and then Larry said, "I know you got a lot on your plate being in leadership and whatnot, so I'm not going to campaign that hard for this thing. I mean I'm not going to go out of my way for it. That wouldn't be fair to you; just know if I lose I will vote for you to be Speaker."

"I appreciate that Larry, rest assured if you win this you got my vote," said Joe. In his mind he was starting to think that he might just vote for Caputo over Larry. Larry gave Joe a quick squeeze on the arm. Once he was gone, Larry slid his drink back to the bartender. "Just give me a tonic with a lime in it, no booze."

Across the room, freshman Representative Lynn Ellington was talking to her mentor Tracy Holcomb. Lynn had interned for Tracy while she was in college, and a mere twelve years later the two women now made up nearly half of the GOPs Women's Caucus in the House of Representatives.

"They seemed cordial," said Lynn as Larry walked away from Joe.

"Don't let it fool you, darling. Larry is playing a game that Humphrey doesn't even know has started," said Tracy.

"I'm not sure, I don't think Larry has much fight left in him for something like this."

"Listen here, Larry Pickard is the slickest and smartest politician you might ever meet. I've known him for over a decade now, and let me tell you, when his eye is on the ball he hits it on the green," Tracy said before taking a drink of her rum and coke. "If he had wanted to, it would have been him conceding to Barack this time instead of McCain."

"No way," said Lynn.

"I'm telling you now, Larry won this thing the minute he got in. Who are you going to vote for?"

"Humphrey," said Lynn. "No way I'd be here had he not sent those checks, not to mention my campaign manager, my field director – they all came from him."

"Ok, me too, for now anyway," said Tracy. "I bet you five dollars right now that before this thing is done we both end up on the board for Pickard."

"That's not a fair bet."

"Why?"

"Because, " said Lynn turning to Tracy. "All I have to do is not vote for Larry and I win. And guess what? I'm not going to vote for Larry Pickard so I've already won."

"We shall see," said Tracy.

CHAPTER 5

Tuesday, December 2, 2008

The next morning Gregory found himself in his legislative office trying to get just a couple extra minutes of sleep. He had to be there early that morning, far too early in his opinion, to meet with the Governor's Legislative Director. Whether their party was in the majority or minority, it was Gregory's responsibility, as House Democratic Leader, to carry all the Governor's legislation. As he struggled to get comfortable on his couch, he had never wanted the Governor to be a Republican so bad in his life. Complicating the matter was the fact that he could not turn out the fluorescent lights in his office without turning off all the lights in his suite. Tom and Alice would be in soon, and he could not bear to hear them bitch this early in the morning about the lights being off. His hangover was bad enough without adding two screaming voices. He turned on his side and closed his eyes. He could feel his body being pulled into a deeper slumber.

Suddenly he felt a blast of wind and the tiles in the ceiling above his head shook as the door opened. It startled Gregory and he shot straight up, wide awake and unsure how long he had been asleep. Charlie was standing in the doorway with his shoulder leaning against the door, his hand still on the knob.

"Got a minute, boss?" he asked Gregory.

"Jesus Christ, Charlie," said Gregory, annoyed. "Dammit son, what time is it?"

"About a quarter to eight," replied Charlie.

"AM or PM?"

"In the morning."

"Ah, fuck," said Gregory. He had only been asleep maybe ten minutes. He was wide awake now; he ran his fingers through his hair. He slipped on his shoes and reached for his glasses on the coffee table. "The hell is wrong with you? Barging in like a damn SWAT team. I mean, damn."

"You sleep here last night?" asked Charlie.

"No, but I didn't sleep anywhere so what's it matter," answered Gregory. "I need coffee."

"No time for that, we have to talk," said Charlie as he closed the door and made his way to the chair across the coffee table from his boss.

"What do you mean, no time?"

"Hey man," said Charlie, pointing at Gregory. "Put your piss-poor mood on the shelf for five minutes. I've got good news." Gregory rolled his eyes and sat back; he extended his hands telling Charlie to proceed.

"Ok, here's what my buddy found out." Charlie pulled a manila envelope out of a briefcase that Gregory hadn't noticed he was carrying. "Seventeen years ago, Joe Humphrey was getting his Pharmacy Degree in Memphis. Everybody knows that, but what people don't know is he was married at that time." Charlie lifted his eyebrows and leaned back in his chair waiting on his boss to praise him.

"So what?" said Gregory. "We all know he's married, his wife used to work for some Congressman in east Tennessee."

"No," said Charlie with a grin, "not her. She's his second wife."

"And . . ."

"And? And? And . . . what more do you want?"

"Charlie," said Gregory, nearly on the verge of exhausted tears. "The Republican Party quit caring about divorce the minute Reagan opined about welfare queens. Give me a break."

"No, no, listen. Alright? Just listen." Charlie put the envelope on the table and opened it. "My buddy went to Memphis and talked to this woman. Her name is Romona, and her and Joe boy were married for two years. She ended it when she found out he was fucking the neighbor's wife, and her boss, and some lady down the street."

"Huh," said Gregory. "That might be something. Was her boss a man or woman?"

"Woman."

"That's too bad. Anything else?"

"No, but I guarantee that's why the son of bitch moved back home to northeast Tennessee." Charlie tapped the table with each word. The two men stared at each other, letting their mental wheels turn as they processed the information. Gregory was about to speak when there was a sudden rush of wind and the ceiling tiles shook. Charlie quickly flipped over the documents in front of him and turned around. Tom was standing in the doorway, wearing an olive suit.

"Good, you're both here. I got some shit to tell y'all," Tom said as he walked in, closing the door behind him.

"Morning, Tom," said Gregory. "Come in, grab a seat. Before you unload on us, Charlie has some info I want you to hear. Charlie, tell him what you just told me, but without the dramatic effects and bullshit." Charlie quickly recapped the information for Tom as he took his seat.

"Wow," said Tom. "Can we prove any of it?"

"Don't matter," said Gregory.

"I think it does," said Tom.

"Don't forget what LBJ said. 'I don't care if my opponent fucked a pig, I just want him to talk about fucking a pig on TV,'" Gregory said with a laugh.

"That's not the line," said Charlie. "It's: 'It doesn't matter if he fucked a dog, I just want him on camera saying he didn't fuck a dog.'"

"It was a donkey," said Tom.

"You sure?" asked Charlie.

"It definitely wasn't a dog," said Gregory.

"I'm almost positive it was a donkey," said Tom.

"Boys, let's not get sidetracked here," said Gregory, lifting his hands. "Point being, let's make him deny it. If he denies it that's good enough. That might pick up a vote for Caputo and bring the Black Caucus back into our fold. Might work, might not, but we can at least play the clips when he runs for Governor."

"What's this about the Black Caucus?" asked Charlie.

"Oh, you weren't here yesterday. Check this out." Tom recounted the information he had received the previous day from Callie. Charlie was surprisingly calm about it.

"Hell, Caputo didn't make any of them chairmen or help them get into leadership. Why should we be surprised?" Charlie said.

"Regardless, we will get them back at our retreat," said Tom. "Which reminds me, we got a room down on MTSU's campus. We'll make it a one-day thing and call it a retreat." Charlie and Gregory groaned.

"Anyway, what did you want to tell us Tom?" asked Gregory.

"Larry Pickard," said Tom.

"What about him?" said Gregory.

"He's running against Humphrey for the Republican Caucus nomination for Speaker," said Tom.

"Oh shit," said Charlie. "That was my guy, I get credit for that."

"No you don't," said Tom. "You were supposed to get him to vote for Caputo, not run against Humphrey."

"Yeah," said Charlie pointing into the air, "but him running against Humphrey means we should get a vote for Caputo if Larry loses."

"And if Larry wins," said Gregory, "we'll have a levelheaded friend in the Speaker's office."

"Yep, exactly," said Tom, leaning back. He and Gregory made eye contact and exchanged exhausted looks.

"What am I missing?" asked Charlie.

"Caputo is done," said Tom.

"If Larry wins, he'll be Speaker and we'll be in good shape; or, at the very least, not in bad shape," said Gregory. "But if Joe beats Larry, we are back to square one trying to find a vote for Caputo and that's a long shot."

"What are you saying?" asked Charlie, who already knew the answer.

"He's saying there's never going to be a Speaker Caputo again," said Tom.

"We're moving the goalposts," said Gregory. "Better to have a Speaker Pickard that we can deal with than risk a Speaker Humphrey that we can't. And Caputo can never know. We can work on this for one more week, and then we have to focus on the Governor's agenda. Actually, you two get to work on his agenda, let me handle this business." All three men understood what needed to happen next.

Most elections are won by convincing a citizen to vote for a politician. They must be convinced the person they are voting for shares their values, and will work on behalf of the voter's best interest not their own. Candidates must go out and meet the voters on their level, communicate with the voters directly. They have to pitch their beliefs and agendas to the voters, help them understand their point of view.

For some voters there is only one issue that matters. A smart politician will be honest with a one-issue voter, admit that they don't agree on that issue, and move on to a voter that cares about more than one thing. A good politician will admit they disagree with the voter without actually saying it; the voter will vote for that politician without ever knowing they disagree. A lucky politician will find that they agree on the one issue and get that vote, even if they disagree on all other matters.

Convincing politicians to vote for another politician in an intra-branch election is different. There is still the need to communicate directly with the individual members who will be voting.

As important, though, is convincing the people who prop up and fund the politicians to support a candidate. Nothing helps a politician make up their mind more than someone with a name they recognize from a check telling them to do something.

Gregory had learned this lesson many years ago. Which is why, instead of reaching out to members of the GOP caucus, he went after the upper elite of Tennessee's economy. He had a few connections to those people, but he needed to leverage those connections immediately. With any luck, he would hit the right pressure points and get the momentum going in Larry's direction. Just a small push on his part might do the trick.

Gregory's first call, his only call, after his subordinates left, was to Thomas Ashford. Thomas owned eighteen different car lots across middle Tennessee. He sold new Hondas, Mitsubishis, Mazdas, Fords, and Jaguars. This also included the used car lots he owned that sold any brand he could find. He was the son of an auto dealer, but his father had only had six car lots, and Thomas had done the work to open the other twelve. Once he hit the age of thirty he was already one of the richest men in middle Tennessee; at least, he was one of the richest who wasn't involved with healthcare. Thomas had always been willing to use his fortune to help get Republicans elected. This was unsurprising: he wanted lower taxes, he wanted to be able to sell a car without having to worry about being sued when it fell apart two weeks later. Every Republican across the state who had run for any major political office had received at least one check from Thomas Ashford. Every Republican, except for whichever Republican who decided to run against Gregory Anderson.

Gregory and Thomas met during their freshman year at Vanderbilt University. Gregory, who had been born and raised in Elizabethton, Tennessee, a small city along the North Carolina border in northeast Tennessee, was a small-town kid experiencing the wonders a big city life in Nashville had to offer for the first time. He was there on a partial academic and a partial athletic scholarship. He had to get a job reshelving the books in the library after basketball practice at night to pay for meals on the weekends.

Thomas had gotten into Vanderbilt with a high school GPA that hovered just below three; he would graduate college with a GPA just above two. He had no scholarships, needed no job, and was able to have a car on campus which was a luxury for a freshman.

The two young men who came from very different worlds found they had a few things in common. They both enjoyed hard liquor, they both enjoyed gambling, they enjoyed football, and the handsome freshmen both had a knack with pretty women. They quickly bonded and became inseparable for the next four years. After graduating they went their separate ways in life. Gregory went to law school at UVA, Thomas took over the family business. They reconnected several years later upon Gregory's return to Nashville and remained friends ever since. Their relationship was politically complicated; Gregory never received money from Thomas, but Thomas withholding funds from Gregory's opponents was just as good.

Smander's was a five-star restaurant just across Rosa Parks Avenue from Bicentennial Park in downtown Nashville in a restored, two-story Victorian house. Its specialty was southern fashion cuisine, although no one really knew what that meant because southern food is just food in the south. Thomas owned a five percent interest in the restaurant which was good enough to have a private booth just behind the basement bar.

Gregory arrived five minutes late in hopes that Thomas would arrive first and get to the booth, otherwise he would have to sit at the bar and wait for his friend to arrive. He had made it clear to Thomas that this was going to be a business lunch when they spoke earlier on the phone. As he walked past the bar, he felt a hand grab him by the elbow. He turned and saw Thomas; the two men laughed and hugged as they greeted each other. Then walked to the private booth.

"You're looking great, for an old man," said Gregory as he took his seat.

"Yeah, well a good surgeon always helps," laughed Thomas. The waitress came to the table and took their drink orders; the two men went ahead and ordered their food since they had the lunch menu memorized. They watched the waitress walk away.

"I tell you this," began Gregory, "nothing much better than a brunette waitress."

Thomas laughed, "It sure does do wonders for the appetite."

"Look, I'll get to the point Thomas," said Gregory.

"Oh boy, this must be serious."

"It's about the next Speaker of the House."

Thomas leaned back in the booth. "Greg. I can't help you with Caputo."

"That's not why I'm here," said Gregory.

"Sure it's not. Everybody in the know knows y'all are doing anything you can to save his ass. And you know I can't support a Democrat, my reputation will be shot," said Thomas.

"Man, Caputo is done. He's not going to be Speaker. We've moved on. Now we are trying to, let's say, lessen the damage," Gregory responded as delicately as he could.

"I'm not following."

"Our goal now is to not have Humphrey become Speaker." Gregory could see Thomas was still not getting it. "Larry Pickard, he's from east Tennessee, do you know him?"

"Yeah, I know him," said Thomas.

"He's running against Humphrey, in their caucus, for the Speaker nom."

"No shit?"

"No shit," said Gregory plainly.

"And you want me to pull some strings for him?"

"Yes, exactly. Look here, Larry actually makes more sense for you. Joe Humphrey is a firebrand, a cultural warrior. He's less concerned about business and such, and more concerned about gays and abortion and prayer in school."

"I'm pro-life and support prayer in schools," said Thomas.

"Bullshit! Since when?" asked Gregory with disbelief.

"Buddy, I've been born again – don't you know?" Gregory stared at his friend. "I'm just fucking with you, Greg. Lighten up," laughed Thomas. Gregory didn't laugh.

"Thomas, the House Dems have been pretty good to you. Not great, but pretty good, and the Governor who was also your mayor at one point, he has been pretty good to you too. But under Humphrey we won't be able to do shit for you."

"Why not?"

"Joe Humphrey will hold everything we want, or even remotely support, hostage to get the votes he needs for his far-right bullshit. Even then, there will be people in our caucus who will refuse to vote for the good stuff because he's forcing through the bad."

"Can't you control your caucus?" asked Thomas.

"Not to be clichéd, but we are in uncharted waters," said Gregory. "I have no idea what the people on my side are going to do. We have enough seats as a minority to cause a lot of headaches and grind things to a halt under Humphrey. But with Larry we can work to get things done. He'll be fair and will put the state, especially the economy, first. We're in a recession. We don't need evangelism right now, we need to get our money moving again. You know that."

Thomas thought about the recent meetings he had with his finance people. If things didn't turn around soon, he was going to have to close a couple of car lots. The thought was too embarrassing to talk about, even with his old friend sitting across from him. But Thomas suspected Gregory knew this, because Gregory was the smartest friend he'd ever had. He got the point.

"Ok," said Thomas.

"Ok?" asked Gregory.

"I'll help get Larry in. I'll make some calls to some other big donors, we'll start writing big checks to him and that'll send a message. I, and some other folks in my circle, will even call some Reps and let them know where we stand. You don't need to know the details, I'll take it from here," said Thomas.

"Ok then," said Gregory. The waitress arrived with their cocktails and let them know their food would be out in a minute. "Hell, I thought it would take more time to convince you."

"A hot shot lawyer like you? Come on." Thomas took a sip of his Jack on the rocks.

"Now what are we going to talk about?"

"You cheating on your new wife yet?" asked Thomas.

"Hell man, we just got married in May," laughed Gregory.

"So?"

"Yeah, but only with my second wife," Gregory smiled as he took a drink.

"Really?"

He shrugged and swallowed his drink. "What can I say? She's been working out."

"You dog," Thomas laughed and tipped his glass to his friend who did the same.

CHAPTER 6

Thursday, December 11, 2008

Every morning Mary Ellen Guess wakes up at six, gets on her bike, and pedals her way into a new day. The exceptions to this are snow and ice, if she's traveling, or if she has a meeting somewhere too early in the morning for her to get ready after her ride, in which case she rides the stationary bike in her basement while watching the ten o'clock news at night.

She enjoys the quiet of her morning rides and the rush of fresh morning air sweeping across her face. She loves how fast she feels, the feeling of speed and power. She knows she can't be going faster than twenty miles an hour, but that is enough for her to escape from her life and work. She loves to feel her long blonde hair blowing in breeze that she is creating with her own force. Occasionally she pretends she is the first woman to win the men's Tour de France, riding into her garage with her arms raised above her head. It's something that won't come true, she knows that, but she still has her eyes set on being the first woman in Tennessee to be Speaker of the House, and Governor. Two dreams that had seemed impossible a year ago, but now they were within reach. She knows how to make those dreams happen and she has a plan. Rather, she had a plan that was working itself out perfectly until late last week when someone decided to mess the whole thing up. She had a suspicion of who, and her ride this morning was with a purpose to confront that person.

The dividing line between the 53rd and 52nd Legislative Districts in Nashville runs down the middle of Woodmont Boulevard and stretches from the 100 Oaks area all the way to the Green Hills Mall where the line then goes south down Hillsboro Pike. This creates an interesting scenario in which one Nashville neighborhood has two State Representatives. Mary Ellen, a former Vice Provost at Lipscomb University, the youngest in the school's long history, lives in a sprawling five-bedroom Tudor just behind campus off of Belmont Boulevard, with her Fortune 500 CFO husband. It is less than a quarter of a mile down Belmont Boulevard, crossing Woodmont Boulevard; in another quarter of a mile on the left sits Gregory Anderson's turn-of-the-century southern craftsman home.

Living in such close proximity, the two State Representatives had become friends, almost like siblings with a decade's age difference. At one point, many years ago, Gregory was Mary Ellen's City Council member. They belonged to the same country clubs and had similar social circles. They even hosted a yearly charitable golf tournament together. It wasn't uncommon to see the two dining together at one of the many trendy restaurants in their neighborhood. Both being moderates in their political beliefs, but being forced into playing the roles dwelling at the furthest reaches of their respective wings in public, the two found out just how much they had in common. They represented the normal Nashville politics in a way that ran counter to the emerging trends in the state.

She could see his porch lights were on, which wasn't out of the ordinary. She slowed down as she approached; her brakes ached and whined in the cold winter morning. Gregory was sitting in a rocking chair on his front porch, still in his pajamas and robe, enjoying his coffee and reading his newspaper. He watched her take her helmet off and lean her bike against his iron fence.

"Good morning there, speed racer," Gregory, ever the morning person when he had a good night's rest, called out to her.

"Don't play nice with me, you slab of shit," said Mary Ellen, breathing heavy from her ride; the clouds from her breath forming in the air like fog.

"Fine then, I take it back," said Gregory as he stood up and dusted off the rocking chair that sat on the other side of the front door . "Have a seat, hateful."

"No, I won't be sitting down for this," she said.

"Why do I feel like my mom is about to lecture me for peeping up skirts at a basketball game?"

"What do you think you're doing? Messing in our caucus business! What if we did this horseshit to you?"

"I don't know what you're talking about, maybe explain it a little bit more."

"You know damn well what I mean! Tom Ashford, your old roommate Greg Griffin, John Bostone, and all the other rich fucks in this city are calling and telling our members they want Larry over Joe. Now why in the fuck would they want one over the other when they know they'll get the same shit from both?"

Greg blew some steam from his coffee, causing his glasses to fog slightly. "That's easy; Larry is focused on business and Joe is focused on lightning rods."

"Good lord, give me a break! You know that shit doesn't matter when you're Speaker."

"You know, for a southern lady you've got a dirty mouth," Gregory said. His demeanor was suddenly serious. He and Mary Ellen had never argued over politics before this moment. Policy, yes, thousands of times. But an argument over the game of politics was new.

"Fuck you, I grew up in Michigan," she said with the stern look she had mastered on her four sons.

"I figured you, being . . . you know," he pointed at her with the newspaper and shrugged, "who you are, would be happy to see Larry as Speaker." Gregory crossed his legs, left over right, and began to rock.

"Don't try to pull that shit on me, I'm not like you--"

"Bullshit. We are the exact same."

"No, I don't have to get my piece of ass a job or promotions and shit to keep them interested." She crossed her arms and leaned against one of the columns on his porch.

"Maybe not, but you don't honestly give a shit about Joe being Speaker, you only care about--"

"I care about keeping my party together--"

"You care that Joe wants to be out of the chair in four years, while Larry might be in it for good--"

"What the hell?"

"You want to Speaker," he said, pointing at her.

"You're damn right, and so do you," she said, stepping towards him and pointing back at him.

"Ha! No, I don't," he rolled his eyes. "You slip some vodka in your water bottle this morning?"

"Yes you do," she said. "That's why you never ran for State Senate, or Mayor, or Congress. You want to be Speaker as bad as I do, but the difference is you're too late. You waited too long for Caputo to retire and now you'll never be Speaker. You've reached your peak, Greg, and we both know it. We both want to be Speaker, but I'm the only one who still has a chance. Meanwhile, you're still doing Caputo's dirty work for no good damn reason!" She crossed her arms and looked down at him. He had stopped rocking and was staring at her silently.

"Do you want to know why I made the call to Thomas Ashford?" he said calmly.

"I don't care," she replied.

"It's not because I want to be Speaker and I'm taking my rage out on the man who's taking my place. Although there may be some truth to that." He paused and took a sip of coffee. "It's not because I particularly dislike Joe, which is also partly true. It's not even because Joe wants to fire everyone who works at Legislative Plaza and bring in people loyal only to him, or because he's going to bring in all that right-wing legislative bullshit and make sure it passes. No, I don't give a shit about any of that. I don't want Joe Humphrey to be Speaker because I enjoy my life the way it is and he's a threat to it. I enjoy the booze, the parties, the women, the arguments, the votes, and he could end all of those things. This stopped being about finding a couple of votes for Caputo a long, long, time ago."

Mary Ellen looked at Gregory as he took another sip of his coffee. She knew he was right about Joe, but she wasn't about to admit it. She walked over and sat down in the other rocking chair. She adjusted her sweatshirt. She was considering what she was going to say, as Gregory handed her his mug of coffee. She grabbed it and took a small sip; it burned and she struggled to swallow it.

"What's in here, whiskey?" she asked.

"Obviously. The sun's up, ain't it?" said Gregory as he rubbed his glasses on his robe and returned to the paper. Mary Ellen noticed the sun had indeed come up during their conversation. She tried to hand the mug back to him but he held up his hand. "You finish it," he said. They sat in silence as Gregory thumbed through the business section. Mary Ellen drank the spiked coffee, letting the whiskey burn her throat and cool her anger. Gregory folded up part of the paper and sat it on the table beside his chair.

"You know," he said, "you could be Speaker in January, I can get you forty-nine votes. That, plus your own vote, and you got it."

Mary Ellen laughed. "Shit, and be Speaker for two years and then out of politics? No thank you."

"No, be Speaker for two years then spend two years running for Governor," Gregory said, turning to look at her.

"And what? Run for Governor as an independent? Fuck that."

"You would be seen as a bridge between the parties; the people here would eat that shit up. Our state is more divided now than ever. Well, except for during the Civil War. And during Reconstruction. Maybe during Prohibition, too. And Women's

Suffrage. Oh, and the Civil Rights Movement. But definitely in last half-century, this is the most divided we've been."

"You really don't see what's happened here do you, Gregory? This state is turning as red as cherries. We are sitting in one of the last strongholds of your party. I'll stick to my plan, and you stick to yours. Joe is scared shitless. Last count he was only up five votes on Larry, and once I'm done with this," she tapped the mug with her fingernail, "he may only be up four."

Gregory laughed and gathered up the newspaper as he stood up. He handed the paper over to Mary Ellen. "Take your time and finish up, I've got to get ready and finish planning our caucus retreat."

"Where y'all meeting? Corner booth at the Waffle House?" she asked with a smirk.

"Maybe you've had enough," he reached down and took the mug away from her. She noticed he was smiling as he went into his house. She laughed and walked down the sidewalk to her bike. She rode home thinking, forty-nine votes plus her own. She could be Speaker. But she knew better; that plan was awful.

CHAPTER 7

Friday, December 12, 2008

Joe liked to eat his lunch on the screened in patio off his living room on days when he did not have to be at the pharmacy, which was most days. His mom and dad had opened two pharmacies when he was a child. After completing pharmacy school and moving back to Colonial Heights, his father promptly retired and gave his half of the business to Joe. Joe and his mother, who ran the actual business and maintained the title of company president, opened three more locations throughout rural east Tennessee in communities that the suits at the major pharmacy chains had never found, and will never find, on a map. Joe worked only two mornings a week and covered shifts for the other pharmacists he employed. For the most part, however, his job was owner of the chain.

He turned on the small TV on the patio, mostly for background noise. He didn't mind the cold, in fact he enjoyed it, but he turned on the heaters to keep from getting sick. He sat at the little table behind the couch and began to eat the leftover spaghetti he had warmed in the microwave. He thumbed through papers his wife had left him to look over. After years of trying to have a child they had decided to adopt. The process was much more complicated than they were expecting, yet they were close. Next summer they might just be parents.

The process had demonstrated to Joe how cumbersome big government could really be. Up until they had decided to adopt a child, his only interaction with the big government boogie-man had been paying taxes, renewing licenses, and changes to pre-scription drug law. He had been isolated from the government overreach into his business by his mother. Over-regulation, over-reach, swollen bureaucracy, had all been words in lines he had memorized and regurgitated to impress admiring constituents. This experience, the simple act of trying to show a child they are loved, simply wanting to give a child a home, had finally given him first-hand experience of the big government he always said he hated. Making adoption simpler in Tennessee was going to be a focal point of his Governor's campaign in four years. Establish-ing adoption reciprocity with other states, one-sheet adoption, one-time fee to end the nickel and diming that surely prevents would-be parents from adopting American children. It would change lives, not to mention bolster his pro-life credentials.

His phone rang as he began to twirl spaghetti with his fork. He checked the name on the screen – Andrew Mansfield, a State Representative from Tracy City and Joe's pick to chair the Busi-ness & Industry Committee.

"Mr. Chairman, how you doing?" Joe jokingly asked as he took the first bite of his lunch.

"Not great, Leader. You got a sec?" asked Andrew.

"Sure do, are you ok?" Joe's voice switched to genuine concern.

"Well, Leader, I'm not even sure how to bring this up. Let me ask you this, you keep up with the newspapers in Nashville? The online ones?"

"No . . ." said Joe as more of a question than answer.

"Well, there's this one, it's got pretty good coverage of politics and such statewide and they put their stuff online. It's called the *Nashville Rag.*"

"Yeah, I check in on that one from time to time," said Joe, taking another bite.

"Anyway, they've got this story up about you. About your first marriage." Joe immediately lost his appetite. He was silent and shocked; he couldn't believe someone had found out about Ramona.

"What's it say?" Joe asked

"Says that the records aren't clear but that unnamed sources are saying you cheated on her, maybe even abused her, until finally she left and then you stopped paying her alimony."

"What the hell? Andrew, with God as my witness I never did any of that shit!" said Joe. "Well, except the alimony thing. But I thought she had gotten remarried, was happy Holly Homemaker now."

"Joe, seems like most of us didn't even know you had an ex-wife. Then it turns out you might have cheated on her? I don't know about this."

"Listen, Andrew, here's what happened. I got with the girl, we dated for like three weeks, and she got pregnant so we got married. She lost the baby, we decided to stay together for a little while after that, but she didn't want to move out here and I was ready to get the hell out of Memphis. That's it! No drama, no cheating, no nothing."

"I believe you, Joe. I'm only calling to let you know about it so you can get ahead of it," said Andrew with concern.

"Thanks, man. I better get off of here and call some people about handling this." Joe stood up to walk his plate back to the sink.

"Alright, buddy. You still got my vote, just so you know," said Andrew.

"Ok, thanks, I appreciate it." He hung up.

He walked down to his basement and into his office. He turned on his computer and went to the *Nashville Rag*'s political section and saw his face with the headline "Man to be Speaker has Checkered Past with Women". He read the article line by line twice, ignoring four phone calls in the process. When he had satisfied his curiosity, he called the Caucus Press secretary Kylie Stewart, who technically worked for Mike Hayes. He felt very little emotion; a numb confusion had taken over. Kylie's phone stopped ringing. He dialed Mike's office directly – if the phone on his desk rang, every phone is his office suite would ring too.

A breathless Kylie answered the phone. "Hey Leader, sorry I was running back as quick as I could when I heard my phone ringing."

"Kylie, I'm assuming you've read this horse shit about me on the aptly named *Nashville Rag*," Joe said calmly.

"Yes sir," said Kylie. Joe could hear her chair strain as she sat down. Kylie wasn't a big woman, but always had a way of sitting that would cause the chair to want to give up. "I tried calling you when they first posted it about an hour ago but couldn't seem to find you. Sir, did they ask you for a comment or anything?"

"No, I don't think they did anyway. They might have reached out to my office but if they did it didn't get to me. Marcy normally refers the press to you."

"Ok, well, this isn't the most reputable news source, so that's not surprising. Plus, releasing it this late on a Friday, that tells me they don't really have any good sources."

"I want to put out a statement, asserting that none of this stuff is true."

"Leader Humphrey, I think that's a good idea. Mind if I get Caroline from the State Party on the call with us and we can workshop this stuff out?"

"No, I don't mind, actually I think that's a great idea," Joe said as he walked back upstairs.

"Ok, give me a sec, I told her I'd be calling her back when I got ahold of you so it shouldn't take too long. Let me put you on hold." Kylie is sweet, Joe thought, but she talks a lot for someone who has made a career out of coming up with concise statements. He went into the kitchen and got a beer out of the fridge. He hardly ever drank during the day, but this was going to be one hell of a twenty-four hours, so he decided a couple of drinks wouldn't hurt.

Kylie's voice broke out of the silence on the phone, "Leader are you still there!?" She was screaming and sounded like she was at an indoor pool.

"Yes, am I on speakerphone?" Joe asked.

"Yes you are, Leader." Joe instantly recognized Mike's voice. "By the way, I read that bullshit they wrote about you. We're going to hand that paper their nuts in a jar." Joe rolled his eyes; he always appreciated the passion and loyalty of his friend but it could be a bit much.

"Is Caroline on?" Joe asked.

"I'm here, Leader," Caroline said with a thick southern accent that had originated deep in Alabama, not Tennessee.

"Ok, what do you think?" asked Joe.

"Well," said Caroline, "I think I know the answer to this, but I still have to ask – is any of this stuff true?"

"No," Joe responded. "Well, none of the juicy stuff anyway. I was married before, that's true, but all the rest is garbage."

"We know, Joe," said Mike. "Caroline, Joe being married before is no secret to some of us. Outside of our little circle some people may know but Joe has kept it private for the most part." Joe rolled his eyes, again.

"That's a good thing," said Caroline. "If people already knew about the previous marriage then that's not big news, we can play it off as 'well of course he was married before, just about everyone knows that.' Now, are you sure there are no court records, or criminal records, that could in any way corroborate the more scandalous parts of this story?"

"Hell no," said Joe.

"Ok, then, here's what we do. We release a statement and give it to a handful of the Nashville press – the real press not bloggers. We point out that your previous marriage is a well-known fact that ended on amicable terms, we paint it as two young people going in different directions. We deny all the other details. Are you still on good terms with your divorce attorney?"

"Yeah, we haven't talked in a couple years. But sure," said Joe.

"Ok then we get him to comment and say none of it is true. And we paint this as the biased liberal media on the local level, who didn't even ask you or your ex about it, and you come out squeaky clean."

"I like it. Do we need my ex-wife to comment? I think she might."

"Let's not," said Caroline. "If the press wants her to comment they can ask her themselves."

"Sounds good to me," said Joe. "Kylie, what do you think?" There was a pause; Joe imagined that Kylie was looking at Mike for permission to speak, because that's the kind of asshole Mike is.

"I like it," said Kylie.

"Alright then, let's do it," said Joe.

The group talked a little longer, exchanged details and phone numbers to get in touch with certain people, deadlines to meet, and when they would talk again. After hanging up, Joe looked at his phone which was filled with text messages and missed calls that all came in during the brief conversation. He hung his head and sighed. Politics could get dirty, he knew that. He wasn't a fan of politics, he enjoyed governing. He looked up and saw his reflection in the TV. He asked himself if he really had the stomach to do this; did he have what it takes to get hit with this sort of bullshit and keep moving, and not be distracted by it? He knew he could hand out this sort of thing, but he hated this feeling, he hated getting hit even though he didn't mind hitting in the least.

His despair quickly turned to rage and anger. He wanted to make the hour and a half drive down to Sevier County, kick in Larry Pickard's door, and ring his neck. His reputation, he thought, was shattered anyway – might as well murder someone. He reached for his phone, knowing that cursing the man out would come with a shorter prison sentence and save a lot of money on gas. As he found the name in his contacts he stopped.

Eight years ago, he had been a freshman State Representative. He had gotten lost on his way to his new office in Legislative Plaza. After doing three laps around the maze of hallways, trying his best to look like he knew what he was doing, he was walked past the cafeteria, Larry walked out of the glass door carrying a cup of coffee and casually throwing the stirring stick away in the trash can without looking. Joe had marveled at how the man looked so natural and at home in that building. Larry looked up and saw Joe walking towards him.

"Hey partner," said Larry sticking his hand out. Joe grabbed it and shook. "What're you doing up here? We don't start for another week."

"Well, small town boy in the big city. You know the story, I need to get the lay of the land and whatnot," Joe said laughing. The two men began to walk down the main hallway.

"How far of a drive is it for you to get down here?"

"Oh, right at five hours," said Joe.

"Yeah, same for me, but that's only because it takes me an hour to get to the interstate from my house." Larry stuck his arm out in front of Joe, like a parent would for a child sitting the front seat before slamming on the breaks in a car, and stopped walking. "I don't know if anybody has shown you around yet, but to the left here, is the Speaker's office." Larry pointed to the grand oak double doors, twice as tall and twice as wide as any other doors in the Plaza. "That's Caputo's office; he's a Democrat the same way lots of us are Republicans, he was born into it, but when push comes to shove he's with us more than he's with his own party. He's an alright guy, don't be afraid to speak to him. Play your cards right, that could be you one day." They started walking again into the lobby area past the escalators.

"I don't know about that," Joe said.

"You might not but I do. Eight Democrats are about to get busted on corruption, we're about to take the White House back, beating a Tennessee Democrat for it, the party nationally is starting to invest in state races, and we'll be in control soon. You've got a safe district; my advice would be to raise a shit ton of money and hand it out to other people running." Larry laughed and patted Joe on the back.

He pointed out the House Committee rooms, the side stairwell that was hidden just behind the coffee makers, the press room which came with a warning to keep quiet when you walked past it. They passed the front door where Larry introduced Joe to the State Trooper who was on guard that day. He briefly pointed out their minority leadership offices and the bathrooms. They turned a corner and talked about what bills Joe was thinking about taking on that year, Larry asked Joe if he drank and Joe said occasionally. They stopped again in front of a shared office suite.

"Well," said Larry. "Nice talking to you, I'll let you get to it. I gotta get back upstairs, you'll figure your way around this place soon enough," Larry winked and shook Joe's hand again and walked away down the hall. Without Joe having to tell him, Larry knew he had been lost, and without having to make Joe admit it, Larry had led him back to his office.

He understood that times and dynamics had changed since then, but Joe could not bring himself to believe that Larry would do something like this. Larry, for all his faults, was a decent person who wouldn't stoop to something this low. He decided to call him anyway. The phone rang twice.

"I was wondering when I'd hear from you," Larry said with a laugh.

Joe smiled. "Yeah, well I wanted to make sure it wasn't you."

"Hell, Joe, I don't have the time or the money to do this kind of shit. I will say this though, this kind of garbage, and I know it's not true, this isn't something you do to try and stop some race like this. If anything it's gonna galvanize people to get behind you. I'm kind of pissed about it myself," Larry laughed again and Joe could tell he was a little drunk. "No, whoever did this thinks you're going to be Speaker and they want to delegitimize anything you try to do. It was probably a Democrat, if not their State Party. You got them shaking, seems like."

"Yeah, well I'm still pissed about it," Joe said.

"Hell, the Canadians have a saying. When you're pissed, get pissed . . . as in drunk," said Larry.

The conversation ended with laughs. Joe could not help but think of how amicable Larry could be when he's drunk, but getting drunk in the middle of the day was unbecoming for the Speaker of the House. He would have to let Mike know about it.

Larry, however, had only acted drunk. He was actually on his way to pick up Harry Sells. Harry was the oldest member of the Republican House Caucus in terms of age, quickly approaching eighty-one. Harry and his wife Ellen loved to eat at the Hadrin's Pharmacy in Lenoir City for lunch every day. Larry had offered to take the two anywhere Ellen wanted to go, but she just wanted their normal lunch spot. It was going to be one of the cheapest votes Larry got.

He had been to Hadrin's Pharmacy once before, when Samuel Hodges was running for Congress some twenty years ago and Larry was one of his campaign chairs. Hadrin's was a good spot for a photo op. Of course, back then the owners were devoted Democrats but they were kind enough to let the Republican Congressional nominee and his entourage eat at their little snack bar on Main Street. Fast forward to now – those same owners were some of Harry Sells' most fervent supporters, devoted donors to the state Republican Party, and sponsors of the pro-life rallies in Loudon County. Larry could not help but wonder if they had left the Democratic Party or if the Democratic Party had left them. Either way, it was the story of the political winds in the south.

He pulled his car into one of the spots on main street and looked at the building. The political allegiance of the owners may have changed but the décor hadn't; nor, for that matter, had main street. He was greeted at the door by no one: it was a seat yourself kind of place. He examined the walls: same knickknacks, same newspaper clippings, same state championship banners for the football and baseball teams. He noted the absence of a banner for the girls' basketball team that had won the state championship five years earlier. He walked through the rows of candy and books on the store side and then into the diner side where he saw Harry and Ellen seated at a table by the window. He changed his expression from serious to friendly. He hated to fake it, but he had to do it.

"Larry, Larry, Larry, it's great to see you," said Harry extending his hand.

"You too Harry," said Larry. "You ready for the crazy to start up again?" The two men laughed.

"Larry, this is my wife, Ellen," Harry said, gesturing to the woman in a long denim skirt with silver hair pulled back into a tight bun seated next to him. "Y'all met before."

"Of course we have, I'd never forget such a pretty face," said Larry taking the old woman's hand and clasping it between his.

"Oh, Larry," she said waving him off with her free hand. "It's wonderful to see you again."
"And you, Mrs. Sells."

"Please call me Ellen."

"I will do no such thing," Larry laughed as the trio sat down. A waitress came over and took their drink order: two black coffees and a sweet tea.

"Now, Larry, I got some news for you," said Harry, chubby elbows on the table and rubbing his hands together. He looked away from Larry.

"Oh boy, this can't be good," said Larry with a chuckle.

"Well, now just hear me out," said Harry. "I know why you're here and I've got an answer for you, but I need to explain things first. I'm retiring from office; this is my last session."

"Oh no," said Larry trying to sound sincere and shocked. Truth was Harry was born closer to the Civil War than the internet, so his retirement was a bit overdue.

"To be honest, Larry," said Ellen in a meek voice, "I've told him he can't run again. The Lord is now counting our lives in months, not years, and it's high time we spent some days together."

"I can respect that," Larry said, looking at Ellen sincerely. He looked at Harry. "And if mama ain't happy, you ain't happy." The group laughed.

"That's true," said Ellen, pointing a bony finger at him with a wholesome smile.

"That brings me to my point, Larry," continued Harry, averting his gaze again. "It got me thinking, what does our party have, and what's it need, now that I'm leaving? We finally got the State House, we got the State Senate, we got some Congressional seats, a US Senator, but we have to start thinking about the future. We need to build a bench of leaders to carry on, and all that. Well, cut to the chase, I'm voting for Joe to be Speaker." Larry felt his stomach turn; he would've bet his house that Harry's vote was his. A path to victory was much harder now, and the margin of error even slimmer.

"Now look," Harry continued, finally meeting eyes with Larry, "I respect you and I want to vote for you, but the fact is we need people who can run for Governor or US Senator in two years, four years, eight years. Joe can give us that. If I was going to be in office another decade, you'd be my guy. Honest to God, you'd be my guy because your ambition would stop with the Speaker's gavel, and you'd give us some stability in the House. You'd probably be Speaker for another twenty years. That's not what we need though. Now the party is competitive, we don't need to run sacrificial lambs statewide anymore. We need people who have the resume to win those races. Look at what we got, we've got one former Governor, and the Lieutenant Governor who's a bit too . . . country, and a couple of dopey Congressmen, maybe a mayor somewhere, and that's it. We can't pluck up some nobody State Rep or some rich businessman to run for the US Senate anymore. We have like two mayors of big cities and a few Congressmen, but we need to protect those seats. We need a Speaker who is willing to run for higher office; they have to be young and ambitious. That's Joe. I'm sorry, old friend, but that's just how I see things now."

Larry was disappointed, down to his bones. Harry wasn't the sharpest political mind, but Larry understood his point.

"I can't say I'm not disappointed," said Larry, disheartened.

"We know," said Ellen.

"But I can respect your point of view," Larry tried to mask his frustration. "Would you know if anyone else feels this way?"

"I haven't talked to anybody about it. Not even Joe. To be honest, not many of us are talking about the Speaker's race at all. We're worried it's going to divide the caucus," said Harry with concern.

"Harry, thank you for telling me, I do appreciate it," said Larry. Harry reached out and patted Larry's hand.

"Do you think," began Ellen timidly, " Do you think that maybe the three of us could have lunch. Just as friends? Not talk about politics now that we got that out of the way?"

"I sure would like that," lied Larry.

"You're still paying, right?" Harry asked with a laugh.

"You rascal," said Larry, faking friendly. "Of course. And, Ellen, I promise no more talk of politics."

The waitress came back with drinks and took their order. They ate their food, talked about grandkids, talked about college football, and the like. Larry ate his grilled cheese and soup, politely making an hour of small talk. He left Lenoir City as soon as he got the change back from the check, and he swore he would never come back.

Murfreesboro is at the geographic center of Tennessee. At one time the small city, located just under an hour's drive southeast from Nashville, had been considered a suitable location for the state's capitol. However it was lacking two things that Nashville had: the first was a major waterway that could be used by politicians to easily reach the Capitol and second was a booming economy. Murfreesboro got a pretty good consolation prize out of the deal; it became home to the aptly named Middle Tennessee State University. The largest college in the state.

The Democratic House Caucus – more specifically, Tom – had chosen a classroom in The Bas Building on the outskirts of campus of MTSU as the site for their so-called retreat. With no freshmen members, there was no need for parliamentary procedure training. Instead the one day, eight-hour meeting would focus on the importance of re-electing Caputo as Speaker, regardless of how futile the effort may be, and to elect their leadership positions. Unlike their Republican counterparts, the Democrats – again, more specifically, Tom – realized the importance of having leadership in place going into such a divided time in the legislature. Nominations and voting would all take place during the last hour and a half of the day.

Things started off smooth enough. Derek James from the Governor's Legislative Office had given the caucus a run down on the legislative priorities that would be coming from his boss. "Bipartisanship, statesmanship, and Tennessee Harmony, that's what the governor wants," Derek had told them. This meant no controversial bills from either party would receive the Governor's signature; a few scoffed at the idea since only a simple majority was required to overturn the Governor's veto. Nevertheless, Derek insisted that the Governor would only be endorsing bills that focused on governing. Derek was well-liked by the caucus members. An intern for former House member Eddie Atrum, Derek had been in the halls of Legislative Plaza for over a decade. The members were proud of the work he was now doing, and so they left him alone.

Charlie followed Derek to give an update on the Governor's inauguration. He had been told to keep his portion brief, which wasn't hard considering Charlie had yet to go to any of the inaugural committee meetings. He did pass along the little information he did have: "Each member will get two tickets. You can have them mailed to you or I can drop them off in your office, up to you." That was that.

The large classroom with auditorium seating and white walls felt empty with only the forty-nine members of the caucus occupying seats. Several staff members had made the short drive down from Nashville to attend, but even with them in attendance the room was barely at half capacity. These were the things Speaker Caputo noticed as he walked to the lectern in the front of the room to deliver his remarks. He couldn't help but remember the years when his party had been a super-majority. In the early 1980s, when he was first elected Speaker, their caucus had numbered in the low eighties. The legislature would bend to his will with little effort back then. He had seen the Tennessee Democratic Party build an empire, and now he was watching it fall.

He approached the podium and stepped up with a smile.

"Thank you all for making the trip today. Sorry everything sort of got thrown together here but we'll get through it." The room laughed. Caputo was well-liked and had become a popular politician because of his plain-spoken style and calm demeanor. Very few of his colleagues in politics had seen his fiery side, though everyone had heard stories. He continued, "I am not going to sugarcoat this, folks. We are hurting, we got our ass handed to us in November and it looks like the tide isn't going to be retreating any time soon. These next two years are going to test us. They're going to test our smarts, and more importantly they are going to test us as a party. But, you know, if we stick together we can stop a lot of the bad stuff the other side is going to try and do.

"You know, I've been Speaker so long that I have forgotten how to be a member," he paused for the laughter and rearranged his notes on the lectern. "But here's what I do remember. A lot is asked of you. You are told how to vote by your constituents, your friends, your family, by lobbyists, and your party." Caputo held up a finger on his left hand after naming each group until all five fingers were up. "That's five different groups telling you what to do, how to think, talking at you about the ramifications. But there's only one thing you've got to listen to," he put down four fingers, and then tapped his heart with his left index finger, "and it's right here. As long as you follow this, you can't go wrong." There were some shouts of 'amen' and words of agreement. Most people in the room thought the Speaker was telling them to follow their heart; Charlie could not help but notice the Speaker was pointing to himself – as long as they followed him they can't go wrong. Charlie appreciated the subconsciousness of the demonstration.

"I know," continued Caputo, "that this is not what we wanted. No one in this room wants to be in the minority. Some of our members here have been in the minority their whole lives and they know what can happen when a monolithic group is in power. It ain't good for the minority. But here's what we're facing. We're up against a group that don't think workers deserve a say in their work. We're up against a group that don't think people who can't find a job deserve to see a doctor. We're up against a group that thinks teachers are paid too much and CEOs are paid too little. We're up against a group that don't think farmers and waitresses deserve a seat at the table they helped set. We can't afford to leave those people behind; we have to stick together and fight for them, not us." There was applause in the room that took a minute to die down.

"I know some of you are considering crossing over the aisle to vote for a new Speaker," Caputo said, changing into a serious tone. "I'm not blind, or deaf. Ok? I may be dumb, but I'm not blind or deaf." He paused for what he thought would be laughter, but there was none. "Let me go ahead and address this head on. Do not do that. Those five groups I mentioned, well four of the five, go on and take the lobbyists out of it. Those remaining four groups elected you for your leadership, but they also elected you to stand up for those people that the other side is going after. Voting for a Speaker who is going to go after them means you lose your seat. If you're going to vote for a Republican, what's going to stop your district from voting for one? Or what's going to stop someone from running against you in a primary and calling you a Republican for four months? If you don't want to vote for me, that's your business, run someone else from the caucus. But don't vote for the Republican nominee and violate everything you stood for during your campaign." Caputo was breathing heavy; he could feel a long-forgotten passion building in his chest. He checked the emotion, deciding it was time to cut his speech short. "And, well, it's getting close to lunch and that's all I have to say. Daniel, you want to tell us what's next?" Caputo walked back towards his seat. There was a mix of polite applause and enthusiastic cheers.

Daniel Burns, Democratic Caucus Chairman, walked to the lectern. He paused briefly to shake the Speaker's hand and give him a pat on the back. Daniel approached the lectern as if it was a stove that had just been shut off and he wasn't sure if it was still hot or not. As he began to speak to the crowd about their late lunch, which had been graciously provided by the Tennessee Lobbyist Association, and the presentations that would be given that afternoon, Gregory made his way over to Xavier Jarvis, Chairman of the Tennessee Black Caucus.

Gregory bent over at the waist so he could be eye level with the seated Xavier. "Jarvis, let me talk with the Black Caucus together during lunch," Gregory whispered.

"And why would I do that?" said Xavier in what was meant to be a whisper but with his deep voice and preacher's cadence, his question was heard by most of the room.

"Because," said Gregory, "I know some of them are planning to vote for Humphrey. We would like a chance to make our case."

Xavier nodded in agreement. Gregory put his hand on Xavier's shoulder as he stood.

Not a lot of work gets done at the State Capitol on Fridays. Even when the General Assembly is in session, Fridays are merely a formality to get through before the weekend. Employees of the legislature show up to spend a maximum of eight hours in the halls of Legislative Plaza before heading home. The exception to this is the legal department, who were often busy drafting formal copies of legislation, researching the Tennessee Code for where the proper bill caption would fit, and finishing projects that had been put on the backburner for the majority of the week.

Fridays when the General Assembly is not in session, are even more dead. Add to that the weird timeframe between Thanksgiving and Christmas breaks where absolutely nothing gets done. The assistants and aides are tasked with answering constituent phone calls, but hardly anyone called their State Representatives when they could just as easily call their Congressman.

On this particular Friday, however, the attitude was leisurely but tinged with dread. Word of Joe Humphrey's plan for turning the branch of government into a Republican operative academy had spread like a virus. Some in the employment of the legislature had already started their hunt for a new job. Most, however, were in disbelief that anyone would be bold enough to pull off the plan, and so they were content to sit and wait. Worst case scenario, they thought, would be a decent severance package from the state.

Rose McKnight had been at the legislature for ten years; it was a stable income with decent benefits, and the job was flexible enough that she could leave early to never miss her son's soccer games or take her daughter to dance class. She had worked for several different members during that time, members of both parties. She had gotten the job from a temp agency but her work was good enough that she was hired full time after her first session. She wasn't particularly political. She had her beliefs which included being pro-choice, pro-gay marriage, anti-tax, and pro-schools, and she kept all of those to herself. She was worried her time at the legislature was coming to an end once Humphrey became Speaker; she dreaded the thought of getting a new job with a boss who kept tabs on her comings and goings. Yet she had chosen to do nothing until she was told she was gone, officially, by the head of Legislative Human Resources. Until that moment, she was content to stay in her little office in the hall beside the cafeteria and mind her own business. Despite electing a black president, it wasn't easy for a middle-aged black woman with no college degree, like herself, to find full-time office work.

For lunch, Rose had brought leftover chicken noodle soup which she had just finished reheating. She sat down at her desk filled with loose papers that were meaningless, but she was too worried to throw away, and turned on the little TV she kept in the corner. Every day she would watch *The Sarah Concord Show*, a syndicated talk show that had just enough drama to keep her interested for an hour. She stirred the soup in the rubber bowl as the intro music began. She left her reading glasses perched on her nose so she could see what she was eating.

As Sarah Concord was giving her show's preamble and introducing the subject of the day (elderly women in loving relationships with men under thirty), Christina Hicks from next door walked in and without saying 'hello' looked Rose in the eye and said, "Did you read about Humphrey yet?"

Rose, in the middle of chewing a soggy carrot, stared at the skinny white woman in her office and said, "Nuh-huh, what he do? Fire us before becoming Speaker?"

"Nooo, girl," said Christina shaking her head. "I just read it online, do you know what he did?"

"Obviously I don't," said Rose with a smile.

"Girl, now listen, you won't believe this." Christina sat down in the blue plastic office chair against the wall in front of Rose's desk.

"Chrissy, if you don't tell me I'll never know," said Rose. She put the spoon in the bowl and wiped her mouth, leaning back in her chair and muted the TV. Whatever Sarah Concord was talking about wasn't going to be as interesting as what Christina had to say.

"Did you know," Christina began, before looking out Rose's office door to see if anyone was around.

"Just close the door if you're that worried about it," said Rose as she stood up and pushed the door. The door made it to the frame but did not shut the entire way. Rose sat back down and gave the woman an imploring look to continue.

Christina spoke in a hushed voice, "Did you know that Humphrey," she said the name with emphasis in case Rose needed to read her lips, "was married once before and got a divorce?"

"Nuh-huh," said Rose in shock.

"Yes-huh," responded Christina.

"You mean, mister pro-marriage got a divorce from someone?"

"Bingo," she said. pointing at Rose with an unlit cigarette that had appeared seemingly out of nowhere.

"When?" asked Rose.

"A while back, like a decade ago."

"Why?" asked Rose. Christina shrugged. "He probably cheated on her, he seems like a cheater." She answered her own question.

"Well, aren't they all?" Christina responded, her voice now at normal volume. She lifted her hands and shrugged. "But, real talk, I don't know why. Maybe he cheated, maybe he hit her, maybe money was an issue, but I don't know."

"Let me get this straight." Rose sat up in her chair and put her elbows on her desk. "He wants to get rid of all of us because he wants to train up young people to protect marriage as an institution, but he's out there tearing that institution down?"

"Yep."

"Don't get me wrong," continued Rose, "you and me are both on our second marriage--"

"Well, I'm on my third now, but yeah," Christina corrected.

"Still, we aren't ones to judge," Rose held up a finger as she was thinking of her next words to prove her point. "But--"

"But we ain't out there saying other people are destroying marriage," said Christina, getting to the point first.

"Exactly," said Rose. She took another spoonful of her soup. She spoke as she chewed the overcooked noodles. "I don't think I can work for that man if he becomes Speaker. I just don't respect him, even before this."

"Me neither, girl," said Christina. "But you know, we might not even get to make that choice."

"You're right, he's gonna fire all of us before we get the chance," Rose laughed.

"No, look here, I think Larry is going to beat him," said Kelly, bouncing the cigarette on her knee.

"No way."

"I'm serious, I think Larry is gonna get the nom over Humphrey."

"How?"

"Well," Christina looked at the floor, "I don't know. Maybe by the grace of God." The two women broke out in laughter. "I just . . . I can't believe they're going to give Joe Humphrey the gavel and let him wreck this place."

"Listen, I've worked for Republicans before and they fall in line," Rose spoke with authority. "If they're told to walk off a cliff they'll do it. Joe is their leader: if he says they're going to vote for him, they will."

"Do you think this divorce stuff is going to stop him?" asked Christina with a little optimism.

"Hell no, you kidding? If anything it'll just give him a soapbox to beat the press with. I bet this will actually put him over the top. They'll all think it makes him look tough."

"So, we're screwed?"

"Yes ma'am, we are," said Rose.

"You know, the Association of Public Employees ain't gonna just let him fire us. They'll put up a fight."

"Nothing Humphrey wants more than to stand up to lobbyists and unions. TAPE won't be able to do shit to him," said Rose. She dropped the spoon back in the bowl. Her appetite was gone.

"They're organizing a protest of some sort, you know," said Christina, returning to her whisper.

"Who? TAPE?" asked Rose.

"Yeah, a walk-out or something. Would you join it? I'm on the fence about it"

"Sure, why not prove that this place runs just fine without us?" said Rose sarcastically. Christina laughed.

"Well, what about we just stop working?" she asked.

"What do you mean?"

"I mean, show up but don't do any work."

"Hell, how is that different than what we do now?" Rose asked; the two women were laughing before she could finish the sentence.

The television caught Christina's attention. A man in his mid-twenties was taking off his shirt, to reveal a hairless chest and six-pack to the applause of the studio audience. An old woman that reminded Christina of the women in the quilting club at her church was seated next to him, smiling and running her fingers over her stomach. "Oh my," said Kelly.

"I. Know," said Rose.

"Where can we find men like that?"

"We're too young for them apparently. Well, at least, I'm too young for them."

"Fuck you," said Christina, adding a little hum at the end of her sentence.

By the end of the day, word had spread throughout the Plaza of Joe Humphrey's divorce. The consensus among all who worked there was that it wouldn't make a difference. Humphrey was a train heading to the Speaker's chair, and it was too late to stop him.

Lunch at the retreat was a catered spread of soggy beef, dry chicken, steamed vegetables, and bread. The only redeeming item was the cheesecake dessert, the entire caucus agreed. While most of the members were eating their lunch inside the classroom down the hallway from the auditorium, sixteen members were sitting in a much smaller classroom across the hall. Every African American member of the Tennessee House of Representatives was a Democrat. There had not been a black Republican at the state house since the end of Reconstruction when the Democrats came back into power and the state essentially became a one-party system. In the mid-1980s, having successfully carved out a wing of state's Democratic Party for themselves, the scant few African Americans in the General Assembly decided it would make sense to band together and form a solid, though small, voting bloc. This gave them a certain amount of power, and as the state became more evenly split between the two parties, the small caucus became even more crucial to win over on any particular vote. The sixteen members of this Black Caucus made it the largest in their history.

Xavier Jones, a Memphis preacher who made most of his money renting out a few small houses that dotted the outlining rural area of Memphis and Southhaven, Mississippi, had spent the past two sessions as the Chairman of the House Black Caucus. He was an intimidating figure at over six foot five inches tall, always dressed in impeccable fashion: pinstriped suits, pocket squares that matched his perfectly dimpled tie. Outside he always wore a felt fedora with feathers sticking out of the band, but inside he would allow his bald head to shine in the light. His mustache was beginning to show signs of his unadvertised age with white hairs peeking out in contrast to the dark hairs that surrounded them.

He was pacing the front of the classroom, the wooden soles of his leather shoes clopping with each step he took. He was debating with his members, who had unanimously reelected him their chairman at breakfast earlier that morning, to give Gregory a chance to speak to them. They had a strict rule in their caucus regarding people from outside addressing them as a group. It took a majority of the members to vote in favor of hearing the person before they could even enter the room. This wasn't an issue when planning their meetings; the guest would simply be listed in the agenda and then the agenda would be approved when the meeting was called to order. Yet in last-minute meetings like this, it posed a problem. There were exceptions: anyone from a higher office (Governor, Lieutenant Governor, Speaker, or any federal office holder) would only need the approval of the Caucus Chairman, and it would be considered rude to not approve their invitation or request, or if the person was there to speak about a piece of legislation, either the Chairman or two other members would have to approve the invitation with a motion and a second.

"Listen to me," said Xavier with his hands pounding an imaginary podium, "it is only fair . . . that we hear the man out!" The caucus was deadlocked; eight members were willing to let Gregory in and eight were not. A tie meant debate over the invitation continued until someone motioned for it to end and a majority approved the motion.

J.A. Dobbins, also from Memphis, responded. "He's had a month to reach out to us individually and has not done so. I see no reason why we should give him a chance now."

Rochelle Frank, from Nashville, interjected to agree. "Amen. He's taken this caucus for granted." Like most caucuses, the Black Caucus observed formal rules for procedure in spirit, but allowed conversation to flow freely, as long as it was respectful. The Chairman was expected to be an active and vocal member who would merely, and judicially, guide the conversation and keep it on topic.

"Taken us for granted?" Xavier twisted his face and turned to Rochelle. "Ro, of all people. 'Taken us for granted?' I guess that fat bank account you got, and all them yard signs with your name on them, got there just because of you, huh?" There were verbal sounds of warning easy, come on now, from the group.

"Don't get me wrong," said Rochelle, "Gregory is my neighbor, he's my friend, he's a brother to me in this party, but he's had his head so far up the Speaker's butt these past few weeks that he's forgotten which tunnel leads out." The room filled with laughter.

"This man," began Connor Macellan, but he had to wait for the laughter to die down before continuing. "This man helped me get to this office, when no one else would. I would have lost my last two primaries if it weren't for him, and so would've a lot of you. Least we can do is let him speak his peace."

"He's had a month, and hasn't so much as called any of us," said J.A.

"He's a busy man, but he's trying to do what's right," said Xavier.

"We, we, know how to do what is right for us," said Tayna Allan from Nashville. Tayna was the longest-serving member of the Black Caucus and the longest-serving member of the House. She had been Speaker Pro Tempore for eight years, the second highest office in the House of Representatives, getting reelected nearly unanimously by members of both parties each time. She had been named in the Tennessee Stud Scandal a few years before, but without enough evidence for a conviction she had beat the charges. She never wielded much power in the House, but she was well-liked and respected, which could be just as valuable. The room hushed when she spoke.

"Tayna, I am surprised at you," said Xavier, stunned.

"I have been Speaker Pro for nearly a decade," she said, "but when I look around the room during leadership meetings, I am not only the lone black, but I'm also the only woman." She stood up to make her point more final. "Gregory has found the time to call and visit nearly every Republican before coming to us. Nearly every Republican. I know this, and so do all y'all. But here we are, seeing him for the first time this morning.

"So, I've got a confession." The room stayed quiet, no one moved, but everyone's pulse quickened. "I figured, if it's alright for him to call the Republicans, it's alright for me too. So, I, myself, called Joe Humphrey last week and traded my vote for their votes. Guess what?" She put her hands together and leaned her head to the right. "They're going to vote for me for Speaker Pro Term again, Joe is also going to make some of us chairman, and he's going to put some women in power. That's more than Gregory, or Bob Caputo, has ever done." The room stayed quiet for a few moments.

Dwayne Reid from Knoxville, the youngest member of the Black Caucus, broke the silence from the back of the room, "What makes you so sure that Joe Humphrey is going to beat Larry Pickard?"

Tayna turned to him. "You talking about that divorce nonsense?"

"Yes, I am," he said aggressively.

Tayna spoke in a condescending tone to the young man. "Honey, they haven't cared about divorce since Ronald Reagan turned a blind eye to black men with AIDS." She sat down and flattened her dress. "I move we close debate on the invitation," she said passively. Several people said 'second' and a few more said 'objection.'

"Alright, let's vote," said Xavier. "All those in favor of ending debate, and thereby rejecting the invitation, please raise your hands." Xavier counted quickly, "that's only eight." There were groans in the room, and Xavier continued. "All those opposed, and thereby continuing debate, please raise your hands." He counted quickly, getting only seven. He counted again, and again got seven. Then he realized he didn't have his hand up. He lifted his left hand. "Vote is eight to eight, debate continues," he said to more groans.

Gregory was standing just outside the door, fuming with anger. He was taking mental note of each voice that was speaking against him, particularly Tayna Allan. He felt particularly betrayed by her; he had been there for her when the corruption charges were filed. He had refused to ask her to resign her office, and he was the one who had convinced the party to stick by her, and he was the one who nominated her for Speaker Pro Term.

Now, when they needed her to stick with them, she was turning her back. The door across the hall where the rest of the Democratic Caucus was eating opened and Daniel Burns walked out. He gave Gregory a quick pat on the shoulder. Daniel knew that if his friend was still standing outside the door, the chances were slim he would get to walk through it.

"Still out here?" Daniel stated, not really asking a question.

"Oh yeah," said Gregory. He crossed his arms and leaned against the wall. "We've got more than I thought who are breaking ranks."

Daniel rubbed his chin. His job as Caucus Chair was to handle business outside the legislature and the inner political workings of the caucus. Where Gregory was tasked with vote-counting, running legislation, and getting members behind a legislative strategy, Daniel was the fundraiser, public spokesman, and principal. Daniel was the face of the Democratic Caucus. He was a natural fit for the job: a young, handsome, and charismatic lawyer, and recent combat veteran. Everyone who looked at him saw a future Speaker of the House. At least they did until last election night; now they could only see a future failed Gubernatorial candidate.

Daniel turned and leaned against the wall next to Gregory. He was a few inches taller than him, and hunched over a little so they would appear the same height. "Can we kick them out of the caucus if they don't vote our way?" he asked. Gregory gave a short laugh and looked at Daniel. Realizing the Caucus Chairman was serious, he changed his tone.

"Well that's your call, you run the caucus, not me," said Gregory. He had kept Daniel up to speed for most of the happenings of the past month; though he'd left out some of the details and spoke to him about it in mostly broad-brush strokes. Gregory trusted Daniel, but Daniel wasn't exactly the most calculating politician. Daniel was black and white, 'get this done now because I said so,' and Gregory was more pragmatic and strategic. Gregory had kept some things from Daniel out of fear that he wouldn't understand how important they were, and would therefore not agree.

"How would I do that? You know the rules better than I do," said Daniel.

"Man, that's what you're supposed to ask your staff," said Gregory, a bit bewildered.

"Yeah, I haven't exactly assembled a crack team," he said. Gregory knew what he meant. Daniel had a staff of four: a Press Secretary named Dawn, a former reporter for a smaller Nashville magazine, a Researcher who was attending law school at night named Ryan, and an Executive Assistant who was supposed to handle the rules of order for the caucus named Steve, and finally a standard issue Legislative Secretary name Bridgette. The only ones who actually knew their jobs and were good at them were Dawn and Bridgette, although Ryan came in handy when trying to formulate legislative strategy. Steve was too often high or chasing interns to care about his work, but his father was one of the top donors to the caucus so Daniel had taken one for the team when he was hired. No one trusted Daniel's staff, least of all Speaker Caputo who had intentionally cut them out of any plans to save his seat.

"Well," said Gregory with a sigh. "To kick someone out of the Democratic Caucus it takes a two-thirds plus one vote of all caucus members – that includes the person you are trying to remove."

"What? Really?"

"Yeah, I mean, they're a voting member of the caucus until they are removed, so they get to vote on their own sentence. It's a fairly standard rule, it's the same for the Republican Caucus," said Gregory, who himself had always been perplexed by that rule. It was like having a serial killer serve on their own jury.

"So, if we tried to kick out more than one," began Daniel, stopping to gather the words to finish the thought, "they would each have two votes to stay in the caucus."

"Yep."

"And," Daniel continued, "if we tried to kick out a member of the Black Caucus from the Democratic Caucus, the entire Black Caucus would probably vote together to keep that person in."

"Yep."

"So they would already have enough votes to stay."

"Yep."

"Well, there ends that game plan," said Daniel.

"Worse yet," Gregory laughed, "it only takes a simple majority to call for a new election for a leadership position."

"So, I try to kick one of them out," Daniel stopped to map out the exact scenario. He laughed as he continued, "They would all vote to keep someone in the caucus, and might get enough of the other members pissed off to pick up nine more to recall me and have a new election."

"Yep," responded Gregory. "Now you're getting it." The two men laughed – what else could they do?

"We could change the rules," suggested Daniel.

Gregory considered this and then said, "We're voting on the rules in two hours, not enough time."

"Shame we didn't hear about this sooner," said Daniel. Gregory nodded in agreement; this had been one of the things he hadn't told Daniel. "Why not send Tom in to speak to them? They would probably hear him out."

"Why? Cause he's black?"

"Well," began Daniel, considering his path carefully. "Yeah."

Gregory smiled and shook his head, "They wouldn't listen to him. They're more in line with Republicans when it comes to gay black men."

"Hold on . . . Tom's gay?" Daniel was shocked.

"Yeah," responded Gregory in a serious tone.

"How about that?"

"He doesn't advertise it or anything."

"Clearly, but good for him for being out," said Daniel. He decided to change the subject. "Oh by the way, did you hear about Humphrey?"

"No, what?"

"Turns out, the dude is on his second wife. Beat his first wife or something like that," said Daniel, feeling some weight being lifted off his shoulders with the change of topic.

"You're kidding," Gregory acted surprise. It didn't fool Daniel.

"I'm not," said Daniel with a smile. "I wonder how the press found out?" Gregory shrugged.

"A mystery we may never know, my young padawan," said Gregory with a laugh. The door to the classroom flew open, and Xavier stuck his head out.

"Chairman," Xavier nodded to Daniel.

"Chairman," said Daniel returning the nod.

"I'm sorry Leader Anderson," Xavier looked at Gregory. "We voted to deny your request for an invitation."

"What?" Gregory was both shocked and angry. "You can't be serious."

"I'm sorry, but I am," said Xavier. He was trying his best to communicate that it was the decision of the Black Caucus and not his.

"Who voted to not let him speak?" asked Daniel.

Xavier looked at Daniel in a confused way and said, "The Black Caucus did."

"Yeah," said Daniel. "But I want to know which members."

"We don't work like that," said Xavier. "We vote as a caucus and speak as a caucus, and unfortunately we have spoken."

"Ok, but as the Chairman of your Democratic Caucus, I want to speak to every black House Democrat, right now, in that room" said Daniel, his anger starting to break.

"Listen, we don't work like that," said Xavier, trying to calm Daniel down. "This meeting, in here, is not your caucus. When your caucus meets, if you want to call us out that's your prerogative. But as the Black Caucus, we would not look too kindly on that."

"Damn it, Jarvis," Gregory started his sentence but was cut off by a sudden rush of wind. The door across the hall opened. Speaker Caputo was standing in the doorway.

"Chairman Jarvis," he said looking at Xavier.

"Yes sir, Mr. Speaker," Xavier said with a smile.

"We're about ready to start up in here again, but before we do I would like to address the Black Caucus," the Speaker was already striding across the hall. He stopped once he reached the doorway to the classroom. He was eye level with Xavier. "With your permission, of course."

"Well, Mr. Speaker," Xavier said, opening the door to allow him to enter. "It would be our pleasure." Xavier held out his hand, welcoming the Speaker into the room.

"Oh, and I want my two boys in there with me," he said, grabbing Gregory and Daniel by their shoulders and pushing them in the classroom ahead of himself. "As my guests, of course."

"Sure thing, Mr. Speaker. But they'll have to stay silent unless addressed directly by a caucus member." Xavier's smile was quickly fading.

"Of course, Mr. Chairman," said the Speaker as he walked into the classroom. He did not say hello, but walked down the middle aisle between the rows of tables until he was standing in the middle of the room. He made a small, slow circle, turning on his heels. He looked at Xavier. "I believe the rules say you have to introduce me."

"Oh right, sorry" said Xavier. "Ladies and gentlemen--"

"I know this," the Speaker interrupted, his voice calm but projected loudly like an actor on stage without a microphone, "because I helped draft the rules when I helped this Caucus get going back in early 80s, two years after I suggested it be founded." The Speaker turned and looked at each of the Black Caucus members as he spoke.

Xavier paused a moment to appreciate the tension in the room, and then started again. "Ladies and gentlemen, with my approval as Chairman of this Caucus, let me introduce our guest: Speaker Bob Caputo, from Brownsville."

"Thank you, Mr. Chairman." The Speaker surveyed the faces in the room again. "I understand that, for the first time since I became Speaker, I need to personally ask for votes from members of my own party. Which is, well, I'll put it bluntly, it feels like a betrayal."

"Speaker," J.A. Dobbins stood up, but before he could make the point Xavier cut him off.

"I will remind the members of this caucus, that we allow our guests to speak uninterrupted. Once they have finished, then we can address them directly," Xavier said, motioning for J.A. to return to his seat. "Please, continue, Mr. Speaker."

"Thank you." Speaker Caputo pointed to Xavier and then turned to face the back of the room. "Look, y'all, I get it. Believe me I do. I haven't exactly been the best guy when it comes to race these last few years. I could have done more for the black community. I should have done more for the black community. But you have to ask yourself, and you really have to wonder, 'will the other side really do any better?' Sure, they'll tell you they're going to build a new school in the heart of your district. But it'll be a private school, invited guests only. And who's going to run it? Some billionaire in Florida that's writing them campaign checks. Oh, and by the way, do you think any white kids are going to be in those classrooms? Nope, they're just going to segregate schools again. They might tell you, 'hey, you want a new hospital in your district? I can get you one!' But are they going to help your people get insurance? Nope. They might offer some new sort of scholarship for your kids to go to college, but guess what? They're going to take away Affirmative Action. If a poor black kid makes C's in high school, they'll tell you he's not smart enough for the scholarship, but they'll sure as hell make sure a rich white kid with the same grades gets in. You know how I know this? Because they've tried. They've tried and they've failed, and they've failed because I've stopped them. So I want to hear from you all: do you think things will be better without me as Speaker? Come on. Lay it on me." Speaker Caputo walked back to the front of the room and stood with his arms crossed.

J.A. cleared his throat and stood up, "Mr. Speaker." Speaker Caputo's eyes widened but his face held a sour look as he stared at Representative Dobbins. "We all know that Republicans will promise one thing and not follow through. Or they'll promise something and only give half the details and then come in through the backdoor to wreck the place. We know that. That is not the issue here." J.A. patted the table with his fingertips with each word, and alternated his gaze between the Speaker's eyes and the floor. The Speaker held his pose and waited for him to continue. "The issue is that I am starting my third term, and I'm from Memphis; Representative Kincannon is starting his fourth term and he's from Memphis; Representative Hawkins is starting his fifth term and he's from Nashville; Representative Vick from Chattanooga is about to start her eighth term; Representative Reid from Knoxville is our newest member, because he was sworn in after me alphabetically, and he's heading into his third term. Then there's the Speaker Pro Term, she's been here longer than you, and she's from Nashville.

"The issue is we haven't had a new black State Representative elected in this state for three cycles. Hell, during that time we've only had one that's won a primary that's not in this room. We're all from one of the big four cities in our state, with the exception of Lawrence over there, but he works in Memphis so he barely counts. The issue is you are not cultivating young black talent across the state. You've just sort of settled that black representatives are going to pop up, like little flowers in the biggest four cities and you can claim diversity. Well, it don't work like that, Mr. Speaker."

"As Speaker of the House, I feel it is my duty to be above political rat-racing like that," said the Speaker in a huff. "I may on occasion campaign with an incumbent, and I might donate money to an incumbent, but I do not recruit candidates. I just don't do that." He pointed over his shoulder with his thumb to Daniel and Gregory who were still standing by the door, barely in the classroom. "That's their job."

Every eye in the classroom turned towards Daniel and Gregory; each face showed they were waiting on an explanation.

"Leader Anderson," said Shawn Maddox. "Boy, you wanted in here so bad. Now you need to talk to us. Give us an explanation."

Gregory glanced at Daniel who offered no advice, and then said, "As Leader, my job is to handle things inside the legislature. I only recruit candidates to open seats if I know them personally. Recruiting candidates is the job of the Caucus Chair." Gregory took a step to his left and then turned his face to the right to look at Daniel. Daniel gave Gregory the best 'fuck you' face he could without seeming rattled.

"Chairman Burns," said Xavier.

Daniel took a step forward, licked his lips, and said, "You're right, we've done a bad job of recruiting black candidates."

"Ok," said Lawrence Mains. "So what?"

"So, I have to do better," he said, knowing that wasn't enough. "We have to do better, as Democrats. We are the party of diversity, and we should act like it." The wheels in his mind began to turn. "We have to create a new system, as a party, to recruit black candidates. Not just for the State House, but for Congress. But we have to start on the local level. We, I mean, me, you all, Leader Anderson, Speaker Caputo, the Senate Caucus, the Governor, and the State Party have to come together to build up a bench on the local level. We have to start getting black county commissioners, city council members, school board members, mayors, and such elected across the state. Not just in Memphis, Nashville, Chattanooga, and Knoxville; but in Johnson City, Kingsport, Hendersonville, Murfreesboro, Jackson, Union City, and everywhere in between." Every head was nodding in agreement. He knew he had to connect it back to the Speaker somehow. He looked around the room for a split second, and then he thought of it.

"But we can't do that, we won't have the resources, if we are busy fighting a bullish agenda in the State House. They've already got the State Senate, they have the numbers in the House, but if we give them the Speaker's Chair, if we just hand it over, well . . ." he took a breath to think of a consequence but none came to mind. He decided to roll with it. "Well, then, we will burn all our oil protecting what we have and forsaking what we want. If we don't get behind Caputo, excuse me, Speaker Caputo, that recruitment plan goes out the window." He finished and took a step back. A mumble began to go around the room.

"You all know he's right," said Xavier to the room while looking at no one in particular.

"But you also know," said Michael Kincannon to both the Speaker and Xavier, "that certain things have been said by some of our members, and they cannot go back on it. At least not publicly."

"So," said Xavier with a shrug, "what do y'all want to do?"

"I am willing," said Tayna, "to vote, publicly, in the Democratic Caucus for Bob to be Speaker of the House, but as the Black Caucus I think it would behoove us if we did not endorse anyone this year."

"I can live with that," quickly responded Speaker Caputo.

"You can?" said Tayna.

"Yes, you are all Democrats. You voting for my nomination in the Democratic Caucus and then issuing a non-endorsement as the Black Caucus – people will just read between the lines there," said the Speaker.

"Ok," said Tayna.

"Ok, well, I'll see you all across the hall in," the Speaker checked his watch, "fifteen minutes."

"Hold on," said Tayna as the three men began to walk out of the room. "Leader Anderson, do you have a plan to get the Speaker reelected?" She asked as if she knew the answer.

Suddenly, deep in the recesses of his brain, a tiny blueprint of a plan began to be drawn up. "Yes, we have the one vote we need, we're just trying to find a few more for insurance." The room fell quiet. "I'll see y'all over there," he said and walked out. He had nearly developed the entire strategy before he crossed the hall-way.

Daniel was about to walk out the door when he felt the Speaker grab his shoulder from behind, and he heard Susan Murphy call his name.

"Chairman Burns, hold on." He turned – Susan's slender figure was standing up, and she stared at him through her silver wire-framed glasses. "You should know, whatever scheme that man has cooked up, you need to be careful." She looked around the room. "We might only be sixteen people out of forty-nine right now, but our seats are safe. We will always be here. You've got thirty-three people across the hall that might not be back in two years, even fewer will be back in four years. This is Tennessee, and we're the party that just elected a black President, don't think for a second that any of your white reps are going to be safe now. Someday soon, these sixteen people right here, we are going to not only be the Black Caucus, but the Democratic Caucus too. So tread lightly, my friend. We aren't going nowhere anytime soon."

Daniel said nothing he just looked at her taking in her warning. He opened his mouth but she raised a hand to stop him. "You better get back over there, we'll be in soon enough." With that Daniel and the Speaker left.

CHAPTER 8

Wednesday, December 17, 2008

The Tennessee State Capitol is a rare working Capitol. Construction started on the building in 1845, but it wasn't completed until 1859. While it was still in its infancy it was thrown into the middle of the Civil War. Changing hands between the Confederacy and the Union, it served as a symbolic reminder of the division within the state itself. One of the few domeless state capitols, the Greek Revival structure with a lantern spire, it looks as though it was carved out of the very hill it sits upon in downtown Nashville. The outside of the limestone building appears to be tan, or white, or gray depending on how the light hits it and the weather. The inside halls are lined with a much darker version of the stone; were it not for the murals painted on the high arched ceilings, it would look as though the first floor was a tunnel in a beautiful mine. Along with House and Senate chambers, the offices for the state's Governor, Treasurer, Secretary of State, Comptroller, and several other executive branch members are housed on the building's first floor.

While the majority of time on a guided tour of the Capitol is spent admiring the legislative chambers, the Governor's office is often the biggest surprise and most memorable part for guests. The chair-railed walls feature on their upper two thirds murals depicting the history, geography, and motto of the state: "Agriculture and Commerce." Commissioned during the Great Depression, the scenes featured include President Andrew Jackson with his slave at his mansion The Hermitage, a paddle boat making its way across a river, Native Americans living a life prior to white settlement, and Desoto's conquest in the western part of the state. The artist, Jirayr Zorthian, even snuck in a self-portrait on the walls. Some of the murals have been the subject of protests. The room even features the actual, literal, seal of Tennessee, a black steel press machine that sits unassumingly in the corner.

Working as the Governor's assistant for the past twenty years, Katy Dill had become accustomed to being stared at by school children and bored adults who pop in on any given day for a tour. She had gotten used to ignoring them, giving a polite nod and hello if she happened to make eye contact. She could close the door if the Governor was particularly busy or having an important meeting in his back office. She was always surprised when a new Governor came in – she was working for her fourth Governor now – how they always seemed to want to interact with those on the tour for the first five months or so, but would then avoid them after that. Often they would instruct her to tell visitors that the Governor wasn't in the office that day. She hadn't voted for anyone in a Governor's race since she got the job, it didn't seem right, and she kept her opinions to herself.

This, she thought, explained her long tenure as the administrative secretary to the Governor's Office despite being a lesbian in the culturally conservative state.

She had arrived this day promptly at 6:45 AM. She always believed, with a third of the state living in the Eastern Time Zone and the other in Central, that if there were Tennesseans at their office in any part of the state, then the Governor's office should be open for them. She walked in with the cup of coffee she had brought from home and placed it on her desk, shaking her mouse to wake up her computer.

She noticed in the lights were on in the back office and the Governor's bodyguard was seated at his little desk in the far corner. She was impressed. She was always the first person in the office for the first three Governors she had worked for, but somehow Governor Wayne Welch was always there before her. The fact that he was here so early after a landslide reelection victory said something about his work ethic, and, she thought, the reason why Tennesseans elected him by the largest margin in the state's modern history. It could also mean the man was busy planning his second inaugural, but she wanted to stay optimistic about her boss.

She sat down behind her desk and gave a polite wave to the bodyguard, Chester, who returned it with a smile. Chester was a polite, handsome, black man, but he wasn't a morning person and Katy knew better than to engage him in conversation before seven. She was willing to give him his space while he got use to the new day. She began cycling through the emails she had received overnight. Requests for meetings with the Governor and events got forwarded to his scheduler, constituents asking for help got sent over to the Director of Constituent Relations, citizens voicing their opinions on an issue got sent to the communications team. She sensed someone standing in the doorway, but didn't look up. Those who worked at the Capitol knew she was programed to ignore people entering the office. If they needed something, they had to call her by her name.

"Good morning, Katy, my dear. How are you?" She glanced up and saw Darrell Clarkson holding his leather portfolio. The short, stout, mustached Secretary of State who had the look of a small-town sheriff in a show about rural hijinks of well-meaning white kids.

"Well, good morning, Darrell, what brings you to this side of the building?" she asked in her groggy morning voice. Darrell had been the Secretary of State for Tennessee for almost eight years, long enough for he and Katy to be on a first name basis.

"I was hoping to get a few minutes of his time, right now, I've got some personal stuff to discuss with him. If I can," he said, moving into the office and standing beside her desk.

"Everything ok?" she asked, concerned.

"Oh yeah," he said. "Nothing serious or sad, just some stuff we've been discussing. It is kind of urgent though."

"Let me see." she clicked to open the Governor's calendar. "He is free until 7:30, I think it'll be ok if you want to go on in. Chester, do you know if he's busy?"

Chester looked up. "No, he's not. He's just reading the morning papers." Chester went back to the screen on his laptop, checking the odds for the upcoming college football bowls.

"Alright, Darrell. Just go in and he'll see you," said Katy pointing with her thumb to the ornate white door that was cracked open.

"Thank you, darling," said Darrell with a salute.

As grand and beautiful as the outer office was, the back office, where the Governor actually does his work, is very ordinary. White walls, blue carpet, dark wood furniture, and wingback chairs. It had struck Darrell as resembling a very nice insurance agency rather than the office of the executive of a State.

The office was only lit by lamp light from the desk and tables around the room. Governor Welch was leaning back in his chair, his feet propped on the desk, coffee mug in one hand while the other was holding a newspaper. He wasn't wearing his suit jacket – Darrell could see it hanging on the coat rack in the corner – and his tie was loose, with his lamb-white hair still seeming wet. "Good morning, sir," Darrell said.

Governor Welch had just put the mug of coffee to his lips when he heard Darrell's voice; he moved it away quickly as he turned to look at the Secretary. "Ah hell, Darrell, you don't have to call me 'sir' or 'Governor' before eight; just call me Wayne, or asshole, whichever feels right." Governor Welch stood up and took off his thick tortoise-shell reading glasses and set them on top of his head as he walked around to shake Darrell's hand. "Let's sit by the window over there," the Governor motioned to two blue wingback chairs facing each other on either side of a small table.

"Sure thing," said Darrell. The Governor smiled as they made their way over. "How's it going?"

"Oh, not too bad I guess. Can't complain for an old man." The Governor sat down and crossed his legs at the knees. "Do you want some coffee?" he asked as he sat his mug on the table between them.

"No sir, I've already had my fill," said Darrell. He opened his portfolio and handed the Governor a piece of cardstock paper. "Governor, this is it. We've talked about it enough, and I think I'm ready to retire."

The Governor read over the piece of paper. "This seems to imply you're done thinking about it."

"I am sir. I'm leaving effective eight AM, January 14, 2009." Darrell had a touch of remorse in his tone.

"Well, I knew this would be coming, but I'm still sad to see you go." The Governor placed the paper on the table. "Obviously, the entire state is indebted to you for your service." Darrell rolled his eyes and smiled and waved a hand dismissing the Governor's words. "I'm serious," he continued, "really, thank you for serving this state. It's not an easy job."

"That's true," said Darrell. "Which is why I am here. I want to talk to you about my replacement."

The Governor shrugged. "That's up to the General Assembly, they pick who's next. I don't really get a say."

"That's true, but not entirely accurate," said Darrell. Governor Welch had made millions in the tech industry, selling software to trucking companies. He had used that money to run for Governor after only serving half a term as Mayor of Nashville. Though he was a good and popular governor, and a smart and crafty politician, some of the quirks and details of the General Assembly were lost to him. Darrell had served three terms in the

State Senate, rising to the rank of Republican Caucus Treasurer before becoming Secretary of State. He understood the process of the General Assembly, and their unspoken rules.

"You see, Governor, while you don't nominate or select the Secretary of State," Darrell shifted a bit in his seat, pulling a flap from his suit jacket out from under him, "your input is sought and is critical. Not in any formal sense, but the General Assembly, when picking a new constitutional officer, wants to make sure they can a) do the job, and b) work with the Governor."

"Ok," said Governor Welch bringing his glasses to his lips.

"Essentially, they aren't going to put someone in place who is going to undermine you. Also, speaking modestly, I'm still pretty popular within my party so they aren't going to pick someone I don't approve of. Now, we are in a unique situation, where the General Assembly is controlled by a different party than the governor. But I was elected unanimously as a Republican by both chambers of the General Assembly, which at the time was controlled by a super majority of Democrats, because the Governor was a Republican." Darrell watched the Governor's face to make sure he was following the logic. "Now, this current crop of Republicans, particularly in the House, they're not going to give you a Democrat as Secretary of State. But what they will do, or rather might do, is give you the Republican you want."

The Governor exhaled. "Hmm," he said pondering the idea. He stayed silent for a moment and then said, "Ok, well, I have a few in mind, but I want to hear who you want."

"Ok," said Darrell. He had been prepared for this question. "Thinking pragmatically, it should be a member of either the

House or Senate – that way they can waive the hearings and put someone in place quickly."

"Agreed," said Governor Welch, reaching for his coffee mug.

"With that in mind, two names come up right away. Both are moderate Republicans, business-minded; in fact they're probably more aligned with your political beliefs than a lot of members in your own party."

"Ok . . ." the Governor was indicating to Darrell to continue without waiting for his response at each point.

"Well, one choice would be Senator Will Ollie. He's starting his fourth term; he runs a major realty business in Shelby County and has experience in local government. He could do the job, but he's just an option – he's not my first choice. My first choice, and this could get dicey because there would be major political ramifications if he accepts, would be Representative Larry Pickard." Darrell said the name as if he was ashamed to mention it.

The Governor sat in his chair, gazing at Darrell. He stayed silent for a minute before saying, "You know, when you mentioned you were thinking about retiring earlier this year, Larry was one of the first people I had thought of for my, let's call it, wish list of replacements." Darrell smiled. It was nice to be on the same page with Governor Welch; he would miss working with him. "Who else have you mentioned this to?"

"No one," said Darrell. "Well, I take that back, I told the Lieutenant Governor, he and I go way back. We're friends, so I actually told him I was retiring for sure, but we didn't talk about names for my replacement. He indicated to me that the Senate would vote for whoever I wanted."

"Ok," said the Governor thinking. "It will be seen as a political bargaining chip to nominate Representative Pickard, as if it's happening to get him out of the race for Speaker."

"I know," said Darrell. "I figured it would be worth telling you because of that. If it's going to be seen as a bargaining chip, why not use it as a bargaining chip?"

"That was my thought exactly," said the Governor, smiling and smacking Darrell's knee. "I'm going to need you to do me a favor, Darrell."

"Ok," said Darrell in uncomfortable agreement.

Brett Kyle was sitting in his little windowless office in the Minority Leader's suite, in the far south wing of Legislative Plaza. He was rubbing his eyes, trying to will them awake. He hadn't bothered to iron his khakis, or his red button-collared shirt, when he got up two hours earlier. He wasn't planning on seeing anyone who would care. He had told Marcy to keep his calendar clear this week. As far as the lobbyists, Republican Caucus members, party officials, and all those in between were concerned, the Senior Legislative Advisor to soon to be ex-Minority Leader Humphrey was out sick today. His desk was a canopy of poorly stacked papers. Resumes to go through, potential pieces of legislation, bills in the final draft stages, bills that needed sponsors. The chalkboards on his walls appeared to be well-organized, but that was just for show; they told the saga of potential committee chairs, potential committee assignments, and new office assignments. There was also the vote count for his boss's race for Speaker. All these things were combining for a nightmare he did not want to face, but if he could just finish one thing he would feel better. Yet after being constantly yelled at, day after day for over a month, by longtime staff members of the General Assembly worried about their future employment, he was beat down.

Somehow he had gotten all the credit for the massive victories his party had achieved in November. He had played a part in it, writing some checks, suggesting campaign timelines, running TV ads, training a few volunteers, but he really hadn't done anything of consequence. He didn't correct people when they gave him the credit, but with all that glory came the added pressure to live up to the image others had given him. He was tasked with picking the new, young conservatives, like himself, who would be employed by the Tennessee House of Representatives, thus getting a leg up in their future careers as operatives. It was up to him to decide which current legislative staff people would be let go; he had ultimately decided that this was too much to ask and it would be easier, and fairer, to just clean house.

Joe Humphrey also wanted to hit the ground running as Speaker; this meant having all Committee Chairs and assignments selected before he was elected. He wanted to announce them during the organizational session on the second Tuesday in January, in his acceptance speech. That task had also fallen to Brett, Which meant every time his boss traded a committee chairmanship for a vote, Brett had to make it work, even when that meant some committee chairmanships had been promised to two or three different members. His boss made the promises, but Brett had to work out the details. A small part of him, which at certain times was a much larger part of him, wished Gregory Anderson would pick off one Republican to vote for Caputo so he would not have to deal with this crap.

Amy Clowney walked into his office and, after placing a cup of black coffee on Brett's desk, she sat down in the small brown armchair in the corner. Brett wordlessly picked up the cup and took a sip. Amy had been given the title of Policy Advisor by Joe when she came on board two years ago. It was a meaningless title; her real job was to fundraiser and run Joe's political action committee (JoePACTN). She was good at that job; Brett looked at her and wished like crazy he had given her the credit she was due. Really, Amy was the reason the Republicans had taken the House in November. She was a petite blonde girl, fresh out of college, with a long nose and big teeth. She was the future of the party, and he knew it. He was lucky, but she was good. She was also kind and understanding, and knew the pressure Brett was under and had chosen not to add to his plate, even if that meant more work for herself.

After several seconds of silence she said, "Did you remember to brush your teeth this morning?"

"Yeah, but forgot my hair," he said running his fingers through it.

"Well, it looks like you've trained it to stay in place. So you're good there," she responded. There was an atmosphere of dread in the small room. They knew the stakes, and they also knew all the work being done could ultimately prove to be a waste of time. "Do we have a vote count?"

"No," said Brett with a chuckle. "The bastards have quit talking about it. They all have their minds made up and they're ready to vote. Some, I would guess, are even lying to us about it just to save face." He leaned back and crossed his legs, ankle on knee.

"I wouldn't be surprised if Joe won with all fifty votes, and I wouldn't be surprised if he lost by thirty," Amy said, holding her coffee cup with both hands and blowing on it.

"Me either," he agreed. "It's a secret ballot, so they can tell us whatever they want and then check whatever box they want. Whoever wins they'll say they voted for them, they're all such pansies."

"If you had to guess," she said before stopping. She thought about the right way to phrase her question as Brett looked at her through bloodshot and bagged eyes. She continued, "what is the vote count that we for sure know? I mean, not factoring in the votes we don't trust one hundred percent?"

"Well, let's see," said Brett. He swirled his chair without changing his posture to look at the chalkboard on the wall to his left. He counted the names for Joe, and said, "We, for sure, have eighteen votes. Definitely have those eighteen. And Pickard has . . ." Brett counted a few more names and then doubled-checked his math, eliminating the ones he thought might be on the fence. "Pickard has twelve, thirteen including his own. Thirteen votes. Yeah, thirteen people had the balls−−"

"Or ovaries," she interjected with a smile. "Representative Ellington is a woman, and apparently for Pickard."

"Right. Thirteen people have the anatomy to tell us they are absolutely voting for Pickard," he said and took a gulp of coffee.

"Jesus, lord," said Amy. "That still means thirty-one people are undecided."

"Oh no," said Brett with more animation than he had shown all morning. "That means there are thirty-one members who have made up their minds, but either aren't telling us or might be lying to us."

"What are we going to do?" she asked. It was an offer to help; she controlled the purse strings. Even if some of the major donors had lined up behind Pickard, a lot of the members had seen her face at their events, wearing shirts with their names on them, knocking on doors in their districts. That carried a lot of weight.

"I don't know," he said. "Wait and see."

"Do you think that ex-wife business is keeping some members from getting behind him, publicly?"

"No," he said with a dismissive tone. "He came out with that statement and that story was dead before we went to sleep that night. It helped that his ex came out with her own statement, I mean it was a bunch of nothing. Most people either forgot about it, or got over it, or didn't care to begin with. Our members are going to stick together. Short of someone murdering someone, they'll support each other." They sat and drank their coffee for a few minutes in silence. "Do you think Pickard has people doing this work?"

"No," she said, quickly and as a matter of fact.

"Really?"

"I know he doesn't. According to his assistant, whatever we come up with for committees and whatnot, he's going to use," she said in a whisper. "He's going to put us on his staff if he wins, it's easier than finding new people." Brett gave a smile laced with satisfaction; at least he was going to have a job working for the Speaker of the House no matter who won. That, coupled with the fact that the Democratic Caucus had been dim enough to re-elect Gregory Anderson, Daniel Burns, and their entire slate of incumbent caucus officers to their leadership positions, meant the Republicans could continue beating the Democrats down for a generation. Amy and Brett had that conversation earlier in the week. The Democrats had been led straight off a cliff in November, and before they hit the ground they decided to stick with the very people who had started the freefall.

"Is Leader Joe coming in today?" Amy asked.

"Yeah, he'll be in after lunch. He wants to make sure everything is ready for the caucus meeting on the fifth. We'll be meeting with Mike's staff in Joe's office at two, I think, to go over some details."

"What are you going to tell him when he gets here?" she asked with concern.

"I don't know," he said with a sigh. He put his face in his hands and messaged his forehead with his fingers. "I'm hoping that invisible hand Adam Smith was yapping about intervenes somehow."

Joe walked into his office suite at half past one carrying his suit jacket over his right shoulder. He had just finished having lunch with the lobbyists for the Tennessee Teacher's Group and Tennessee Education Society. He had listened to their legislative agenda for the upcoming year and given them insights on what might, and what might not, pass the House. Truthfully, Joe knew none of it was going to pass, and if Larry Pickard wasn't running against him for Speaker, he would have told them so. Yet the TTG and TES held some sway over certain members in his caucus, and with the vote margin so thin, according to Brett it was still too close to call, pissing off the wrong lobbyist could cost him, or Larry, a vote or two. And a vote or two might just be the difference.

Marcy was standing at her desk when he walked in. "Sir," she said, and it struck Joe as odd. She always called him 'Joe' unless there was someone important around, but his office was empty. He gave her an inquisitive look.

"'Sir'?" he said. "Marcy, what's wrong?"

"The Governor and Secretary of State had lunch together in the Plaza cafeteria," she said in an urgent tone.

"So?" Joe responded dismissively. "Good for them, I went to the South Eastern downtown with a couple of lobbyists. It was delicious, but thanks to stupid ethics rules, because of corrupt-ass Democrats, I had to pay for my own." He began to walk past her desk into his office, and she grabbed his arm.

"They're coming down here to talk to you." She gave him a worried look.

"They're coming here?" he asked.

"Yes, Joe. Here, your office."

"Did they say why?"

"No, but they'll be here any minute."

"Huh, that's interesting," said Joe. It was strange for the Governor to meet a member of the General Assembly in their office rather than the Governor's office. The unofficial rules dictated that members go to the Governor, regardless of party. "Ok, I'll be in my office. Send them in when they get here."

"Ok," she said. "Brett put some bills that need your approval on your desk, look them over, try to look busy."

Joe laughed. He didn't need to try to look busy, he was busy. Still, she was right, it wouldn't hurt to make it look like business as usual. He hung his jacket on a hook in the wall beside his desk and opened one of the blue files that contained a rough draft from the legal department of a bill he might carry. Of course, as Speaker, he knew he would not actually have any bills of his own. He would have to find someone to run them through the legislative process for him. This bill concerned speed limits around churches with daycare facilities, essentially designating the church as a school zone. He read over the bill and made a few notes, then he picked another bill. This one preempted local governments from regulating payday lenders. The next bill instituted a two-year waiting period before a former teacher could run for the school board. Joe made his way through eight different bills, marking what he believed were grammatical errors with a blue pen, and making notes and writing questions for the legal department with a red pen. He was lost in the legislation, and unaware of the time. He had found a groove going through the bills; below his harsh and cutthroat politician exterior was a policy nerd. He experienced an authentic surprise when Marcy knocked on his door.

"Sir," she said with only her head crossing the threshold into his office. "Governor Welch and Secretary Clarkson are here and would like a moment of your time."

"Of course, send them in," he said as he stood up from his desk. He could see the two men standing in the lobby of his suite past Marcy's shoulder. She turned and motioned for them to come in. Joe was, as always, surprised by how tall the Governor actually was. He always seemed shorter on television, but standing next to the old man Joe barely came up past his shoulder.

"Governor, a pleasure as always," Joe said extending his hand. Governor Welch gripped it tightly.

"Leader Humphrey," he said with a smile. "How's the ship sailing?"

"Straight and true, I reckon," said Joe. He extended his hand to Secretary Clarkson. "Well, Mr. Secretary, it's nice to see you back in the Plaza."

"Ah, Leader Humphrey. You ready for Christmas?" said the Secretary with a smile.

"Shew," said Joe with a grin. "I tell you what, I almost forgot about the holiday coming up with all the mess flying around. Let's sit over here at the conference table." Joe pointed to the dining room set a local artisan in Kingsport had built. Joe had paid too much for it, but it fit into that space in his office so nicely. The Governor and Secretary went to the table and stood behind their chairs. Joe knew it would have been rude for him to sit behind his desk while the two high ranking government officials sat in chairs reserved for lobbyists and constituents; the two men knew it would have been impolite to sit down before their host. Joe took his jacket off the hook and put it on. "Marcy," he called out.

"Yes sir?" she said from her desk just outside his door.

"How long till my next meeting?"

"At two thirty you have a leadership meeting in Chairman Hayes' office to finalize the details for the caucus meeting on the fifth. That's in about forty-five minutes," she said. She turned around in her chair to look into his office. "Want me to call and say you'll be late?"

"Yes please," said Joe, slipping his arms into the jacket. "But don't tell them why."

"Yes sir, I'll do it," she said as she closed the door. She, of course, had every intention of telling them why her boss would be late.

Joe walked over to the table; he picked the seat directly in front of Governor Welch. He pulled the chair out and as he sat down, he encouraged his guests to do the same. "Would y'all like some water or coffee or anything?"

"Oh, no thank you," said the Governor. "We're fine. Listen, Leader Humphrey, we know you're busy so we won't be long."

"Please, if you're both here it must be important," said Joe. "What can I do for you two? Something about your inauguration?"

"Oh no, I've got an entire committee handling that," said the Governor. "This is about actual business."

"I'll jump on in here," said the Secretary. "Leader Humphrey, I'm retiring. It might seem like short notice to you, but I've been talking to the Lieutenant Governor and Governor Welch about this for a few months. I don't want the General Assembly to consider me when they vote, and I will not accept a nomination. I'm ready to ride into the sunset, so to speak."

"I'm sorry to hear that," said Joe sincerely. "I've enjoyed working with you and think you've done a fantastic job in your position. You will be missed a lot around here."

"I appreciate that," said the Secretary looking down at the table.

"So, I assume you're here then to tell me who you all have in mind for a replacement?" asked Joe.

"That's right," said the Secretary.

"Governor Welch," said Joe, "I just want you to know our caucus isn't going to make you work with a Secretary of State that you don't approve of, provided that you're open-minded about who you like."

"Yes sir," said the Governor. "I figured as much. I do appreciate you letting me have some say."

"Leader Humphrey," said the Secretary, "I've talked quite a bit with the Governor and Lieutenant Governor about who I think would be best to replace me, and they have both given their blessing to my choice. I would have included you in the discussion but between you and Representative Pickard, not to mention Speaker Caputo, I just . . . well, I didn't want to be seen as influencing the race."

"Don't worry about it," said Joe. "I know, things are complicated in the House right now. I get it, you didn't want to be seen trying to tip the scales. It's fine. But as Minority Leader – well, really Majority Leader –this would fall under my jurisdiction. So, I think you're in the clear."

"Ok, good," said the Secretary. The three men laughed uneasily.

"So, who is the lucky guy or gal?" asked Joe.

"Senator Ollie," said the Secretary.

"Huh, William Ollie?" said Joe. The two men nodded their heads in confirmation.

"We all feel," began Governor Welch, "that he has the experience, temperament, and the nonpartisan capabilities to do the job effectively."

"He would be a fine choice." Joe had a sudden idea. He leaned back in the chair and rubbed his chin. "Yeah, he would be alright. Have you asked him yet?" He needed to think fast for it to work, but couldn't quite think of the opening.

"Not yet," said Secretary Clarkson. There was a long silent pause. "So, you're in agreement?"

"Hold on, now, I didn't say that," exclaimed Joe. He was desperately trying to think of what to say.

"What's the problem, Leader Humphrey?" asked the Governor with concern.

Joe needed a reason to say no; he decided to start talking and maybe it would come to him. "Senator Ollie has a pretty solid voting record, to my knowledge," he began. "I doubt we would need a hearing. Although with the margin so slim in the House, the Democrats could force one." Maybe that would do it.

"No, we don't believe so," said the Governor. "I think I will be able to keep my party in line. They won't want a hearing, nor will they want to nominate their own candidate. I think I can get them there."

"I might have some concern over his nomination being used as a political football in the Speaker's race," said Joe, feeling a bit better about this line. "Like we get to the floor and suddenly they, the Dems, insist they won't vote for him without a hearing unless we elected Caputo as Speaker."

"Again, Leader Humphrey," said the Governor with a touch of frustration. "I don't believe that will happen. Even if a few of them think of it, Senator Ollie is from Shelby County and is well-liked in Memphis. I don't think the Black Caucus would let their fellow Democrats hold up the nomination of a prominent

Memphian to such a high-profile position. They, at the very least, would vote with Republicans to waive the hearing."

Memphis, that was it, he had it. "Yeah but who would take Senator Ollie's seat in the Senate?"

"That would be up to the Shelby County Election Commission," said Secretary Clarkson, knowing this answer was part of his job. "Whoever they pick would serve for two years, finish the term, and then the people in the district would elect someone new."

"Exactly," said Joe. "The Shelby County Election Commission is mostly Democrats."

"That's true, but standard procedure and precedent would suggest they select a Republican to replace a Republican," said the Governor.

"With all due respect, procedure and precedent are not the law, Governor Welch," said Joe, leaning forward with his arms on the table. "The Shelby County Election Commission could pick a Dem to fill that seat, in a district that is pretty much evenly split between the two parties. Then, in 2010, Republicans would be running against an incumbent Democratic State Senator. Now, I'm sorry, but for us to vote for somebody, they would have to come from a county with a Republican County Election Commission."

"Come on, Leader," said the Secretary. "All the counties with Republican Election Commissions are represented by hardline, far-right members of our party. They would grind the work of the state to halt. That's not fair to the Governor, the General Assembly, or to the people of this state."

"What if we pick a mayor?" asked the Governor. "Or, maybe someone from the private sector?"

"Someone from outside the state government would certainly require a hearing. We have to make sure they understand how the state works," said Joe.

"What about promoting someone within the Department of State? Like an undersecretary?" suggested the Governor in a pleading manor.

"Sorry, but if it's not someone we already know and trust there has to be a hearing. Not to mention, you'll be running the risk of a floor fight because the Dems might smell blood in the water and try to pull some shenanigans," Joe knew the conversation was going his way.

"Ok," said Secretary Clarkson. "You tell us. What person can you think of, that's up here right now, so they wouldn't need a hearing, who comes from a county with a Republican Election Commission, and is moderate enough to actually work with both the General Assembly and the Governor?"

Joe pretended to ponder the question for a minute, then said, "I can only think of one name, but you aren't going to like it."

"Who?" asked the Governor coldly.

"Now, really think about it," said Joe. He lifted his hands to brace for an attack. "Larry Pickard fits that bill."

The Governor laughed, "You can't be serious?"

"I'm afraid I am."

"Joe," said the Secretary. "Like I said, we want to stay out of the Speaker's race. Picking Larry puts us right in the middle of it."

"Y'all know I'm right, and, you can't honestly tell me that he wasn't on your shortlist before he decided to run for Speaker." Joe looked at the two men daring them to disagree.

"Even if he was," began the Governor, "and I am not saying he was, but even if he was, picking him now would be seen as some sort of corrupt bargain with you. Like John Quincy Adams with Henry Clay, I'd get nothing done."

"No," said Joe dismissively. "Look, sure, it would solve a lot of headaches in my caucus, but everyone would understand the choice because Larry would be a great fit. Plus, it would be Darrell that would make the suggestion and we would be the ones that hire him. Not you, Governor."

"Sure, and you get to waltz into the Speakership free and clear." The Governor wasn't hiding his disgust at Joe's suggestion.

The Secretary shook his head and looked at Joe. "I don't think so, Leader."

"Pick Larry and I'll pass ten of your bills," said Joe quickly, eyes beaming directly into the Governor's.

"It would take more than that," said Governor Welch. He moved to stand up, but Joe put his hands up to tell him to wait.

"Ok," said Joe. "Fifteen bills. That's most of your legislative agenda."

Governor Welch sat down; Joe could tell the man was now intrigued. "My legislative agenda is going to be nearly thirty-three bills."

"Seventeen," said Joe calmly.

"Twenty," said the Governor.

"Eighteen, but nothing that's a hot button. Only stuff that isn't seen as far-left, I still have to sell it to my caucus," said Joe.

"Fine, eighteen," said the Governor. "And, my budget passes."

"Fine, but only if it doesn't increase spending by more than two percent." Joe could feel the wind starting to blow at his back.

"Five percent." The Governor didn't move; the room became deathly quiet. A phone from some office nearby began to ring just within earshot, and it was the only sound.

"Eighteen bills, and a three percent increase in the budget," said Joe. He held out his hand to seal the deal.

Governor Welch looked at Secretary Clarkson, "What do you think, Darrell?"

"Larry was my top pick before he decided to run for Speaker," said the Secretary. "If this is what it takes for him to get the job, then so be it. I'm good."

The Governor looked at Joe and smiled. He took Joe's hand and shook it, the three men stood up and laughed. "Congrats," said Governor Welch, "Mr. Speaker."

Joe felt tears beginning to moisten his eyes; he blinked rapidly to recall them. "Don't say that yet," he said through his laughter. "When are you going to tell Larry?"

Secretary Clarkson checked his watch, "Well first, we need to tell the Lieutenant Governor. Then I'll call Larry tonight before supper."

"Ok," said Joe. "Y'all let Speaker Caputo and the Chief Clerk know, we do the nominating on the first day before we elect the new Speaker. We will actually vote on it the next morning."

"Yeah," said Secretary Clarkson with a smile. "I'm aware of the way it works."

"Of course," said Joe. "Well, I won't keep y'all any longer." Joe walked the two men out of his office. They stopped and talked to Marcy for a minute before the Governor and Secretary left the suite, walking towards the Lieutenant Governor's office.

Joe walked back into his office and closed the door. He walked to the middle of the room and lifted his fists in the air before covering his face with his hands. He laid down on the couch against the wall and laughed as the tears began to roll. It was over. He was going to be Speaker. Which meant he might be Governor. Then, who knows? He didn't want to think that far ahead; he wanted to take in this moment and enjoy it.

The Governor and Secretary walked out of Joe's suite and stopped to exchange some pleasantries with the State Trooper guarding the entrance to Legislative Plaza, where Chester was waiting patiently for his boss. He then began to escort the two men down the hall. There were a few tourists from Mountain City wandering the halls of the Plaza, and the Governor stopped to talk to them and take a few pictures. As they passed the Speaker's office they waived to Carroll who was sitting dutifully at her desk.

As they passed the entrance to an empty committee room, the Secretary whispered to the Governor, "I thought your budget only had a one percent increase?"

"It did," said the Governor with a smile, "but now it'll have a three percent increase. Also, we were only planning on running twelve bills in our legislative agenda. I got to tell my people to get to work."

"Man," said Darrell. "You were right about how desperate he is; I didn't think you were right about it this morning, but now I see it. You probably could have asked for a constitutional amendment to serve a third term."

The two men laughed. They were at the Lieutenant Governor's suite. Governor Welch turned to the Secretary of State and said, "I learned a long time ago: when someone is offering you more than you thought you could get, you take it and don't get greedy." They walked into the Lieutenant Governor's office, who quickly agreed that Larry Pickard was the right man for the job.

CHAPTER 9

Monday, December 22, 2008

There was snow on the ground in Nashville. At least, Nashville's version of snow. As Tom drove into the parking garage underneath Legislative Plaza, he couldn't help but think that a few men with feather dusters could remove all the white flakes from the sidewalks downtown. He pulled into his spot in the garage by the elevator, but he took the stairs up into the Plaza because they were closer to his office. As far as he could tell, he was the only person in the building. The empty lots downstairs and empty chairs in every office he passed validated his feeling. He couldn't help but notice the emptiness of the Plaza and how that only gave credence to Joe Humphrey's plan to fire and replace everyone. Christmas break did not actually start until the next day, and Tom seriously doubted that everyone had requested the paid time off for today. Although, he supposed, there was also the possibility that everyone took the day off and got an early start to the holiday, assuming the worst thing that could happen to them was getting fired.

He got to his office and sat in his chair. He unplugged the phone on his desk and didn't turn on his computer. Instead he just sat there, evaluating the situation they were in. Their plans to influence the GOP Caucus nomination for Speaker hadn't worked. Their hit piece against Humphrey had backfired. They had done a decent job of getting the big money Republican donors to throw their support behind Larry, but that seemed to only make him more attractive as a replacement to Secretary Clarkson. Yes, Secretary Clarkson. That was the wrench thrown into the moving gears they were not expecting. Maybe Humphrey already had the votes he needed to win the nomination, but maybe not. Now, they would never know. Then, of course, Governor Welch endorsed Larry for the position the day it was announced. The details of the deal between Humphrey and the Governor, Tom did not know, but he had noticed more and more bills coming to his desk from the Governor's office. They also said they were restructuring the budget. Tom was sure the extra legislation and the new budget were part of whatever deal the Governor struck with Leader Humphrey to get his rival out of the race. What he didn't know was whether or not Governor Welch had been kindhearted enough to also save the state employees who worked at the Plaza. Leader Anderson insisted he didn't know the details yet, but the Governor would fill him in after his inauguration on the first Saturday in January.

Tom sat silently at his desk thinking all these things over, trying desperately to think of a new way to improve their odds. Reelecting Caputo as Speaker still seemed like a far-fetched idea, despite Leader Anderson supposedly having a secret plan to do so. It was too late to get the GOP Caucus to nominate someone else; their nominations were closed and Larry had officially withdrawn. Tom and Charlie had come up with a doomsday plan on Friday night after drinking too many three-dollar pitchers at the Front Page Bar on Union Street. Their Caucus had forty-nine votes – why not nominate a Republican for Speaker? They could for themselves, plus the forty-nine Democrats would be enough to win. Then the Speaker would really owe them. It was a flimsy plan, more unstable than finding the one vote for Caputo. But why not just throw it out there during the meeting this morning? It can't be worse than whatever asinine plan Gregory had cooked up.

He heard Charlie's door open next door. A few minutes later his coworker popped his head into Tom's office. "Hey man," said Charlie. "Want some coffee?"

"Sure," said Tom. Charlie disappeared and returned a few minutes later with two styrofoam cups, handing one to Tom.

"Good weekend?" asked Charlie as he sat in the wingback chair in the corner of Tom's office.

"Not bad," said Tom. "Got some Christmas gifts for my family. Other than that, I just tried to stay busy and not think about how fucked we are."

"Yeah," said Charlie. "Sounds a lot like my weekend. Minus the gifts for the family, also you probably watched a lot less porn than I did." They sat quietly and sipped their coffee. Then Charlie said, "So, what do you think the Leader's grand plan is going to be?"

"I'm not sure," said Tom. "Probably hiring a terrorist to blow up the Capitol during the Governor's State of the State."

"Well," said Charlie. "As long as we keep Tayna Allan out of the Chamber when it happens, that might not be bad. I'd sign up for Tayna being Governor." They laughed and returned to silence.

"Hey," said Tom, "do you remember what we talked about Friday night?"

"That white guy at the bar you want to smash with?" asked Charlie. Tom had forgotten that he had spent at least a drunken half hour talking to a man who he was convinced was gay too. Turned out, he was just very well groomed.

"No," said Tom burying the memory. "The other thing."

Charlie narrowed his eyes and puckered his lips; he had entered into deep thought. "What other thing?" he asked.

"Our doomsday plan?"

"No, refresh my memory."

Tom sighed, and then whispered. "We get one Republican to vote for themselves and we give them our forty-nine votes?"

"Ah shit!" exclaimed Charlie. "I remember that. No! That's a bullshit plan."

"Why?"

"Think about what all has to happen," said Charlie sitting up straight. "Caputo has to withdraw his nomination, the new guy would have to be willing to get kicked out of the Republican Party, then they would have to make the same exact promises to the Black Caucus, we don't even know what those promises are by the way, they would have to be ok with working with a Democratic staff because I seriously doubt any Republican in this state would work for them, and our side would have to be ok with voting for a Republican."

"Does that sound more, or less, crazy than asking a Republican to get kicked out of their party for voting for Caputo?" asked Tom.

"Same," said Charlie. "It sounds the exact same level of crazy. It's a wash of crazy."

"Let's just bring it up to Gregory," said Tom.

"No."

"Bring up what?" said the voice of Gregory from the conference room.

"Nothing, sir," said Charlie.

"Guys, let's meet in my office in ten minutes," said Gregory.

"Ok," said Tom and Charlie in unison.

"Now you've fucking done it," whispered Charlie to Tom as Gregory disappeared into the reception area.

"What's wrong with suggesting it?" Tom whispered.

"And stab Speaker Caputo in the back, directly, like that? Not even nominating him?"

"It's worth discussing, at least between the three of us," whispered Tom.

"No, let's both shut the fuck up about it," whispered Charlie as he stood up and left Tom's office.

Tom and Charlie walked into Gregory's office together. The two young men were waved in and wordlessly told to sit down on the couch while Gregory had set up shop in a chair in the lounge area of his office. Gregory had a small stack of files on the coffee table.

"Boys, Christmas is coming up," is he how he chose to start the meeting.

"What did you get us?" asked Charlie.

"A shit ton of work," responded Gregory without cracking a smile. "Anyway, this means we only have days, not weeks, to come up with and execute a plan to keep Caputo Speaker." Charlie and Tom both leaned back against the couch. Tom rolled his eyes. Charlie was more vocal with his annoyance.

"Ah shit, Greg," he said. Gregory's face showed signs of surprise. "I thought we agreed there wasn't going to be a Speaker Caputo?"

"Yeah we did, back when we thought we could knock out Humphrey with another Republican." Gregory was defensive with his reply. He had more to say but Tom cut him off.

"We still can," said Tom. Charlie gave Tom a worried sideglance.

"No, no," said Gregory. "That ship is long gone. We are back to getting Caputo reelected, and I have the plan to do it," he tapped the files on the table in front of them.

"Fine," said Charlie, his tone unpleasant. "Let's hear it. But I warn you, I'm not going to like it. Humphrey is going to be Speaker and we should start getting ready for that, but, sure, let's see what you've got cooked up."

"Now, look," said Gregory ignoring Charlie's negative attitude. "Humphrey thinks he has this thing sewn up now. But we got something, or actually some things, that he doesn't. Do you know what?"

"Forty-nine votes," said Tom. His heart started to beat faster and his disposition changed. Maybe, just maybe, he thought, his boss had already come up with the same plan they had.

"That's right," said Gregory pointing at Tom. "And what do they got that we don't?"

"Fifty votes, more commonly known as a majority," said Charlie. He had already grown tired of the conversation.

"Sort of, the answer I was looking for was a large caucus," said Gregory. He picked up the pile of files. "That means, they're going to have internal caucus, and ambitious young members, and angry old members. I remember there being about five or six different little cliques in our caucus when we were a super majority." He shook the files. "Here. These are what I think their groups are going to be. All we got to do is pick one, just one group, identify the leader, get them all to vote for Caputo and in return we'll vote for whoever they want to be Speaker Pro."

"No," said Tom.

"Absolutely, the fuck, not," said Charlie.

"Are you insane?" asked Tom. "The Black Caucus would never stand for this. They'd recall your leadership position, right now, if they knew you were even suggesting stabbing Tayna in the back like this. What the hell?"

"Listen, I've thought this through," said Gregory, trying to regain some footing. "We wouldn't just be getting one vote, but closer to twelve, from their entire little group. Tayna would lose her position, which she doesn't really deserve, and we'd keep the Speaker for two more years."

"You'd have a better shot at making Tayna Speaker and giving Humphrey the Speaker Pro office," said Charlie. "Put the Black Caucus to the side for a bit. What would the State Party think of this? You'd get primaried so fast you wouldn't stand a chance!"

"For saving the Speaker? I doubt it," said Gregory.

"You're wrong, Leader," said Tom. "I'm sorry but this is a stupid and desperate plan. Caputo is done."

"Do you two have anything better?" said Gregory, throwing the files back down on the table with anger.

"Yes, actually we do," said Tom. He took a deep breath. "We sh——"

"We should start studying what other Democratic minority caucuses across this country have done to win legislative battles," interrupted Charlie, putting his hand on Tom's knee.

"That's not——" Tom tried to continue but Charlie talked over him.

"You've already done the leg work, Leader Anderson," said Charlie, picking up one of the files. "We need to get ass-deep into the legislation and figure out which of these groups of Republicans we can get to vote with us on any particular issue. Abortion, gay stuff, education, healthcare, real estate, whatever the fuck it is. It's easier to find one of them to vote for or against a bill than it is for one of them to vote for Caputo. Or to vote for any Dem for that matter. Plus, with Pickard leaving the day after we start, his replacement won't be up here until after the two weeks we recess. We'll have an even split for the first few days. That's what we should be planning for."

"Charlie," said Gregory. He rubbed his forehead and then continued, "You're right. Ok? You're right we should do that. I want you to do that, but that's the backup plan. That's what we'll do if all else fails. Actually, we'll have to do that anyway. But we're going to have to try my thing first."

"There's one other option," said Tom.

"Tom, stop," pleaded Charlie.

"Let's hear him out," said Gregory, condescendingly.

"We've got forty-nine votes," Tom began. He paused. He knew he may only get one shot to explain this correctly; he didn't want to waste his chance. The tension in the room had risen quickly. "We have forty-nine votes, and this whole time we've been operating under the assumption that we need one person to vote for Caputo. What if, instead, we offered one person forty-nine votes for themselves to be Speaker?" Gregory squinted and cocked his head in a shocked and confused manner. "Our forty-nine votes for them, plus their vote for themselves – that person becomes Speaker and owes us big time." Charlie crossed his legs, covered his mouth, looked away, and stayed silent.

"Are you serious?" asked Gregory.

"Yes," said Tom reflexively.

"Do you think that Bob Caputo is going to vote for a Republican over himself?"

"I'm saying we, as a caucus, nominate a Republican and not Bob Caputo."

"Oh," said Gregory spreading his arms and leaning forward. "This just keeps getting better."

"I think he would go for it, if we timed the question right," said Tom.

"And when would that be?" asked Gregory sarcastically.

"The Monday before session starts."

"My God, you want to ask the longest-serving Speaker of the House to remove himself from consideration and vote for a Republican to replace him . . . the day before the vote happens," Gregory asked with a laugh.

"Yes," said Tom. His answer came almost before the question had been asked. "And we wouldn't tell our members until the

meeting prior to going to the floor for session to be gaveled in."
Gregory rolled his eyes and removed his glasses. "It's our only
play left."

"The hell it is," said Gregory. "I've already thought of this,
Tom. I didn't tell anybody because I didn't want to look like a
fucking dumbass in front of people, something you clearly aren't
worried about. And what do you think the TNDP, or the DNC,
is going to say if that were to work?"

Charlie spoke up, finally. "Look around, Greg! The State
Party is nowhere to be found; they've been missing in action
since last August. The DNC wrote Tennessee off the minute
this state picked Bush over Gore. They don't give a shit about
us. Meanwhile, the Republican State Party Chair is a member of
their House Caucus, the RNC is crawling all over the place from
Mountain City to Memphis. Democrats don't give a shit about
us. We're on our own!"

"So you agree with Tom?" Gregory asked Charlie.

"No, I think his plan is equally stupid to yours," said Charlie.
"Christ, I'm the only one here that's thinking right."

"My plan picks someone out of obscurity, makes them
Speaker. Saves every job up here, from the janitor to the Chief
Clerk, and they'd be completely dependent on us for help because Republicans would abandon them. We could negotiate
chairmanships, office assignments, leadership roles--"

"No," said Gregory in a stern voice.

"But, sir--" pleaded Tom.

"I said, no, Tom." Gregory was calm now. There was a tense
silence. "Charlie, you start doing your thing. Tom you help him,
and forget that bullshit you just offered up. I still like my plan, so

I'll go at it alone; that way you two don't get blowback because despite this moment, I know this could ruin you two and I don't want that. Get the fuck out of my office. And Merry Christmas."

Tom and Charlie left. Charlie went back to his own office to start his project, realizing now he should have been doing it from the beginning. Tom left the Plaza; he was sick of it, he was going home. On the way he would make a mental list of every person he could call about getting a new job.

CHAPTER 10

Sunday, December 28, 2008

Gregory had spent the past four days in his hometown of Elizabethton, Tennessee. A small city, closer to the state capital of North Carolina than Nashville, hidden away in the low valleys of the Appalachian Mountains. Gregory did not often share with his friends back in Nashville that he had grown up here. It wasn't that he was ashamed of it, quite the opposite, he was extremely proud to have grown up poor in the mountains. It was because when people in Nashville saw him, a successful attorney and politician, in thousand dollar suits, with slick hair, a nice tan, expensive cars, a big house, and a much younger wife, knowing that he started out a poor mountain kid could give people an impression he did not appreciate. It was the idea of new money, as if because he started from a low rung on the social ladder, he must have done something illegal to get to this point. Unless his hometown could be advantageous to his ambitions, he kept it a secret. Plus, after more than thirty years in Nashville, that city was his hometown now.

He had arrived at his mother's house on Christmas Eve. Just him on this trip; his wife had gone to be with her family for the holiday, and Gregory preferred not to spend time with them. Being a few years older than his father-in-law made for awkward conversation. Gregory's mother had been diagnosed with a form of dementia a few years ago, and as she lost her memory he lost even more of his connection to home. His two sisters, one a nurse and the other a bank teller, had been tasked with being her caregivers. Gregory supported their effort financially with no questions asked.

Christmas Eve dinner was rough; his mother had sat at the table not speaking while the rest of the family discussed their lives. Christmas Day, his mother was far more present when the entire family – brothers-in-laws, nieces, and nephews included – came over for lunch. Seeing his mother remember her grandchildren made the discussion among he and his hardcore Republican brothers by marriage more bearable. Gregory was surprised to learn that no one he had talked to in the area, whether in his family or not, knew that the Republican Party was now the majority despite the fact that Carter County was a Republican stronghold. It was as if the people there had gotten used to playing the victim and weren't ready to give it up, that and while they all had opinions on politics, none of them seemed to keep up with what was happening beyond the new President.

He spent the rest of the trip caring for his mother, giving his sisters a break. He was disconnected from everything else in the world during those last three days. This was, after all, the woman who raised him and his two younger sisters on her own. His father had died before Gregory was out of third grade, and now his mother was set to go. Sometimes he would think to himself he should visit more often, but when he did, he felt as though the time there was going to tarnish the memories of his mother. He didn't want to remember her like this: slow speaking, unaware of her surroundings, this wasn't his mother and he felt very little obligation towards her in her present state. But he knew his sisters needed the break and he was there to help, for once.

Now he was heading back to Nashville. He hadn't spoken to Tom or Charlie, or anyone attached to his political life for that matter, since the meeting in his office on Monday. Being away from the situation, he slowly realized how foolish his plan actually was, but he wasn't ready to give up on it just yet. He wanted to at least offer it up to a Republican before he abandoned it entirely. Charlie was right, they should be planning for the upcoming session in a strategic way. They had focused so much on step one that steps two through one thousand were now floating down river. Still, he had one shot. One Republican Representative that he knew he could ask and keep a secret. He was going to have a cup of coffee with him before heading home. Home to Nashville.

Zach's Place sat in an old yellow brick building at the corner of East Elk Avenue and Post Office Street in the downtown area of Elizabethton. The family-owned diner had become a local institution during its fifty-year existence; a place where frozen food could be defrosted and cooked quickly on demand. It was now in the hands of the third generation of the Zachary family; a local politician named Keith ran the show. Keith Zachary and Gregory Anderson first met the summer before their sophomore years of high school. They attended a basketball camp that summer at local Milligan College and quickly realized they had compatible personalities. As they made their way through high school, Gregory at Happy Valley High and Keith at the rival Elizabethton High School, they remained friendly but not quite friends. After graduation Gregory went on to play Division One basketball at Vanderbilt, and while most of his time was spent on the bench, Keith went to Milligan and played the most games in the history of the small college. They had lost touch, occasionally seeing each other when Gregory came to town for a visit. Four years ago, while Gregory was positioning himself for a run at House Majority Leader, Keith, who had been Vice Mayor of Carter County at the time, ended up winning the Republican primary for State Representative in District Four. Winning the Republican primary there meant one would win the general election by default – there were maybe twelve Democrats in the district. Gregory and Keith struck up a new bipartisan friendly relationship; being small-town men at heart, in a big city they felt comfortable with each other.

Gregory parked his car around the corner on Post Office Street. He enjoyed walking through the cold mountain air, clearing his lungs of the stale air of decay from his mother's house. Zach's Place, he had been told, had recently undergone some renovation. Yet when he walked in, it looked just as it did when he was in high school. He surveyed the small restaurant and did not see Keith. The place was surprisingly empty, then Gregory remembered it was Sunday morning and most people were still at church. He started to move towards a table in the corner when the door to the kitchen opened.

"There he is," said Keith walking through the door. He was wearing slacks and a white button-up dress shirt; Gregory thought the outfit was risky for a man who works in a greasy restaurant. His thin grey hair was slicked straight back, showing just how far back his hairline went on his head. His normally pencil-thin mustache was bushier than normal.

Gregory smiled, waved and held out his hand for a shake, all in one motion. He said, as Keith took his hand, "Hey partner, how you been?"

"Not bad, not bad. Better than you I suppose," said Keith with a laugh. "Want coffee or food?"

"I'll take a black coffee," said Gregory.

"Ok, I'll grab it. Please, have a seat anywhere you want."

Gregory picked a table near the kitchen; he hung his jacket on the bag of the chair as Keith disappeared through the kitchen door. Gregory hollered, "Why's the place so empty?"

"Ooohh," said Keith. "We don't open till one on Sundays typically. To be honest, I was dressed for church when I remembered you said you were stopping by. You and me got the place to ourselves for a while."

"Shoot, son, you didn't have to come in just for me," said Gregory.

"Oh no, it's fine," he said as entered the dining area with two mugs of coffee with steam floating up from them. "I wasn't looking forward to the service today anyway. The Sunday after Christmas is always the worst. You want more Christmas stuff from the preacher but he's there to remind you that the world has moved on from the birth of Christ and it's time to start getting ready for His death. It's a real bummer, you know?" Gregory laughed and agreed.

"Place looks good," Gregory said, despite not being able to tell what was new and what was old.

"Well, thank you. We repainted and got new floors, but we picked the same tiles and same paint color so it feels familiar, just new," said Keith looking around at the yellow walls. "We're getting new tables and chairs in the summer. But, yeah, same tile, and we took a piece of the wall over to the Lowe's down there. They put it on this machine and it matched the old color perfectly, it was pretty incredible."

"Really?" Gregory faked his interest; he knew how the color-matching process worked.

"Oh, yeah man. They can do it for any color," Keith sipped his coffee.

The two men sat in the empty diner talking about their lives. Gregory updated Keith on the state of his mother, Keith offered his sympathy. Keith talked about his kids, who were now in high school. Keith invited Gregory back to the area for the Happy Valley versus Elizabethton High School basketball game in January; Gregory said he would try. They talked about Keith's new apartment in downtown Nashville, one that he was going to share with Peter Newman from Riceville. Keith said he was going to try to make it down for the Governor's inauguration. They talked a bit about some policies, and the new United States Congress. Finally they got to the topic of the General Assembly.

"Look now, Gregory, I know it's going to be tough for you and Speaker Caputo to be in the minority." Keith was trying his best to express sympathy for his friend. "But y'all can still get a lot of stuff done."

"Oh, I know," said Gregory.

"I mean, hell, y'all only need one vote." Keith held up one finger to emphasize the math. "Just one, and brother, y'all can pass any bill you want."

"Oh, we know, Keith, we've got plans." Gregory adjusted the way he was sitting in the chair. "I think the Governor and Humphrey have already struck a deal on some bills. As long as Joe Humphrey lives up to the deal, I think we might be ok."

"I don't trust Joe Humphrey for nothing, but he ain't gone back on any promises he's made to me yet," said Keith in a whisper.

"Oh really?" said Gregory.

"Oh, yeah. Really, I've never known him to go back on his word," said Keith. He quickly added, "aside from the normal political bargaining things, you know."

"I meant," Gregory began and then stopped to think about the phrasing. "I was talking more about the part where you don't really trust him."

"Well, trust isn't the right word. I meant more . . ." Keith went silent to think, he moved his hands in circles to help the process. "I was meaning more that I just don't like him."

"Why's that?"

"He's young, and he thinks he can be President. Shit, I don't like people like that up there. I like the people like you and me, the ones who are there to do the work of the House, and who aren't out for themselves."

"Were you going to vote for Larry?" Gregory asked cautiously.

"Oh, shoot yeah. Larry was going to be my guy," Keith said with some enthusiasm. "I didn't want Joe to be my Speaker. Him and his whole sleazy crowd, no, thank you."

"Then why not vote for Caputo?" Gregory asked almost breathlessly. Why hadn't he thought about asking Keith sooner? He had the exact profile they were looking for; he wanted to kick himself for not thinking of it sooner. Yet his hopes were quickly dashed.

"Oh I couldn't do that. You see, we have to take an oath after our nominating meeting that says we will only vote for a Republican or face a fine, or expulsion, or something like that." Keith seemed adamant about the issue. Gregory decided to swing for the fences.

"Well, let me ask you this," he took a breath and whispered. The two men were alone, but the extra caution of speaking softly seemed like the right thing to do. "Let me get this out and then, if you want, we can never talk about it again. We've got forty-nine votes; if we added your vote, Caputo could win. In return, I can get you the Speaker Pro office."

Keith's eyes went wide. He looked over his shoulder to check the kitchen making sure it was empty. He leaned to the side to look out the front windows, making sure no one was on the street. Then he shook his head, "Boy . . . you're getting desperate. You have to be desperate, or crazy, to suggest a damn fool thing like that."

"But it's not that crazy," Gregory could feel himself pleading.

"Look here, let's assume I agreed to this. Which I won't, and never will, but just to prove this here point. Let's say I were to agree. I run against not only my party's nominee for Speaker Pro but also Tayna Allan. No way I get enough of my caucus to break ranks to vote for me, which I would have to because there's no way your Black Caucus votes for me, and most of your House Caucus isn't going to vote against Tayna. I mean, come on man, think about it."

"It could work," said Gregory, defeated.

"It couldn't, I'm sorry but it couldn't." Keith leaned back and shook his head. "Plus, I think there's a pretty good chance Joe makes me a chairman of a committee."

"Ok, but Caputo would absolutely make you chair of any committee you wanted."

"I'd rather skip the drama, stick with my party, and take my chances with Joe. Now, I'm sorry but I have to insist we drop this." Keith was raising his voice. "And, as your friend, I'm going to tell you to drop that idea altogether." Gregory dropped his head.

"You're right, I know you're right," Gregory said, as he kept his head down and shook it.

"It's alright, bud," Keith patted Gregory's hand. He was speaking to Gregory as his friend now, not as a fellow politician. "You aren't used to losing, but you've lost. Time to get ready for the fight, you've wasted enough time trying to stop what was going to happen no matter what."

Gregory looked up, "You're right, I'm sorry man, I just, I don't know."

"Hey, it's ok," said Keith. "Me in your situation, I probably would have done the same thing. And you know how I know?"

"How?"

Keith smiled and popped out his front two teeth, "Because you're the son of a bitch who knocked my teeth out." The two men laughed.

"Yeah, I did," Gregory tapped his nose, "but you broke my fucking nose the next year."

"Well, I had to get you back," Keith exclaimed. They laughed and shared old basketball stories for another hour.

Once the restaurant staff began to show up, Gregory made his exit with a handshake and a promise to get dinner at a nice restaurant when Keith got to town for session. Gregory walked back to his car.

He passed the hours of the drive back to Nashville with an audiobook, but it was on for background noise. He knew, deep down, the fight was over, but for some reason he couldn't bring himself to accept it. Tom, Charlie, Keith, even some of the staffers who foolishly thought their jobs could be saved if their bosses voted for Joe were against him now. He hated that he hadn't stood up to the Speaker after the election; he should have told Caputo to handle it himself. As he made his way back into the city, he resolved himself to start fighting to protect his caucus and their staff. He was giving up on Speaker Caputo, once and for all.

CHAPTER 11

Saturday, January 3, 2009

The weather had actually cooperated for the Governor's Inauguration. It was a cold day, but thankfully it was dry and sunny. The wind that swept through the ceremony provided cold bites of chaos. The fountain plaza that sits on top of Legislative Plaza and in front of the War Memorial Building had been packed. Governor Welch had taken his second oath of office and delivered his remarks from a stage on Charlotte Avenue, which had been shut down to traffic, with a massive red flag behind him featuring the state's unmistakable white tri-stars in a blue circle. It was a picturesque moment: Governor Welch on stage with the political leaders of the state seated behind him, mixed with his family and pillars of the community. The columns of the Capitol behind the stage had been wrapped with red, white, and blue streamers that had somehow stayed put through the wind. The Governor gave a rousing speech on the difficulties the country was facing, but he noted how Tennessee always led the way and this time would be no different. A hopeful, optimistic, and idealistic message that resonated with all in attendance. At the end of it, everyone in the crowd, regardless of political affiliation, felt united and ready to link arms to boldly face their uncertain futures.

Mary Ellen disappeared shortly after the applause for the Governor had ended. There were other events she could attend, but she had gone to the prayer breakfast at Lipscomb University that morning and had been at the main event. She wanted to enjoy the afternoon before having to drag her husband to the inaugural ball at the convention center.

She walked the three blocks from the plaza to the Cades Hotel Downtown as unassumingly as possible. She rode the elevator up to the fourth floor, walked down the hall, and softly rapped on the door to room 403. Larry Pickard, who had sat on the stage next to his soon-to-be-predecessor Darrell Clarkson, had somehow beaten her to the room. He opened the door, still wearing his suit but he had removed his tie. She put her hands on his shoulders and ran them up his neck, behind his head and pulled his face to hers. Their lips met. He moved his fingertips over her hips, across the small of her back, then down to her rear, grabbing it with both hands, pulling her into the room. He shut the door with his foot. She dropped her bag on the ground.

He unzipped the back of her red dress and began to pull it off her as he led her to the bed. Just before laying down, she moved her dress past her waist, over her legs, on to the floor. She stepped out of it and her high stiletto heels as she laid down in one smooth motion. She took her hands and fluffed her long blonde hair out so it sprawled across the bed, as he held himself above her and kissed her neck. He moved his lips down to the skin between her neck and shoulder, and felt her shake slightly as he moved on to her shoulder. His lips followed his fingertips as they easily, gingerly removed the lacey blue bra strap from her shoulder. He worked his way down her chest, her stomach, he kissed her left hip on the bone before moving to the upper part of her hairless thigh. She was the only woman he had ever been with that shaved her legs above the knee. He was on his knees on the floor as she laid on the bed, her fingers running through his hair.

As he moved to the center of her body, she sat up and pushed him away slowly. She kissed him, running her tongue against the roof of his mouth, and removed his jacket. He felt the skin on her back, soft and smooth, as she unbuttoned his shirt one button at a time. She felt his bare torso with wisps of chest hair; she enjoyed the sensation of the roughness of his chest hair mixed with softness of his skin. His pectoral muscles had started to go flabby but she didn't mind; she had never minded.

She laid back down with her hands on the top of his head, pushing his face to the space between her belly button and panty line. He exhaled slowly on her skin while letting his nose gently trace the path down to the top of the lacey blue panties. He moved them down slightly, tenderly kissing the spot of flesh. He enjoyed the fact that the top and bottoms of her underwear always matched as a set. That, too, was something he had never experienced before her.

They finished an hour later. She rolled off of him, collapsing next to him on the king-sized bed, exhausted. He rolled over to face her, propping his head up on his fist and stared at her as she gazed up at the ceiling, catching her breath.

"Hello, how's your day?" he said with a smile; they were the first words they had spoken to each other that day. She laughed and rubbed her eyes. She got up and walked over to her bag, pulling out an oversized cardigan sweater. She put it on, it covered her chest and flirtatiously fell to the top of her hips. She pulled it closed with her hands, returning to the bed and got under the covers. Larry quickly slipped on his boxers and joined her under the sheets. She placed her head against his chest, her arm around his abdomen, and he wrapped his arm over her shoulder as she put a single leg between his. He felt her breathing return to normal and then become heavy as she fell asleep.

He watched as a small stream of drool began to ooze out of her mouth onto his chest. He marveled at her beauty; she was eleven years his junior. Yet her beauty wasn't his main attraction, it was her mind and her potential. He was drawn to her power, her future, from the moment they had met. She had been drawn to his boyish good looks, his innocent smile, his way of thinking about the world as nothing more than a stop on the journey of existence. He turned on the TV, and as she slept he watched the second half of a ball game happening in a much warmer part of the country.

She woke up still in his arms. "What time is it?" she asked, barely opening her eyes.

"Quarter till four," he said muting the television.

"Hell," she said, still groggy from her nap. She rolled out of his embrace and laid on her stomach with a body space between them. She gathered all her strength and pushed herself out of bed. She walked to the bathroom, removing the cardigan on her way. Larry watched as her body glistened with sweat; she found a towel and began to wipe herself off.

"What time do you have to be somewhere?" he called to her.

"I'm meeting Tracey at her loft on Second Avenue at five. A bunch of us are getting ready for the ball over there." She walked back into the room and began to get dressed.

"Is hubby picking you up from there?"

She rolled her eyes. "He's supposed to, but who knows. I need to call him; we might just meet at the ball." She walked over to him holding her hair up with one hand, and he zipped her dress back up. "Your wife not making the trip?"

"No," he said with a sigh. He turned off the TV and stood up looking for his pants. "I'm taking my daughter instead."

"How sweet, a nice little father-daughter date."

"Something like that, one of her friends from UTC lives in Nashville. She's staying with them; she's going to be here at six and we'll leave from the hotel."

"That's nice," she said with a smile. She found her earrings and put them back in. "I talked to Lynn Ellington at the inauguration, she's pissed at you."

He laughed out loud while sitting in the chair, slipping his socks back on. "She'll get over it. Joe still needs to keep her happy. She's the pro-life leader now."

She pulled her hair back into a tight ponytail and looked at him. "A lot of us are pissed at you."

He looked up at her while he buttoned his shirt. "Why? Joe was going to be the only option before I got in. Things are back to normal, the way I see it."

"Yeah, he was, until you jumped in." She sat down on the bed, leaning back on her elbows. "You got in and a lot of us felt relieved. We all understand that it's Joe's turn or whatever, but he's such a fucking dictator. Quite of few of us aren't looking forward to him."

"He's a dick, leave off the 'tator.'" Larry smiled at his attempt at humor. Mary Ellen didn't flinch. "Look, I thought I had a shot but the vote count wasn't breaking my way."

"How in the fuck would you know that?" Mary Ellen stood up. "Jesus Larry, you barely tried! You had lunch with a few people, shook some hands, or whatever bullshit you did. But you never really put any effort into it."

"That's not true."

"Like hell it's not!"

"It's not," he said walking past her into the bathroom.

"Name one thing you did that I didn't mention," she said as she followed him into the bathroom. She crossed her arms and leaned against the door frame.

He was holding his toothbrush but stopped looking for the toothpaste. "Look, even if I had been in the lead of the vote count, which I wasn't, I still would've dropped out to be Secretary of State. It's a safer bet and a bigger job."

"Cool, so, fuck the rest of us, I guess."

"Why do you care so much? You're the one that told us it was Joe's position," he said, pointing the toothbrush at her.

"Larry," she said putting her hands to her sides, "you don't get it. I was fine with Joe. Sure, it won't be that great for four years but whatever. But I, personally, believe in you. I thought, for some damn reason, that you might actually make a good Speaker."

"Fuck that," he said turning away; he found the toothpaste in the toiletry bag. He turned back to her. "It should be you, Mary Ellen. Everyone, every single last damn one of us knows that you should be Speaker."

She shook her head. "It's not my turn"

"Oh, what the fuck does that even mean?"

"It means, if I'm going to be the first woman to be Speaker of the goddam House I've got to play the game the right way! I can't decide to jump in and piss off a bunch of men who think they could do it better than me! I don't get the luxury of just up and deciding it should be me – doing that ends my political career. So, I have to wait. I fucking hate it, but it's the reality I deal with."

He stared at her for a moment, and then said. "That's bull-shit."

"No, it's not. It's the truth."

"You are Chairman of the fucking party; you don't have to wait on anyone."

"I'm Chairman because I played the exact same game with the Republican executive committee, but that's a party thing, not a caucus thing." She looked at him wordlessly, feeling exhausted again. She rolled her eyes and shook her head, "I've got to go." She slipped back into her heels.

"Hold on, Mary Ellen, just wait," he said remorsefully. He knew he had crossed some line, but he didn't know which line or how.

"No, serious, it's time to go. We both have to get ready." She threw her sweater into her bag and put her coat on.

"I'll see you tonight, I guess," he said, watching her move towards the door.

"Sure," she said turning back to him. "We'll exchange polite handshakes, make small talk, and pretend we barely know each other. Enjoy your fucking night," she said as she opened the door and let it slam close behind her.

"Fucking hell," whispered Larry to himself. His adrenaline was still running high, but all he could do was brush his teeth with a bit too much force.

CHAPTER 12

Monday, January 5, 2009

Hannah Collins was sitting at the small desk in the House Committee Cloak Room, which was more of a closet than room. Filled with wires, small fans, and rhythmically beating lights, the Cloak Room had been co-opted by the Legislative IT department nearly a decade ago when the demand for internet access in every office was finally agreed to by Speaker Caputo. The little space connected the back hallway, where the Majority Leader's office sat, to the large House Committee room, big enough to hold a committee of thirty and an audience of over one hundred, which bore the creative name of "Committee Room 3".

What the Cloak Room did have was a small desk typically reserved for a Sergeant at Arms who would be stationed there during a committee meeting and would only allow Members and Staff to enter through that door. It was at this desk that Hannah was sitting, double checking the numbers in her ledger, making sure they all added up to the correct number of ballots submitted. She was an accountant, the owner of Hollins Standards. She was also a staunch Republican who was often tapped to serve as Treasurer on political campaigns throughout middle Tennessee. She considered it an honor to count the ballots for the Republican House Caucus at their nominating meeting, where the new House Speaker – a Republican House Speaker – would be elected. More or less. She double-checked the numbers one more time; she knew they were right. Finally, she checked her numbers against the numbers that were totaled up by Tucker Pyle, the soon-to-be-former Caucus Secretary, just before her. The numbers were a perfect match. She put the ballots in a banker bag and closed the ledger. This was her moment.

She walked out of the Cloak Room into Committee Room 3. The room had been so loud and full of voices while she was tabulating the votes that she could pick out every word being said. Yet as she walked down the steps, past the four layers of desks at the front of the room, and to the podium front and center, the room fell quiet. She laid her ledger down on the lectern, and looked around the room. Blinded by the lights from the cameras of local news channels, the State Party, and the RNC, she held a hand up over her brow and watched as the caucus members and the media found their seats. Scheduled caucus meetings, that were official and not spontaneous, were required by ethics laws to be open to the media. This was a law that was only followed occasionally, since most caucus meetings were not scheduled. Hannah didn't mind; she wanted proof that she was part of this moment in history. She saw Mike Hayes walk past her and smiled. She gave him a thumbs up to indicate she was ready to proceed. Mike took his seat in the middle of the top row of the desk behind Hannah. He hit the gavel.

"I now call this meeting back to order," he said into the pencil-thin microphone, banging the gavel again. Hannah pulled out the sheet of paper with her lines on it.

"Mrs. Collins, have you completed the tabulations of the ballots of all present caucus members?" asked Mike in a stern and professional voice, with the cadence of someone imitating an auctioneer.

Hannah checked her lines on the sheet, and read them timidly, "Mr. Chairman, I have completed the tabulations."

"Mrs. Collins, do your tabulations match with those of the Caucus Secretary?"

"Yes, Mr. Chairman. The tabulations are identical."

"Mrs. Collins, have the ballots from the caucus members been out of your sight since they were submitted?"

"No, Mr. Chairman. They have been in sight and in my possession since they were submitted."

"Mrs. Collins, does the total number of ballots submitted match the number of caucus members present when a roll call vote was taken in order to satisfy a quorum?"

"Yes, Mr. Chairman. The number present matches the number of ballots submitted."

"Mrs. Collins, do you swear, or affirm, before this body, and God, that the numbers and results you are about to share are, to the best of your knowledge, legitimate, and without bias, the results of fairly offered contest?

"Yes, Mr. Chairman. With God as my witness, I swear."

"Mrs. Collins, please read the results of our intra-caucus elections, noting only the winners and losers and the margin of victory. I will remind you that we keep the vote totals for each candidate for office confidential. The margin of victory is to be announced, however any member may request to count the ballots themselves within the next twenty-four hours, after which time the ballots will be destroyed. Furthermore, when Mrs. Collins calls a winner of an election, the winner is to proceed to the front of the room and stand to the right of Mrs. Collins facing the body. Please hold all applause until all offices and results in this portion are announced. Mrs. Collins, you may proceed."

"Thank you, Mr. Chairman," she said. She moved the yellow sheet of paper underneath her ledger book. She adjusted the microphone slightly; she took a sip of water from the glass next to her. She began to speak, unsure if the microphone was amplifying her voice. "In the race for Caucus Treasurer, Ms. Lee Jason has been elected uncontested. In the race for Caucus Secretary, Mr. Buddy Hill has been elected uncontested. In the race for Assistant Floor Leader, Mr. David Jones has been elected uncontested. In the race for Floor Leader, Ms. Tracy Holcomb has been elected over," she paused momentarily hearing gasps in the room, and looked up as a hum of voices began to whisper in surprise shock of the last result. She heard Mike bang the gavel behind her.

"Order," said Mike, giving the gavel another smack. "Our apologies, Mrs. Collins, please continue."

She looked back down at her ledger book, found her spot and continued, "Ms. Tracy Holcomb has been elected over Peter Newman by four votes. In the race for Caucus Whip, Mr. Ron Evans has been elected over Mr. Craig Holly by fifteen votes. In the race for Vice Caucus Chair, Mr. Afton Krammer has been elected over Mr. Andrew Mansfield by eighteen votes. Finally,

Mr. Mike Hayes has been," Hannah paused and smirked – Mike Hayes wasn't only her personal State Representative but also her friend – "reelected uncontested. Mr. Chairman," a small smattering of applause broke out. Mike was quick to gavel it dead. Hannah laughed at the interruption. "Mr. Chairman, that concludes the intra-caucus election results," she said, quickly finding the yellow sheet of paper, "I yield back my time."

"Thank you, Mrs. Collins. Congratulations to the victors, and thank you to all who chose to run. I hereby declare these votes valid and, without object, consider their elections certified." Mike banged the gavel and smiled. Hannah looked over her right shoulder and saw a small row of finely dressed people standing there. She mouthed congratulations to them, they politely nodded; Lee Jason shook Hannah's hand and mouthed the words 'thank you.' Mike hit the gavel three more times, ending the applause.

"Mrs. Collins," he continued, "I now ask that you read the results for the election of House Republican Leadership." After offering the same preamble, Hannah proceeded.

"Thank you, Mr. Chairman," said Hannah. She returned to the ledger book and read, "In the race for Assistant Republican Leader, Mr. John Liston has been elected over Mr. Tim McCray by twenty-one votes. In the race for Republican House Leader, Mr. Tucker Pyle has been elected uncontested." She looked back at the yellow sheet of paper, and said over the growing applause, "Mr. Chairman, that concludes the election results for the House Republican Leadership. I yield back my time." The applause grew steadier as the two men, one quite old and stocky the other young and tall, made their way to the front of the room.

Mike returned to the gavel with three slow whacks. "Thank you, Mrs. Collins, congratulations to the victors, and thank you to all who chose to run. I hereby declare these votes valid and, without object, consider their elections certified," Mike said, this portion faster the second time and only gave the gavel a little tap before quickly moving on.

"Finally, Mrs. Collins." There was applause and Mike let it carry on for a moment; he jokingly lifted the gavel with a smile, causing laughter to fill the room. The atmosphere had suddenly turned electric. "Finally, Mrs. Collins," Mike repeated as the noise faded, "I now ask that you read the results for the election of House Republican Nominees for General Assembly Officers."

"Thank you, Mr. Chairman." Hannah could feel herself smile and lighten up. The energy in the room was having an effect on her. "In the race for the Deputy Speaker nomination, Mr. Al Grindstaff has been elected uncontested." She turned around and looked at Mike, who waved a hand telling her to continue over the applause. "In the race for the Speaker Pro Term nomination," she referred back to the yellow paper to read her line, "Mr. Tucker Pyle has withdrawn his name, no other names were nominated. There will be no Republican nominee for Speaker Pro Term." This was met with sarcastic groans and boos followed by laughter. Everyone in the room knew the agreement between Joe Humphrey and Tayna Allan. Most approved of it. Anything was on the table to ensure Joe's victory.

"And finally Mr. Chairman," Hannah smiled and looked around the room; she intoned the next line in a lower voice as the sound in the room had vanished. "The one y'all have been waiting for." There was laughter and some applause. "In the race for the Speaker of the House nomination, Mr. Joe Humphrey. . ." There was an outburst of excited screams and yells mixed with applause at the mention of the name. She paused before realizing Mike wasn't going to gavel the noise down, so raised her voice so it could be heard over the crowd, "has been elected, uncontested!"

The sound of elation filled the room and could be heard throughout Legislative Plaza. Hannah applauded and turned back to look at Mike who was also standing and applauding. Joe made the slow walk to the front of the room; the joy on his face was genuine. The tears in his eyes were proof that he was nearly overcome with emotion. Once he reached the front and shook Hannah's hand along with everyone's hand who had been elected to office, Mike waited a few extra moments and then pointed at Hannah. Mike returned to his seat and hit the gavel.

"Mr. Chairman, that concludes all elections for this meeting. I yield back my time."

"Thank you, Mrs. Collins. You are dismissed and relieved of your duty having been complete." Mike hit the gavel, but it didn't do anything to quell the noise. "If y'all don't calm down, we are never getting out of here." The applause ended and laughter picked up, but was quickly hushed. "The Chair now recognizes the Honorable Mary Ellen Guess, State Representative and Chairman of the Tennessee Republican Party, to administer the caucus oaths."

Mary Ellen had been seated on the front row. She walked slowly to the lectern and momentarily bathed in the applause directed at her. She waved, and then held up her hands for quiet. Mike was now in line with the other victors waiting to take his oath; he had one arm draped around Joe, and could not gavel the noise away. She opened a folder that she had carried with her and spoke. "Raise your right hand and repeat after me." She waited while the line of people lifted their hands.

"I, state your name, do swear, or affirm, to represent the values, vision, and ethics of the Republican House Caucus, and represent, to the best of my ability, my people, my country, and the Republican Party, in the office for which I have been selected, so help me God." After the group had repeated the last words, a quiet fell over the room. Mary Ellen broke the silence by leading the crowd in a round of applause.

Mike walked back up to his seat and hit the gavel. "I will now ask the Honorable Mary Ellen Guess to administer the caucus oath to the entire body."

Mary Ellen turned to the second page in the folder, she took a deep breath and smiled as she looked over the room and read out the oath. When she was done, the room was once again filled with noise.

Mike quickly said, "All business of the scheduled meeting being complete, I now declare this caucus meeting adjourned!" He loudly hit the gavel several times for emphasis and then quickly descended the stairs to join the celebration.

The reporters had their story; the field and the fate of the House of Representatives was sealed, as were the next day's headlines of 'Joe Humphrey Set to be Next Speaker: House Republicans place two women in power to the Democrats' one.' Most caucus members remained in the room for another hour; Joe snuck out after twenty minutes. He had a meeting across the street with Rachel Garrison, the Director of Legislative Human Resources.

CHAPTER 13

Tuesday, January 6, 2009

On the second floor of the State Capitol, across the vast limestone hallway from the Senate Chambers, sits three doors. One leads to the Capitol Library, the last room to be completed in the building. It was constructed with the intention of being used as an actual library, but quickly became obsolete for the purpose. The two-story room still houses shelves full of books, historical artwork important to Tennessee, a bust of Sequoyah, and massive portraits of all three presidents and their first ladies. The lower level of the room is used for press conferences, caucus meetings, luncheons, and other gatherings. The upper balcony, off limits to the public, is used for storage of the tables and chairs used in the room. The rod iron spiral staircase connecting the two levels was purchased from a Sears Catalogue in the early twentieth century when builders were desperate to just finish the building. On either side of the library are the ceremonial offices for the Speaker of the House and Speaker of the Senate, more commonly known as the Lieutenant Governor. These office spaces are rarely used by their modern office holders. As soon as the construction of Legislative Plaza had been complete, the two speakers moved into their new subterranean office spaces. The ceremonial offices were used during long days of session as a hide-out, occasionally for extraordinarily important meetings, and for photo opportunities. Each ceremonial office featured two rooms: a small entryway where an assistant or secretary might sit but was normally unmanned except on the days when the legislative bodies had floor sessions, and a larger office complete with a handcrafted wooden desk and a conference table large enough to seat ten people.

For the past twelve years Duncan Blaine had served as the Chief Clerk for the Tennessee House of Representatives. He had been selected for the job by Speaker Caputo after serving for two years as the Parliamentarian. The job came with a near-six-figure salary, on the condition that Duncan served as both the Chief Clerk and Parliamentarian. The job was more intense than it would appear from the outside. Yes, the most public aspect of the job was the Parliamentarian side. Standing at the well in front of the Speaker in the House chamber, he was the guy who would read the bill titles, read the amendments, make sure motions were properly made and seconded, and ensure votes were taken and resolved in the correct manner. He was the expert in the rules of order for the Tennessee House of Representatives, and his responsibility was to make sure those rules were followed.

The other side of his job, the Chief Clerk side, was more banal. In this role he made sure the chairmen for each committee were trained in the rules of order. He accepted bills that the Representatives wanted to run and filed them. He assigned each bill a number and assigned them the proper committee to hear the bills. This could be a very powerful tool in the wrong hands. So powerful, in fact, that most states would send bills to an assignments committee to prevent any funny business from happening, but Tennessee left that responsibility solely in the hands of the Chief Clerk. He could, without question or explanation, send a bill to any committee he saw fit. Meaning he could kill a bill by sending it to a committee that would kill it, or give a bill a fighting chance with a more favorable committee assignment. The only check to this to this power was for a member to call for a vote on Rule 54, then with a two-thirds majority, the member could essentially pick the committee that would consider their bill. No one had ever called for a Rule 54 vote since he had become Clerk. There were statutes and laws he was supposed to follow when assigning a bill to a committee, but those were mostly for show.

Every two years, after each caucus had nominated a member to run for General Assembly officers, Duncan would call all the nominees and the House Party Leaders to a meeting in the Speaker's ceremonial office. Some would show up, most did not. Here he would run through the agenda for the first day of session, guiding them through the election of officers and the constitutionally required resolutions. He would then give a brief run-down of the events of the second day, when constitutional officers for the state would be elected in the morning, followed by the Governor's State Address in a joint session that afternoon.

This would be the sixth time he had held the meeting, but it was the first one that he wasn't looking forward to. As an employee of the House, he worked at the privilege of the Speaker of the House. With a new Speaker, that privilege would be going to someone else. Duncan, like all the others in the orbit of the Speaker's power, had resigned his fate to the hands of Joe Humphrey. Yet he could not bring himself to start looking for a new job; this place had sucked him in and he was going to fight as it tried to spit him out.

Duncan was the last to arrive at the ceremonial office. He walked in to find all the politicians standing around, laughing, talking, and sipping coffee as if they were at any random social gathering in their districts. He wasn't surprised. Out of all the things he would miss about this place, the insincere friendships and exchanges among the members would not be one. He knew these people hated each other. He knew the last thing Speaker Caputo wanted to do was be in a room with Joe Humphrey; he knew that Gregory Anderson would stab Mike Hayes in the neck with a full fountain pen if given the chance. Yet because they were programmed to respect their fellow office holders, they were more than willing to put on happy faces.

"Ah! Duncan!" exclaimed the Speaker upon the Clerk's entrance. "We were just talking about that time, you'll remember, when you kept cutting off John Baumer's microphone when he would speak!" The group laughed; Duncan did his best to join in the fun, though he was in no mood for it.

"I remember that," he said. The look on the others' faces implied they wanted to hear more. "The night before, at the firefighters' fish fry, he had drunk all the good gin, and he needed to pay for his sins. What can I say?" They laughed again. Joe patted Duncan's shoulder, and then gripped it slightly.

"Duncan, I want to introduce, well re-introduce you to somebody," Joe said, leading his gaze to a short stocky man. "You might remember, this is Gerald O'Connor." Gerald held out his hand, Duncan took it.

"Why, yes, sure I do! Member from two years back, right?" Duncan asked.

"That's right," said the man in a heavy east Tennessee accent. "I left because I hated the drive, but now I live here so what do I know?"

"Listen, Duncan," said Joe. "Should things break my way next week, Gerald here is going to shadow you for session and learn the tricks. Then next year we're gonna see if maybe he might want to take over as Parliamentarian or Clerk, but maybe not."

Fuck that; I'll quit the day you win, thought Duncan. What he said was: "Sounds alright, welcome aboard Gerald."

"Thank you, sir," said Gerald.

"Ok, if y'all don't mind, let's go on and take a seat and get through this," Duncan said motioning towards the conference table. The group took their seats, segregating themselves based on party. Democrats sat on Duncan's right, with Republicans to his left, and Gerald sitting directly across from him.

"Alright. So," Duncan began. He opened the file he had been carrying containing agendas for the first two days of session, handing the stack to Speaker Caputo who took one and passed it around the table. He clicked his pen. "Now, most of this is essentially set in stone. The order of things is, you know, the way it has to be done. But we can rearrange the way we do things a little." He waited as the members looked over the papers before continuing.

"So, we'll start with the opening. Speaker Caputo will gavel the House to order, and we'll take roll call. With roll call, if we have a quorum, the Speaker will declare us in session. Now, this is the Organizational Session, it does count as the first Legislative Day for the General Assembly but we won't consider bills until we come back from the two-week recess. At this point, on day one, he will call a justice from the state Supreme Court to the well to administer the oath of office to all members duly elected. Then we will move onto new business, which will comprise of passing two House Joint Resolutions and approving the temporary House rules. The House rules come first, it's a voice vote. We are going to vote on the same rules as last year; if the Speaker elected wants to change them, they can do so during the two-week recess by appointing a committee to change them, and then a simple majority to adopt the new rules." Duncan stopped to see if Joe wanted to say anything. Joe was sitting cross-legged and nodding. He looked at Duncan with a passive shrug suggesting he was fine with the rules from last year being temporarily put back into place.

"Next is nominating constitutional officers for the state of Tennessee. State Treasurer, Secretary of State, Comptroller, those people. That will be the first reading; we won't actually vote on any of them until the second day, just in case someone objects and because they have to be publicly nominated for at least twenty-four hours prior to their election. That will be done with a House Joint Resolution. The second is a House Joint Resolution inviting the Governor to give his State of the State on day two. We'll have to suspend the rules to do that, because it's supposed to be held for three days for people to read, but since the address is the following day this year we're going to wave that rule. So, those two HJRs will be moved and rules suspended for both at the same time."

"Quick question on that, Duncan," said Tucker Pyle. Duncan had never liked Tucker. The man was a lapdog for whoever was in power on his side, and he always acted like the smartest person in the room, unless whoever's ass he happened to be kissing was in that room too.

"Yeah," said Duncan.

"Who is actually making those motions? I mean typically it's the majority leader, but by this point the Majority Leader and Speaker are from two different parties. So I'm just wondering, you know, it seems a little confusing." The eyes of the table turned back to Duncan.

"Well, actually," said Duncan looking down at the agenda. He stopped to think. He was reading through the rules of order in his mind, turning page after page until he found the answer. "Actually, these motions are made by the Floor Leader for the majority, which at this point would be you," Duncan said, pointing to Tracy Holcomb, the lone woman in the room. Her face was full of surprise.

"Oh, I don't know about that," she said.

"No, it's supposed to be the Majority Floor Leader," said Duncan, daring anyone to question his parliamentary knowledge. "But you can do what Nathan has always done."

Nathan Murray, the Democratic Floor Leader spoke up. "Yeah, I always defer to the Majority Leader to read the procedures. If he can't, for whatever reason, then I would do it myself but normally I would defer."

"I've never heard you motion to defer," responded Al Grindstaff.

"If you tell me beforehand, you can defer to anyone you want, as long as they're ok with it," said Duncan.

"Ok," said Tracy contemplating her options. "I think I want to do it, if that's ok?"

"Well, it's your call Representative," said Duncan quickly. "You don't have to ask anybody's permission."

"Ok, then, yeah I want to do it," she said, drawing laughs from around the table. "Can you write down what I'm supposed to say?"

"Yes ma'am," said Duncan. "You'll get the script every week because you'll be moving bills from first reading to second reading and then to committees. Stuff like that. There will be a lot of them, so I'll write it down for you, so you can keep track."

"Oh, bless you," she said with a chuckle.

"Don't mention it, it's my job." For now, he thought. "Any other questions on this part?" He looked around the table; he couldn't see any signs of confusion. "Ok, y'all have been through this before, sort of, so I think you'll understand everything. We are blazing a bit of a new trail here with the switch in parties, but these first two days are probably all going to be mostly the same as always.

"Now let's move on to the General Assembly Officers elections. So, the HJRs have been properly moved. Speaker Caputo will call on me to move to the next item which will be––"

"Oh wait," said Al Grindstaff again, "will Larry Pickard be voting for all this too?"

"Yes," said Duncan. "He'll be a member until just before the Governor's address. He'll be sworn in by a justice of the Tennessee Supreme Court in between the morning and afternoon sessions on day two, and resign between the morning session and being sworn in. Until then he is a duly elected member of the body and has all the same rights as any other Representatives. He will resign his office, officially, to whoever wins the race for Speaker."

"Ok, just wondering."

"No, it's fine. Now's the time to ask," said Duncan before returning to the agenda. "Ok, then the next item will be 'Election for officers of the one hundred and sixth Tennessee General Assembly, House of Representatives.' The Speaker will say something like that and then I'll call the first office to be elected. This is the fun part; historically we elect Deputy Speaker, then Speaker Pro, and last Speaker of the House. They'll all follow the same format. The Speaker will call on a member from each caucus, starting with the majority, to nominate someone. Whoever he calls gives a little speech that ends with the nomination, and then someone else is called to second the nomination. Then it goes to the minority party, same deal. Then it's opened for anyone to nominate anybody."

"Can we not do that?" asked Mike.

"Which part?" asked Duncan, slightly confused.

"Open it to the floor for anybody to nominate anybody?" asked Mike, looking around the room.

"Well, no," said Duncan. "It's a requirement of the rules."

"Oh," said Mike with his mind at work. "I'm asking because, we haven't nominated anybody for Speaker Pro. We feel that

Tayna has earned the right to keep that post. I'm worried that someone in our caucus might try to nominate someone without our approval." A small murmur of concern went around the table; for the first time Duncan realized that Tayna Allan wasn't at the meeting. Duncan couldn't tell if the concern was for Tayna's nomination or that she might have cut a deal with the Republicans. Duncan tried to stay out of the political wheeling and dealing – that would be something else he would not miss about this place.

"If that is a concern, then perhaps you should let the Democrats go first in nominating that office? After they nominate Tayna for Speaker Pro, someone else we all agree on can move to close the nominations. As long as someone seconds the motion and nobody objects, that will stop the nominations," offered Duncan.

"That'll work," said Mike.

"Ok, just let me know who will close the nominations," said Duncan, looking around the table. "This portion is very scripted, so we need to know who to recognize for the motions to nominate, the seconds, and to close the nominations."

"Right," said Mike. "I think it would be a nice touch if someone from our side closed the nomination for Speaker Pro."

"Would you like to do it?" asked Jon Green, the Democratic selection for Deputy Speaker. The question was directed at Mike.

"Sure, yeah, I'd be honored to," Mike responded.

"Works for me," said Duncan looking around the table for objections. There were none. "Now, are we changing the order of things so that the Dems are nominating first for every office or not?"

"No," said Speaker Caputo sharply. "I, uh, I would consider it a personal favor if you all deferred to us in just this one case, and let us go last for the other two." The Speaker was looking at Joe Humphrey. It was as close to begging as anyone in the room had seen Bob Caputo come to, and it caused all noise and movement to stop.

Joe nodded silently with a small, caring, smile. "Sure," he said, "of course." He held the smile. Duncan could not see any sincerity in Joe's actions, and he immediately tried to think of what the man's ulterior motive could be.

"Thank you," said the Speaker, unable to look at anyone.

"Ok," said Duncan quickly. "So we will nominate Deputy Speaker. Republicans first, then Democrats. Then Speaker Pro, Democrats first and then Mike will move to close nominations. Then last will be Speaker. Republicans first and then Democrats. Let me know later who will nominate and who will second. Quick note, well reminder really, there might be a need for a recess before we vote for Speaker. Really, the need might come up before any of these votes, to get your caucuses in order. It only takes a majority of the members present to do that if there is an objection to it. Proper manners say you typically don't object to a recess in between votes, but that's up to y'all in the moment." He looked at the nodding faces.

He continued. "For Speaker Pro, with one nominee we can do a voice vote. The other two we will call the roll, by district, and light the votes up on the big board. Voting for a Republican will be indicated with a green light, voting for the Dem will be a blue light, and if there is a third they will get the red light. If for whatever reason there is a fourth, they'll get a white light. A fifth? Then we're screwed." This line got a laugh; it always did. "I'll be calling the roll pretty quick, in order of district, so tell your people to be ready."

"Not for the Speaker," said Caputo. "Whoever wins, well, they deserve to soak it in." The room went quiet again. The Speaker was looking at the table. "Take your time with that one." Joe smiled with pity at the Speaker who still wasn't making eye contact with anyone. Duncan knew Bob Caputo well enough to understand the Speaker wanted to make a list of every Democrat who voted against him in his last race for Speaker of the House.

"Ok," said Duncan. "I'll slow down a tick for the Speaker vote. Moving on, after the votes for all offices are taken, we will swear everybody in. Reverse order, Speaker first, then Speaker Pro, then Deputy Speaker. Each elected officer can address the body after being sworn in. Unless we want to swear them in after each vote? We have done that before."

"I don't like that," said Joe. "Let's swear them in one at a time after all officers are elected. That way each person can take their time with their speech." Yeah, why share the spotlight you egotistical ass, thought Duncan. Everyone seemed to be in agreement with Joe.

"Sure," said Duncan. "We'll have a judge on hand to do it. After the oath, the new Speaker will make a speech, and then they will take over. All they'll get to do as Speaker that first day is their speech and then adjournment till the next day.

"Day two, in the morning. Roll call and call to order. Representative Holcomb will place bills on first reading. Then we will vote on the consent calendar; this will feature the two HJRs from day one. We'll vote on them together at the same time since no one is going to object to them. There may be some other business but we won't know until we're closer to the date, but I'll fill in the elected Speaker the night before. Then the Speaker will appoint two ad hoc committees, one to tell the Senate we have concluded House business and we're ready for them to come over for the State of the State, and one to go to the Governor extending the invitation. Those committees are completely up to the Speaker. Once the Senators, Cabinet members, Supreme Court Justices, and whoever else are in and situated, the Lieutenant Governor takes the gavel and opens the Joint Session. Then the Governor comes in and does his thing. Lieutenant Governor then moves to adjourn. And that's that.

"Day three is more or less back to regular business, moving bills to second and third readings so y'all will have something to do when you come back. But I'll talk to Rep. Holcomb and the Speaker about all that after the State of the State."

"Well, alright," said Gregory, who had been uncharacteristically quiet throughout the meeting.

"Yep, quick and easy," said Duncan.

"Easy as pie," said Joe awkwardly.

"Oh, and by the way," said Duncan, suddenly remembering. "That first day, members can have one, just one, family member over the age of eighteen with them on the floor, but as many children under eighteen as they want, as long as they are the child of that member. Get those names to me and the Sergeant at Arms so we know how many people are going to be in that mosh pit."

"What about special guests?" asked Joe with concern.

"What do you mean?" asked Duncan.

"I mean like, people not from Tennessee but who are office holders, or political figures of some type, and the media." The room was split down party lines: Republicans were curious about the answer while the Democrats were curious about the guests, but neither side said anything.

"In those cases," said Duncan, "the Sergeant at Arms and myself would have to approve them. Media will only have to apply for a pass. Other special guests we will probably limit to, I think, it's twelve per caucus. Just give me their names. I'll do a quick background check and have them bring some form of identification day-of once they're approved. But get me the names ASAP."

"Ok," said Joe. "That covers it for me."

"Me too," said Gregory.

"Me three," said Daniel Burns, Tracy, and Mike in unison. The fake laughter that filled the room was like a fork in a microwave to Duncan.

"Leader Anderson," the Speaker said as he stood up from the table, "stick around for a bit once everyone's gone. I need to bend your ear in a private."

That was how the meeting ended. As he walked back to his office in the House chamber, Duncan was desperately trying to think of ways to catch a stomach virus that would put him out of commission for three weeks.

Rachel Garrison was standing in the cloak room of Committee Room 3. Through the small window in the door she could see the room was nearly full. The digital clock on the back wall read, in burning red, numbers 8:59 AM. One more minute. She felt her stomach harden then fill with tingles. She had been dreading this since November, when Joe Humphrey had told her his plan. She had considered quitting; she hadn't taken this job all those years ago just to fire everyone. She had taken it because the money was good and the work was easy. Yet she knew if she quit, someone else would take the job and do the deed. What kind of person would take a job knowing the first thing they would have to do is fire nearly every single person that works for them? Not the kind of person she would trust. Anyone who works for the House of Representatives works for the Speaker of the House, and this was his call. The clock read nine, she ran her fingers through her long dark hair and slipped back into her two-inch navy heels. She walked out.

She looked at the faces of the people in the room; she recognized some of them, but did not know the names of any. It was probably a good thing – you wouldn't want to name a chicken before you chopped its head off and fried it. The room was packed, standing room only, and silent. Legislative Assistants, Committee Researchers, Legal Staff, the staff from the Clerk's Office, even the Sergeants at Arms. They were all there. She laid her folder on the hearing table that faced the chairs for members, she chose not to use a podium.

"Good morning everyone, no sense in beating around the bush, let's jump right in," she could feel her voice shake as she spoke. Her vision filled with light; for a moment she thought she was going to pass out. She leaned her butt against the table and crossed her legs at the ankles. She tried to smile. "Can y'all hear me in the back?" she asked. The heads in the back nodded. "If you can't, we could probably use one of the microphones over here." She was stalling. She didn't want to do this. There were a few words of confirmation from the back of the room. Now or never, she thought.

"Ok, there have been rumors about employment in the House with the new incoming Speaker. If things go the way it looks like they're going to go next week, we've decided it would be best if we addressed those rumors now. Some are false, but some are true." She looked down at the ground. Then she thought better of it; she knew these people deserve to be looked in the eye.

"Let me start by saying this, if you work for a member of the leadership for either caucus you won't see any changes. Officers will still have discretion over who they hire. Keep in mind, being a committee chair does not mean you work for leadership. If you work for a chairman some of these changes may apply. The first major change that is probably going to happen," she stopped herself. "Not probably, the first major change that is going to happen is that anyone who works a salary position within the House of Representatives must have at least a bachelor's degree." There was a hum of voices; she put her hands up and asked for quiet. "Please, let's stay quiet until the end. This is important information." She waited as the audience began to quiet itself. "Ok, salary positions will require a bachelor's degree, not associates, and you cannot be in the process of getting the degree. You have to have it, regardless of your major or field of study. And no one will be grandfathered in." There was louder groans and louder voices. "Please!" she said with her hands raised. "Please! Let me get through this!" The noise died down. Her voice was beginning to break with frustration.

"Next, everyone is going to be hired on a two-year contract. That means every two years, you will have to reapply for your position or a new position. All hires will have to be approved by the Speaker – that goes for everyone who does not work for leadership. That will start in two years, so going into the next General Assembly of 2011. Oh, but if you work for a committee as a researcher or assistant, you'll have to apply for those jobs during the two-week recess and then the Speaker's office will hire and assign, and that will start this year."

"Ok, so for those of you who do not have a college degree," which is roughly ninety percent of you, she thought, "you will stay on until they come back from the two-week recess. So that first Friday before they come back, I think it's January 30th, that's the last day. During those two weeks we are going to try our best to place you all in other departments within the state, and match you with jobs that are available in the private sector," – which is in the middle of the greatest economic downturn since the Great Depression – "but we can't make any promises. During that time, those two weeks, if you no longer qualify for employment with us you have to stay on for those two weeks. If you quit or don't show up, we can't help you find a job or offer you severance or approve your unemployment. That's also the time where we are going to ask that you let the people that have been hired to shadow you to get a sense of the job." The noise from the group rushed out in anger and fear, like a stampede of cattle who had finally found an open gate. Rachel tried her best to calm everyone down, but no one was listening. She finally walked over to the members desk. She pulled out a microphone that had been retracted into the table; she pushed the little red button beside it to turn it on.

"EXCUSE ME!" she yelled loud enough to cause feedback in the speakers that were in the ceiling. The voices quickly died down. "Thank. You. Now. I am here to answer questions," There was an outburst of voices asking desperate questions all at once. She held up her hand, "BUT!" she yelled into the microphone again; the crowd went calm but the anger in the room hung in the air as if it were humidity. "But . . . I can only answer them one at a time. So, we will start up here in the front row, going from my left to my right. One at a time, if you have a question you can take a turn. One at a time. Everyone please listen because someone might ask the same question you have."

"Do we have to be here?" said a male voice from somewhere in the back.

"No you don't," said Rachel. "If you don't want to be here you can leave; if you have a question you can email me and I'll respond. Maybe try not to call since I'm going to have to respond to so many questions." She watched as a handful of people made their way out. Some were angry, some gave her dirty looks, some walked as though they were prisoners being led to their execution, knowing there was no way out. "Ok," said Rachel. "We will start here with you," she pointed to an older woman sitting in the chair furthest to her left on the front row.

The older woman stood up and said, through a voice on the edge of tears, "How definite is this plan?"

Rachel's heart broke in that moment. Should she be honest or give hope? "The question is," Rachel spoke into the microphone, "how definite is this plan? And the answer is, barring some sort of unforeseen circumstance in the race for Speaker of the House, and I mean it would have to be something pretty drastic, this plan is one hundred percent going to happen." She expected there to be more angry noise, but the old woman simple sat down and the room fell quiet. Rachel looked around; the anger had washed away and the room had been eroded down to despair.

Rachel looked at the next woman and pointed, "Do you have a question?" Rachel would be in Committee Room 3 for another four and a half hours, diligently answering their queries. By the end, no one blamed her for what was about to happen.

CHAPTER 14

Friday, January 9, 2009

Gregory walked into his office suite. As he had anticipated, Legislative Plaza was near-empty. There were members, a few staffers from the Senate, a couple of lobbyists trying to get in a few meetings before the big rush, and some upper level leadership people still hanging around. For a Friday the place could be considered busy, but on the House side of the Plaza it felt empty. Session was starting next week, there should be action, but if there was any action happening it was on the Senate side. What he hadn't anticipated was getting to his office, after ten in the morning on a weekday, and being the one that had to turn on the lights. That was something new. He felt defeated. He was defeated. He sat down behind his desk and did nothing. He stared out of his door, looking into the area Alice normally occupied, and longing for someone to walk through.

"This must be what it's going to be like now we are the minority," he mumbled to himself. He thought about how useless his position was now. Yes, he would still get the Governor's bills, and, sure, some of them would pass, but it wasn't the same. The lobbyists wouldn't need his vote or voice like they had before. There would still be mixers and the parties, but people would not be pulling him to the side trying to get in a quick word. The good times had rolled, and this is where they stopped. He sat there, in silence, just looking out his door.

He lost track of time. He had perked up the first couple of times he had heard noises in the hallway, but no one had walked in; the noises had only walked past. He just sat there, trying to soak it all in before it all dried up.

"Hello there, you son of a bitch," a voice said. He looked up, Alice was standing in his doorway wearing blue jeans and an orange Tennessee Volunteers sweatshirt.

Gregory smiled – at least he would get to keep Alice for another two years. A gift from the now-mighty Joe Humphrey. "Good morning, Alice."

"Morning? Huh. You're serious?" Alice put her weight on one hip, Gregory heard it pop. She looked at her wrist as if she were wearing a watch, which she wasn't. "You mean afternoon?"

Gregory checked the actual watch on his wrist; it was half past noon. "Yeah, I guess I do."

"Boy, I never thought I see the day when you would look so washed up."

"Well," said Gregory leaning back and putting his feet on his desk, "what else is there to do now?"

"Well," she said mockingly, "you could start by apologizing to those two boys that work for you?"

"What?" said Gregory with confusion.

"What?" she said in a lowered voice, it was a poor imitation of Gregory.

"Tom and Charlie? Why would I apologize? For what?"

"You know, these walls," she knocked on the wall separating his office from hers, "they're awful thin. I hear everything y'all say in here. For the most part I ignore it. I let it go in one ear and out the other, but some of it sticks. Let me tell you, while this place was burning down you decided you wanted to try and put out the flames. The only two who followed you were Charlie and Tom. And what did you do about that?" She waited for him to respond.

Gregory was off balance. He hadn't expected a lecture from Alice. He thought for a second. Then said, "I listened to them and tried to do what was best."

"Bullshit," she said quickly. "Best for who? Not for me. Not for you. Certainly not for them." Her eyes narrowed. Gregory suddenly felt empathy for her children. She was animated and spoke with her hands. "You did what was best for Bob Caputo, you went and fought his battle instead of fighting your own. You played a game for him. You did that because you got stuck in this fishbowl, and now your bowl is getting tossed out the damned window." She stood there silently, letting her words sink into Gregory. "Now look what you done. You got two boys who actually admire you, pissed off. Gregory, they were the only two who jumped off the cliff with you, but guess what? You grabbed a branch halfway down and they went splat right on the ground. So, the fuck are you going to do about it?"

She was right. He hadn't seen it happen as it was happening, but he had led his team straight into a den of wolves and they got torn apart for nothing. "Where are they?"

"They're eating lunch by the fountains up top."

"It's freezing," said Gregory with some surprise. "Why are they up there?"

"They smoked some pot out by President Polk's grave, then got hungry and ordered a pizza; that's where the pizza guy met them." She said this as if it was a normal occurrence.

"Goddammit," he said. He grabbed his coat and walked out of his office. Before he went out of Alice's door he turned around and said, "Thank you, Alice. I needed to hear that."

"You're welcome, Leader Anderson," she said as she sat down at her desk.

"And, Alice," he continued, "you can't talk to me like--"

"I'll talk to you however I damn well please," she said interrupting him. She had already started to check the voicemails. Gregory tapped the door with his knuckles. He walked out into the hallway, to the left, then out the side door that had a set of stairs that led directly to the fountain plaza.

Tom and Charlie had their backs to him, facing the War Memorial Building. They seemed to be looking at the half-naked statue of the Greek god that sat in the courtyard of the War Memorial Building. Gregory had never bothered to learn which god it was, but it was certainly holding the goddess Nike. He knew that much. He walked over to the two men; there was no sign of pizza.

"Hey guys," he said taking a seat beside Tom. "Alice told me you had pizza."

"Well, she lied," said Charlie.

"She also said you were high," said Gregory.

"Do what?" said Tom.

"She said you were smoking pot over by Polk's Tomb up by the Capitol," said Gregory pointing in that direction.

"Oh, yeah," said Tom with a sad smile. "That part is true, but it's worn off now. Now we're cold."

"And there was pizza," added Charlie. "But we ate it already."

Gregory laughed. He tried to find the right words to say, but none were coming. So he just started talking: "I ran for office because it seemed like the next step in my career. Not my political career. I didn't give a shit about that. I mean my law career. Figured, when I was on the Metro Council for Nashville I saw an uptick in clients, so if I was in the General Assembly I'd be set for life. I never planned on being in leadership. Hell, I thought I'd be up here for two terms then hang it up, but it turns out I was pretty good at this. I could argue and make these grand speeches on the fly. I understood the law, I understood how to make deals. The whole leadership thing just sort of happened. And as soon as it happened, I got used to it. I got complacent. Never in my wildest dreams did I think we would lose the House. I got desperate to try and hold on to something. To try to make being in the minority seem normal. I thought having Caputo stay on as Speaker would make it feel ok, but that was never gonna happen. I'm sorry, y'all. This whole thing is my fault. It's over now, anyhow. Speaker Caputo told me, himself, to just drop it."

They stayed quiet. Then Charlie sniffed. Tom said, "Are you crying?"

"No," said Charlie sniffing again. "My nose is running."

"Shit," said Tom. "You are crying."

"No I ain't, you're still high," said Charlie using the sleeve of his jacket to wipe his nose.

"Maybe, I don't know," said Tom. "What I do know, Leader Anderson," Tom turned to face Gregory, "is that none of this is your fault. Burns is Caucus Chair. Y'all promoted him too quick, he didn't know how to run the races with Obama on top of the ticket."

"Still," said Gregory. "I shouldn't have signed us up to try to save Caputo."

"You didn't," said Charlie. "We signed ourselves up."

"Why did I get reelected Leader? Why the fuck did I agree to run again?" asked Gregory. He felt hot tears boiling over against his cold skin.

"Because," answered Tom, "everyone in our caucus trusts you. Even the Black Caucus. They don't like Burns, and they're mad at you. But they trust you to lead them through this. We all do. At least, that's my take on this situation."

Gregory wiped the few stray tears that managed to escape. "Regardless, it was a bad plan," he said. "And it wasn't even a fun plan that went bad. It was just a bad plan."

"There was no good plan," said Tom.

"Mine was pretty good," said Charlie. "We should've been planning to be in the minority this whole time."

"That's not a good plan," said Tom.

"It's a sensible plan," said Charlie. Gregory's phone began to ring.

"Sensible isn't good," said Tom. Gregory pulled his phone out of his pocket. "Who is it?" asked Tom.

"Oh," said Gregory. "It's Keith Zachary. We're supposed to have dinner tonight since he's in town now." Gregory ignored the call. "I'll call him back later. But, yeah, Tom's right, sensible doesn't mean good."

"Ok, but sensible is sensible which is better than bad," said Charlie.

"Sensible is eating your vegetables and not dessert," said Tom with a hint of resentment.

"Yeah. And?" said Charlie. Gregory's phone rang again. "You got voicemail, don't you?" asked Charlie.

"I do," said Gregory. "Boys, I'm going to take this. It might have something to do with mom."

"Yeah, go head," said Tom with a sudden concern for his friend.

Gregory took a few steps away and answered. "Hey, Keith. Everything ok?"

"Sort of," said Keith. He sounded like he was in the middle of the spin cycle. "Lelia is getting fired."

"Who?" asked Gregory. He felt relief that this call wasn't about his mother taking a turn for the worse, but he was also confused, again.

"Lelia, my assistant," said Keith with some urgency. "She don't have a college degree and Joe ain't going to make me a chairman. So, she's done. She's been up there eight years, and they're just dumping her."

"Oh, sorry to hear that," said Gregory. "Yeah, pretty much all the assistants are gone."

"All of them?" asked Keith.

"Yeah, man, all of them."

"You around anybody?"

"I'm outside, in downtown Nashville. Lots of people are around."

"I mean," Keith was starting to sound a bit frantic. "I mean, is there anyone around that you might not want to hear us talk about certain sensitive things."

"Oh," said Gregory finally understanding. Rumors about Keith and his assistant had popped up here and there, so him being upset made sense to Gregory now. Keith was about to come clean. "No, no one can hear us. If they can they won't understand. So, shoot."

"Is that Speaker Pro deal still on the table?"

Gregory's heart sank, he knew better now. "Afraid not, no way we could make that work. Tayna is going to be Speaker Pro."

"Well good, cause I don't want to be Speaker Pro Term. I want to be THE Speaker," Keith said breathlessly. Gregory turned around quickly. He wore his shock on his face. He looked at Tom. "Did I lose you?" asked Keith.

"No, I'm here," Gregory said. Tom looked up at Gregory. They made eye contact.

"You get me your forty-nine votes, and I'll give me my own vote, and we'll work something out. I want to be Speaker and end this madness," said Keith. Tom saw the look on Gregory's face; he nudged Charlie who looked up and recognized the look too. They sat there, not breathing, and clueless.

Son of a bitch, thought Gregory. It could fucking work.

"You there or did the call drop?" yelled Keith.

"I'm here," said Gregory. He could feel his heart beating faster than he could ever recall. It could actually, truly, work, he said in his mind on repeat.

"Ok, don't stop talking until we hang up. I'm shaking I'm so nervous about this," said Keith.

"Where are you?" Gregory asked him.

"Cookeville, about an hour out from Nashville," said Keith, as if Gregory didn't know how far Cookeville was.

"Ok, what time will you be here?"

"I have to pick my sister up in Carthage then I'll be going straight to my apartment in Hermitage."

"Ok," said Gregory trying to think of the next steps. It could work. "Get your sister, but don't tell her about this."

"I can do that."

"Go to your apartment, and then come over to my place for dinner. By yourself, don't bring your sister."

"What is she supposed to do?"

"I don't know," said Gregory with some frustration. "Tell her to go see a show or something, whatever, tell her you have a super-secret meeting with a lobbyist. Make something up, but come to my house for dinner. My wife is out of town. It'll be you, me, Tom, and Charlie. If this is going to work no one outside of us four can know about it for now. Have you told anyone else?"

"No, and I won't. I promise."

"Ok, be at my house at six. We'll hash out the details there."

"Ok, what are we having?" asked Keith. Gregory rolled his eyes.

"Pizza," he said.

"Ok, I like sausage and cheese on mine. Nothing else."

"Fine," said Gregory rolling his eyes again. "See you at six o'clock sharp and tell no one."

He hung up the phone and walked over to Tom and Charlie, trying to act natural.

"Everything ok?" asked Tom with concern.

"Yeah, everything is great," said Gregory. "Charlie, your plan was shit."

"It's not, we figured it out. It's boring, but ok. That's what we settled on," said Charlie defensively.

"No, it's hot smelly-ass roadkill," said Gregory. Charlie was about to say something, but Gregory continued, "we're going with Tom's plan."

Tom laughed, "You must've caught a contact high, I always thought that was a myth. The Republican Caucus got their nominee."

"Not that plan, your other plan," said Gregory. He watched as Charlie, and then Tom, got the point.

"Seriously?" asked Charlie.

"Yeah, I just found someone who wants to do it," said Gregory.

"WHO?!" screamed Tom as he jolted up to his feet at attention.

"SSSHHHH!" Gregory put his finger to his lips. "You'll find out at dinner tonight, my house, be there at six o'clock. I can't tell you who yet, but I want the both of you to grab your stuff from the office and get out of here. Go to Charlie's apartment, and start coming up with a game plan of how we convince our caucus to go along with it."

"What about Caputo?" asked Tom.

"Yeah, how do you plan to get him on board?" asked Charlie.

"Not sure, but I'll think of something," said Gregory. He smiled, then laughed, he patted their shoulders. "We're in the shit now boys! See you at six, my place."

"What are we having for dinner?" asked Charlie.

"Oh my God," said Gregory. "Probably fucking pizza."

"But we had pizza for lunch," said Charlie.

"I don't want to fuck a pizza," said Tom.

"I like mine with pepperonis, onions, and pineapple," said Charlie.

"That sound disgusting," said Tom.

"Oh my God! See you at six," said Gregory. It could work, he thought.

CHAPTER 15

Monday, January 12, 2009

Speaker Caputo had procrastinated packing up the things in his office. The pictures lining the walls, the awards in the cabinet that most politicians would throw away, the framed pieces of legislation, the tables, the couch, the chairs, the rugs – all of it was where it had always been. Whether he was refusing to accept what others viewed as inevitable, or if he was just unwilling to move, his office looked the same it had always looked while Gregory, Tom, Charlie, Xavier, and Daniel waited for him to show up. The Legislative Plaza was once again deserted, partly because people had given up working there knowing that the operations of the state would carry on without them, and partly because the next day was the first day of session. This meant everyone in that world would be there tomorrow; the members of the General Assembly, the lobbyists, and the activists would all be there every day until session was over. Typically, this left legislative assistants with the feeling of being invaded but this year they all couldn't help but already miss it.

Xavier checked the massive watch on his wrist and sighed. He shifted his weight in the tiny chair, careful not to wrinkle his grey suede sport coat or his black slacks.

"Would you be more comfortable over here?" asked Tom pointing to his spot on the couch next to Charlie.

"No, I would be more comfortable if this old man would just show up," said Xavier.

"Hey," said Charlie in a whisper. "Did you ever think you would live to see a man be late to his own funeral?" He looked around the room; the faces looking back at him were confused. He continued, "Cause now we have." There was silence, and suddenly Xavier got the joke and laughed. Then the punchline hit Daniel who gave a polite smile.

"I don't get it?" remarked Tom.

"Me either," said Gregory.

"He means," said Xavier whispering, "this is like, you know, Caputo's political funeral, so to speak. And he's late for it." Xavier lifted his eyebrows and nodded his head waiting for the gears to click in Gregory's head.

"Oh," said Tom dryly. "Sure. Yeah, that's real funny."

"Yeah," said Gregory. "I get it, but I don't think it's funny."

"Lighten up, man," said Daniel tapping Gregory on the knee. Gregory flinched a little; he was nervous.

The meeting between Keith, Gregory, Tom, and Charlie, had lasted nearly six hours. By the end of it they had a plan. They knew they needed to keep the circle of knowledge small; they weren't going to let the House Democratic Caucus know it until the pre-session caucus meeting that takes places a few hours before session is gaveled in.

Bringing Xavier in on the plan was Charlie's idea, and it was good one. Once they got it through Keith Zachary's head that the entire plan would fall apart if they couldn't get the Black Caucus on board, he agreed too. Tom paid Xavier a visit at his house on Saturday afternoon. Xavier hated the idea of voting for a Republican, any Republican, but he hated the thought of Joe Humphrey being Speaker even more. Tom had to show Xavier a picture of Keith to get him to realize who they were talking about. "Harmless," Xavier said when Tom pointed to Keith in the House Directory. While he couldn't promise he would be able to convince the rest of the Black Caucus to sign up, Xavier agreed to do what he could to make it happen. He was hoping some Obama magic would come to Tennessee during the next two years and maybe they could pick up a few more seats, win back the majority. Keith Zachary would buy them those two years. Deep down Xavier knew that wasn't going to happen, but a lot could change in two years.

It hadn't been hard to convince Keith of Daniel's value. Daniel's military experience was all Keith needed to trust him. Like most northeastern Republicans in the state, Keith had an appreciation for the military that bordered on a fetish. Gregory wanted to let Daniel know because the Caucus Chairman's ability to argue a case on the fly was going to be crucial. Plus, the House Democratic Caucus Chairman deserved to know if the caucus wasn't going to vote for a Democrat. Daniel, to his credit, got behind the plan relatively quick. His only condition was that Speaker Caputo, himself, had to withdraw his own nomination before the caucus. "I don't think he'll do it," he had told Gregory over the phone on Sunday. "I mean, he's going to give up that easily? Not even force a vote? This is his chance to be eulogized on the House Floor. But if he does, then I'm in." Although, much like Xavier, Daniel had to find a picture Keith in a Blue Book to figure out just who he was voting for on Tuesday.

Now, here they all were, minus Keith who was busy touring the Country Music Hall of Fame with his sister, waiting for Speaker Caputo to meet with them. Meeting with the Caucus Chairman and House Party Leader the day before session starts was standard procedure. The Speaker had seemed unconcerned about Xavier, Charlie, and Tom sitting in on the meeting when Daniel had called and asked him about it that morning.

The backdoor to the Speaker's office flew open, rattling the frames on the wall. "Sorry, folks," said the Speaker walking in. Gregory noticed the man looked worn down, even more so than he had looked during the meeting with Duncan. He wasn't wearing a suit but instead had on khakis and a long-sleeve navy polo; he had a five o'clock shadow, and his hair looked longer and curlier than normal. The other men in the office stood up, Speaker Caputo motioned them all to sit down as he took the last remaining chair between Xavier and Daniel. He slouched down in the chair, rested his head against the back of the red leather seat, stretched his legs out and crossed them at his ankles. He pointed at Gregory, as if signaling him to start.

"Mr. Speaker, we hav--" began Gregory.

"You know," said the Speaker, interrupting Gregory. "I've come to a decision, and I got to give credit to my press secretary Carrie for coming up with this--"

"Yeah, where is Carrie?" asked Charlie looking around the room. "Actually, where is all of your staff?"

"Oh, well," said the Speaker. "Carrie is at home getting ready for tomorrow. Anthony, my policy guy, you know, well, he is over at the TNDP headquarters. He's going to be doing some policy stuff for them starting next week. Glenn, you probably heard, he took a lobbying job back before Christmas. My attorney already got another job at some firm. Carroll is down in the garage smoking."

"What's going to happen to Carrie?" asked Tom.

"If y'all will let me finish, please," said the Speaker holding out his hands. He wasn't frustrated in his tone, more pleading. Whatever was happening was painful to him. "Carrie is going to stay on for the next two years; I'm paying her out of my own pocket. You know how when Hank Aaron retired, or Michael Jordan, they did a stadium tour? Each city they played in got a chance to tell them 'good-bye'? Well, Carrie and me talked last night, and I like that idea. Turn the next two sessions into my going-away tour. I'm not going to run for reelection in two years, I'm gonna let someone else take this seat. I think, as a party, we can hold on to it. I don't want to be up here and not be Speaker. I'm going to catch seniorities, I think that's what it's called. Just be up here and enjoy my last two years, not worry about anything."

The other five men seated around the circle exchanged nervous glances. The Speaker's decision to retire could affect his response to the plan to make Keith the House Speaker. The minds of Tom and Charlie went straight to the assumption that Bob Caputo's ego would want to be nominated one more time, hear the nomination speech, accept it, and go down swinging. Xavier thought it would help their cause; if the man is going to retire, why not just retire and step away with an unblemished record in Speaker races? Daniel saw both lines of thinking, though he tended to agree with Tom and Charlie. Gregory waited, listening to see what the Speaker would say next.

"I guess, what I'm saying boys," the Speaker continued. "Nominate me. Don't nominate me. I don't really give a shit. But," he said, sitting up in his chair, pointing at no one in particular, turning his head to make eye contact with each person as he spoke, "but, if I were y'all, I would find a way to use the forty-nine votes we do have and toss them to someone who is not Joe goddam Humphrey."

The surprise that filled the room couldn't be seen on any faces, except for Tom whose mouth dropped open; although Charlie's eyebrows shot up he held them there as if they were naturally that high on his forehead. The rest played a very cool poker face.

"Oh, Mr. Speaker," said Xavier with concern. "We couldn't do that; you deserve to have one last nomination." Xavier winked at Charlie.

"No, no," said the Speaker. "Y'all really need to think about what I'm telling you. Our forty-nine people plus one of their own votes . . . it might work."

"Sir," said Gregory following Xavier's lead, "really, let us nominate you so that you get that last recognition on the floor."

"Y'all need to listen to me," said the Speaker, wagging his finger in the air. "I don't know why we didn't think of this sooner, but it could work."

"But session is tomorrow," said Tom. "We don't have time to find a Republican who would vote for themselves, much less whip the votes in our own caucus."

"He's right," said Charlie. "We talked to a lot of them about voting for you, and they're all committed to voting for their nominee."

"See, now, that's where your mind isn't keeping up with mine," said the Speaker, pointing at Charlie. "You talked to them about voting for me. You didn't ask them if they wanted to be Speaker." Caputo looked around the circle, he could not understand what they weren't understanding about his plan.

"Mr. Speaker, really sir––" Gregory was cut off by Speaker Caputo.

"Now, listen here Greg," said the Speaker, lifting his hand to keep Gregory from continuing, "every single son of a bitch up here would trade their first-born child to be Speaker. Every single one. Even you three here. If you offer it to any of those Republicans down the hall, they'll take it. We just have to ask." The group went silent. They exchanged glances communicating to each other if they thought it was safe to proceed. The Speaker interpreted these glances as tepid agreement. "You know I'm right," he added in a whisper.

Daniel cleared his throat. "Mr. Speaker, for this to work, and I want to be clear I'm not agreeing to it or saying it would work––"

"It will work," interjected the Speaker.

"Ok," continued Daniel, "that's your opinion, but before I agree or disagree, you need to understand. If we nominate a Republican, you have to withdraw your name before the caucus. You have to do that; we can't do it for you."

All eyes focused on the Speaker, waiting for his next words. He rubbed his knees and shook his head. He took a few deep breaths and then spoke. "I know. I know. God, I know. I think I'd rather not be in the mix than be in it and lose my last time trying, you know?"

"I totally understand," said Xavier, patting Caputo on the back.

"And you, Jarvis," said the Speaker. "For this to work, you have to get your people to toe the line."

Xavier gave a small laugh. "My people don't really tow lines, sir. But if we are doing this, and it has to be all of us on board," he paused and pointed around the circle, "then I think maybe my caucus could get behind it."

"Ok," said the Speaker. "*Shew.* If y'all are willing to try to get this done, I'm willing to stand up in front of the caucus tomorrow and withdraw my name. Simple as that." He gave a shrug.

"Ok," said Xavier.

"I'm in," said Daniel.

"I don't like it, but it could work, so ok," said Charlie.

"Me too," said Tom. With that all the eyes fell on Gregory.

Gregory shook his head, feigning defeat. "Well . . . who did you have in mind?"

The Speaker smiled. "I'm glad you asked, Greg," he said. "Now, anyone we pick is going to be good to our side, obviously, but we might as well pick someone who will be better. I've got three names. Stuart Noel, Darren Hope, or Creed Edmunds."

"No," said Xavier.

"Jarvis," said the Speaker with a hint of agitation. "You've got to at least think about it."

"I have, I did. Just now, and we can't use them."

"Why not?" asked Caputo, who had become more animated with his anger.

"Because they're your friends," said Xavier expecting the answer to suffice.

"And? What's wrong with that?" Said Caputo.

"What I'm saying is, if you thought of this plan, then we have to assume there is a possibility that Humphrey and/or Hayes have too," said Xavier calmly. "They know that the first people you're going to turn to are your friends, that little circle of Republicans you got. Joe and Mike are going to be watching those guys like hawks. I wouldn't be surprised if those greasy assholes hired PIs to follow your buddies around. They're waiting for someone to break rank and they're betting it's one of the people in your circle. Asking them will tip off Humphrey and then the plan is ruined." There were nods of agreement.

"He's right," said Gregory. "Look, Creed and Darren, hell even Stuart, would make good Speakers, but they're too risky to ask now. We need someone less assuming. And we can only ask one person. If we ask more than one then that will only increase the likelihood of this getting out."

"You're right," said the Speaker, looking at Gregory. He tapped Xavier's leg with the back of his hand. "So are you."

"So who do we pick?" asked Daniel.

"Where does Carroll keep your Blue Books? We can thumb through last year's House members," said Charlie.

"In the cabinet behind my desk," said the Speaker. Charlie went to the cabinet, he opened it and grabbed six Blue Books. He noticed a small bronze vase; he looked inside and saw some condoms. He shook the image of a naked Bob Caputo from his mind and closed the cabinet. He walked back over and handed out the books. They began to turn the pages.

"What about Charles Beckett?" asked Daniel.

"No," said Tom.

"Hold on, I like Charles. Why not him?" asked the Speaker.

Gregory responded, "Sir, time is of the essence. We can't debate each name." The Speaker nodded in agreement. They began to turn pages.

"Andrew Mansfield?" asked Xavier.

"No," said the Speaker, almost reflexively, to the surprise of everyone.

"Patrick Pope," said Charlie.

"No," said Tom. "We'd cover more ground if some of us started in the back."

"Ok," said Caputo, taking the bait. Everyone waited as he turned the pages. "Who's this guy?" The Speaker held up the page and point to Keith Zachary's picture. "I don't know if I've ever seen him. What's his story?"

"Oh, that's Keith Zachary, from Elizabethton," said Daniel nervously as the others held their breath.

"You know him Greg?" asked the Speaker.

"I did back in high school, we're still friendly," he responded.

"Oh, never mind," said the Speaker. Panic set in on the group.

"Now wait," said Tom. "How friendly are you?"

Gregory looked at Tom, sensing the signals. "Well, we aren't best friends. I see him when I visit Mom, we might grab a meal or two when he's up here. We aren't that close."

"Interesting," said Tom.

"We said no friends," the Speaker reminded the room.

"Right," said Daniel. "But they aren't friends, so they wouldn't expect us to ask him."

"And," said Xavier holding up a finger, "it wouldn't seem out of the ordinary for you to be talking to him."

"Suppose not," said Gregory. Charlie and Xavier nodded. The other three looked at the Speaker.

"Can we trust him?" asked Caputo.

"Yes, I think so," said Gregory.

"You think?" asked Caputo.

"I trust him more than any other option," said Gregory confidently.

The Speaker leaned back and joined in the nodding of heads. "Ok," he said. "Ok, Greg, you ask him. Do it softly, just float the general idea out and see what he says. If he agrees, tell me in the morning and I'll withdraw. If he doesn't, well, we'll come up with a plan b tomorrow."

"Alright," said Gregory.

"This does not leave this room, y'all hear?" said Caputo.

"Sounds like we got a plan," said Xavier.

CHAPTER 16

Tuesday, January 13, 2009

5:30 AM

Joe and his wife Alyssa were sitting at the small table in the kitchen of the townhouse Joe had purchased in the Germantown neighborhood of Nashville, just across Jefferson Street from Bicentennial Park, down the hill from the Capitol. Alyssa had been wary of the place when she first saw it: aside from the expense of a mortgage on a three-bedroom, twenty-five hundred square foot brick townhouse, the neighborhood did not suit her small-town sensibilities. Yet Georgetown was clearly on the verge of gentrification, and so the value would only increase. Joe had also made a compelling case that, as Speaker of the House, he would need a more permanent place to stay in Nashville since he would be spending most of the winter and early spring there. A place that was within a reasonable distance from the Capitol. A place that was big enough and nice enough to host parties, General Assembly Members, and the occasional out of state diplomat. A place that had enough room so, when they did finally adopt their child, there would be enough space for the kid to have their own room and for Joe to have an office. Alyssa had to admit, this particular townhouse was perfect. Joe had dreamt, during the occasional moments when he would allow himself to dream about his place in history, of turning the townhouse over to the state and creating a "Speaker's House." A home where subsequent Speakers of the Tennessee House of Representatives would get to live during their term with the gavel. The Humphrey House. This was going to be the first landmark Joe would have in the state, but he would not allow himself to dwell on the thought too long.

Wearing plain, unwrinkled cotton t-shirts, Alyssa's covered by a white crew neck Volunteers sweatshirt, and sweatpants, the couple gave the impression of a family in a stock photo who had just risen from bed. In fact they had been up for an hour, and had changed into the outfits. Alyssa had straightened her hair and done her makeup, and had applied just a touch of foundation to Joe's face as he was combing the gel through his hair. The small camera crew, sent by the RNC at Joe's request, was there to document the day as it unfolded naturally. Yet Joe and Alyssa wanted to be camera-ready.

The light from above the peninsula in the kitchen hadn't been enough for the crew, so they had moved their shot of the couple having breakfast, oatmeal for Alyssa and yogurt with strawberries for Joe, to the table with a better light fixture. They were doing their best to act naturally.

"Let's start from here, act like you all have just sat down to eat breakfast together. You know, like a normal morning," Simon gave the commands as if he were directing a blockbuster motion picture. His accent gave a hint of the upper midwest. He wanted this documentary to be good; it was going to be shown at the

RNC convention in 2012 and at multiple conferences leading to the 2010 midterms.

Joe and Alyssa looked at each other and gave sheepish laughs, acknowledging the awkwardness of the moment. Alyssa brought her knee up to her chest and placed her foot on her chair, trying to look casual. She moved her silky blonde bangs out of her eyes, looked at Joe, and said, "So . . . any big plans today?" This got a laugh from Joe and the five-person camera crew. Simon instantly noted the moment for the film's trailer.

"Maybe it would be better if I asked some questions," said Simon. "It's still early, you know."

"Yeah, let's try that," said Joe eating his breakfast. His stomach was a mess of nerves, but he knew he needed to eat.

"Alyssa, when you met Joe, did you know you were going to marry him, and that he would play such an important part in Tennessee politics?"

"Oh, I knew I was going to marry him," she said placing a hand on top of Joe's. "I was in love with him the moment I saw him. As for the politics stuff. I knew he was a passionate person, and I knew he wanted to have a positive impact in the world. Our views and beliefs aligned perfectly, and I was ready to help him change our state. I didn't realize he would be Speaker of the House," she said imitating surprise. "I didn't sign up for that." This got another laugh from the room. "I'm joking, obviously, but I didn't realize how much other people believed in him. I knew I believed in him, I still do, I think he can do anything. I knew he had the potential to do something great like this, and I'm just thankful other people have seen it too. I'm very happy to share him with the rest of the state." Joe smiled and turned his hand over to hold her fingers in his palm, stroking them with his thumb. He leaned over and kissed her on the cheek.

Simon asked other softball questions about their life together: what it means to be a Republican, what it means to be the first Republican Speaker of the House in well over a century. Then he asked, "Joe, what's the agenda for today?"

"Let's see," said Joe finishing his last strawberry. "At seven we have caucus meetings. I don't know what the Dems will be doing in theirs, but in ours we will have a sermon from Justin Porter. He's a preacher and member of our caucus from Greenville. Then at nine, Speaker Caputo will gavel in session and take roll call. We have to swear in the members, nominate some constitutional offices, and handle some general business. Then we move into nominations for Speaker Pro Term, and there's only one person running for that. Then Deputy Speaker. Then Speaker. At some point, we will take a recess, probably after the Speaker Pro election, to caucus and make sure everyone knows what's happening. Although, I wouldn't be surprised if the Dems call for a recess after Speaker Pro and Deputy Speaker elections, both of them. They're trying really had to find a way to save Speaker Caputo, but our caucus is in lockstep right now. Who knows though, they might try to nominate another Dem to try to sway one of our people."

"Do you think they'll do that?" asked Alyssa.

Joe turned to her. "I wouldn't be surprised if they nominated a Dem who isn't Caputo, but again our people are locked in. I'm extremely confident in our side sticking together," said Joe looking at the wall, recalling where he was in the day's agenda. "They'll do a roll call for the Speaker, call each name by district.

Then the new Speaker gets sworn in on the floor, gives a speech, we handle a few more things, and then we're done."

"Easy-peasy," said Simon.

Joe laughed. "Yeah, easy-peasy." He blinked and stared off in the distance. This was really going to happen; he was going to be Speaker. It had taken years of hard work, political gaming, back-stabbing, fundraising, hand-shaking, even the occasional campaign finance violation, but now . . . everything was easy-peasy.

"Last question, then we'll fade into the background and let you all do your thing," said Simon writing something in his notebook. "Joe, do you know what suit you're going to wear?"

Joe and Alyssa both laughed. Joe shook his head, "No, truthfully, I haven't had time to think about it. I've been so busy. Probably something dark blue or grey. I would wear black but Alyssa here advised against it."

"Yeah, don't wear black," said Alyssa. "A really dark blue or grey looks so much better, and it gives the appearance of black without making you look pale."

Joe laughed. "Geez, thanks. Anyway, either dark blue or grey. Maybe a white shirt, I might wear a blue shirt if I go with the grey suit. And a red necktie. I guess the big question is, a striped tie or a plain tie?" he said, looking at his wife.

"I think you should wear a tie with a pattern," she said.

"No," he said with a smile.

"He hates ties with patterns, I love them. He either goes with a solid color or stripes," she said looking at Simon standing behind a camera.

"That's true," said Joe. "I'm leaning towards a solid red tie, though." The truth was, Joe had picked out the suit just before

Thanksgiving. He had it tailored made, a deep dark navy blue that bordered on black, a white shirt, and a red necktie with black and gold stripes.

6:45 AM

Gregory walked into his office, his mind spinning, clouded with everything that was set to happen. He set his coffee mug on top of the small stack of blue files containing the Governor's bills that he should have gone through weeks ago. He made a mental note to hand them off to Charlie tomorrow. This scheme, if it worked, might actually help the Governor's agenda. If it failed, Governor Welch's second term was doomed. Regardless, today was the battle and tomorrow he would bury the dead. He took off his jacket and hung it on the coat rack by the door. Past Alice's desk he noticed the door to the conference room was slightly ajar. He could see movement through the frosted window in the door. He decided to check it out.

To his surprise, he found Tom and Charlie sitting opposite from each other at the conference table. A large stack of bills were between them, with smaller stacks of the bill folders surrounding them.

"Good morning," he said in his deep morning voice. The pair looked up.

"Oh shit," said Tom in surprise. "We didn't hear you come in."

"What are y'all doing?" Gregory asked.

"Well, these," said Charlie motioning to the bills surrounding them, "are bills from the Governor."

"You're kidding me," said Gregory.

"Afraid not," said Tom.

Charlie sighed. "Apparently Governor Welch has decided to flood the market with as many bills as possible to see what works."

"My God," said Gregory in shock. As the House Leader for the Governor's party it was up to him to file the bills, and then either carry the bills as his own through the House or assign them to other members. "There must be two hundred."

"Two hundred and eighty-seven, actually," said Charlie. "I picked out like six of them for you to carry yourself. I've already picked who is going to carry some of the others. There's only a few more to get to and Tom is helping me."

"Would have been nice for the Gov to mention he was unloading on us like this," responded Gregory.

"He did," countered Charlie. "Really, he just told me. Well, his staff did. Anyway, it's not as bad as it looks. Most of these either eliminate old laws or codify administrative practices. Nothing major."

"How long have you been working on this, Charlie?"

"About two, maybe three weeks," he said. Gregory suddenly felt a sense of gratitude for Charlie he hadn't felt before. Charlie had been doing his job, as assigned, while he, Gregory, had spent most of the past few weeks lamenting the fact he couldn't save a man's job he should've lost a long time ago. Charlie had kept the ship from running aground; Gregory owed him a lot. Charlie continued, "Tom is going over some of the early filed GOP bills I flagged, just double checking my interpretations to make sure they're as bad as I thought."

"They're all bad," said Tom. "Real bad. Prohibiting gay partner visitations in prison, like forty different abortion bills, a statewide school voucher authorizer, penalties for school districts that prohibit prayer. All stuff their side goes nuts for and our side stands for."

"Don't be too rough on them, we would do the same if it were us," said Gregory. "This is their first real chance to bite the apple, and they want to eat the whole thing in that one damn bite."

"Anyway," said Charlie. He leaned back in his chair and stretched his arms and yawned. "We got here about five, thought this would kill time."

"Xavier should be here soon," said Tom.

"Speaker too," added Charlie.

"Yeah, we should probably make coffee," said Gregory.

"Already did, bossman," said Charlie.

As if on cue, the Speaker and Xavier entered the room together. Xavier smiled and took a seat next to Charlie. Speaker Caputo stayed standing at the other end of the table.

"Are we good, Leader Anderson?" Caputo asked looking at Gregory.

"He's in," said Gregory referring to Keith.

"Ok, are we going to get him over the limit?" Caputo looked to Xavier.

"I think so. Might have to twist some arms," Xavier said.

The Speaker looked around the room. "How do we let the man know if we got the votes?"

Charlie was quick with the response. "We got it worked out."

"I trust you, but I want to know how. We can't walk up and say it to his face." Caputo had some worry in his voice.

"I'll let him know after the recess, before the nominations," said Charlie. "If we've got the votes, I'm going to walk past him and give him two quick pats on his back." Charlie rapped his knuckles on the table two times in quick succession. "If we don't got the votes, I'm going to walk past him and rub his shoulders. Nonchalant like."

"Won't that be obvious? How often do you rub this man's shoulders?" asked the Speaker.

"It's not like a backrub," said Charlie. "It's like, you know, when you walk past someone and want them to know you're there so you squeeze their shoulders, that kind of thing."

"Still seems like that might give it away," said the Speaker. He had a tense look in his eyes.

"It won't matter," said Xavier. "If Charlie squeezes the man's shoulders, it means it's not gonna happen and no one will ever know."

Speaker Caputo thought about it for a moment, "I guess you're right, Jarvis. What time is caucus?"

"Less than an hour," said Gregory. "Seven-thirty in the Governor's Conference Room."

"I thought it was the Old Supreme Court Chamber at eight?" asked the Speaker with confusion.

"Republicans are going to use the Old Supreme Court Chamber," said Xavier. "They're letting the press in and need the space."

"We changed the time so it can be considered spontaneous and keep the press out," added Tom.

"Everybody on our side knows?" asked the Speaker.

"Yeah, Daniel talked to all of them personally," said Tom.

"Sorry boys, I'm struggling without the staff right now," said Caputo.

"It's just a few more hours," said Gregory.

The Speaker looked up at the ceiling and nodded. His eyes began to glisten. "Yeah, a few more hours," he said, his voice breaking. There was an awkward silence as the room gave the Speaker time to recover. "Ok, I'll see you in Governor's Conference Room. I'm going to head up there now, try to avoid people." He left without saying another word.

"Poor old man," said Tom after the Speaker left.

"Fuck him," said Charlie. The room stared at him. "I'm serious. Fuck that dude. He made us bust our ass to try to save his job, and now he expects us to praise him as some sort of martyr. No, if he wanted praise or sympathy or whatever he should have done more for our people while he had the gavel." No one responded; they agreed silently.

7:30 AM

The Governor's Conference Room, located just off the lobby in the Governor's suite on the Capitol's first floor, had the same appropriately boring décor as the Governor's office, except with hardwood floors instead of carpet. The conference table only sat twenty people; those seats were reserved for the early birds of the House Democratic Caucus who had arrived before the meeting was set to start. The other members were standing around the room facing Gregory, Daniel, Xavier, and Speaker Caputo who were standing at the head of the table. Ryan, Daniel's Researcher, was busy checking names off a list. He looked up at his boss and shook his head no; he held up two fingers.

Daniel spoke up, "Ok, people, we are waiting on a few more folks then we'll jump in." The hum of voices trying to sound optimistic barely noticed Daniel's announcement. Everyone in the room knew the events to come could divide the caucus, but they did not know the plan. Daniel returned to the leadership cluster with his arms crossed; they were the only group not saying anything in the room.

After several minutes Bill Sanders and Jerry Cole walked into the room, laughing at something that had been said just before entering. Ryan found their names on the list and checked them off. He looked up at Daniel and gave a thumbs up with an exaggerated nod of his head. Daniel returned the gesture and pointed to the door telling his assistant to leave, which he did, closing the door behind him. Ryan was unaware of the topic that was to be discussed. This was a members-only meeting.

Daniel walked up to the table and knocked on it to call for silence; the message was received. "Ok, let's get going," he checked his watch, "we only have about seventy-five minutes, and we'll probably need every second."

"Are you going to hand out an agenda for this meeting?" asked Jane Dunn who was seated at the opposite end of the table.

"No," said Daniel. "There's only one item: our votes for Speaker." There was some uncomfortable shifting in seats. Some members chose to look away from Caputo. "This conversation never leaves this room, understand?" Daniel looked for signs of agreement. "I'm going to turn it over to Speaker Caputo to let him say a few words."

Daniel took a few steps back and the Speaker took his spot. He rubbed his fingertips along the wood grains of the table. He suddenly realized he might have avoided this moment in his life had he ran for Governor; maybe his portrait would be hanging on the walls of the Capitol's first floor. Instead every decision he'd made had led him to this last humbling and defeating moment.

"You know," Caputo said meekly. He was unable to finish that sentence. His voice cracked and tears began to sting his cheeks. J.A. Dobbins noticed, and began to clap. Soon the entire room had been engulfed in an applause somewhere between pity and gratitude. The Speaker used the moment to regain his composure. He held up a hand for silence. "It has been," he said before stopping, feeling his voice wavering again. He looked up at the ceiling and took in a deep breath. He looked back down at the faces, knowing some of them were happy to see him go. "It has been my honor to be Speaker," he said in a whisper. He took another deep breath, "But now it's somebody else's turn." He shook his head and gathered his strength. Then, in the most stern and steady voice he could produce, he said, "Which is why I am withdrawing from our caucus' nomination for Speaker." A whisper cut through the room. "Thank you," he said, his voice breaking again. He walked back to stand between Xavier and Gregory. Xavier put his arm around Caputo's shoulder; he felt the old man holding his breath to fight back tears.

Daniel returned to the spot at the table, but before he could say anything, Tyler Kelly asked the question that was on the mind of many. "You aren't going to tell us to vote for Humphrey, are you? Because I won't be doing that, no sir." There was a chorus of agreement.

"No, I would never ask you to do that," said Daniel. "I'm asking you to vote for Keith Zachary."

"Who the fuck is Keith Zachary?" asked Jim Miller. The voices in the room rose in agreement with his question.

Gregory stepped forward with a Blue Book in hand, opened to the page with Keith's picture. He handed it to Holt Michaels who was seated closest to him. "Pass that around, Holt," Gregory whispered.

"Keith Zachary is the lone Republican willing to vote against Humphrey," said Daniel. "He's willing to vote with us, as long as we all, every one of us, vote for him."

"Ooooh, no."

"Nope."

"Absolutely not."

"No way." These responses from the members had been expected.

Daniel held up his hands asking for silence, after a few moments it was given to him. "Leader Anderson knows Rep. Zachary better than anyone else. He's spoken to the man. He has Keith's offer. Give Leader Anderson a chance to lay it all out and answer your questions."

The room stayed quiet as Gregory stepped forward. He unfolded a piece of paper from his pocket and held it up, "This," he said waving the paper, "is the offer Keith is putting on the table for us." Gregory held the paper and began to read a long list of committee chair names.

"But wait. There's more. Each vice chairman of full committees gets to pick half of their committee's members; the other half is picked by the chairmen, or chairwoman. Every committee will have one party serving as chair and a member of the opposite party as vice chair, with the parties switching roles for subcommittees. Beyond that, every Democrat can keep their office if they want. With one, obvious exception. Also, all legislative staff members will stay where they are, unless the member wishes to make a change." Gregory folded up the piece of paper and put it back in his pocket. "Questions?"

The room was quiet. Most faces already showed signs of agreement.

Joshua Hyde spoke up, "When did you all come up with this?"

"Fair question," said Gregory. "This plan has been in development for a while now. The details have come together over the past few days."

"Sounds alright to me," said Ryan Landry. "Can we trust him? He's not going to backstab us, we aren't being set up?"

"I've known Keith since I was a kid," Gregory responded. " I trust him. Plus, the moment we nominate him he has to commit."

"And you're ok with this?" asked Shawn Maddox, looking at Xavier.

"Yes," said Xavier. "I support it one hundred thousand percent."

"I've got a question," said Tayna, who was standing in the back looking at Gregory. "At the retreat, you said you had a plan to save Caputo. Was that a lie?"

"Yes," said Gregory being half-honest.

"Then why should we believe this now," said Tayna. "I'm personally half-inclined to recall you this moment." There were some harsh noises of disagreement met with a few voices of support. "I'm serious. Look, let's be honest, some of us have made our own deals with Humphrey, and you are asking us to take those back now? You already admitted you lied to us. I really think we might need a new Democratic Leader."

Gregory thought about the questions for a moment, then answered. "If Joe's end of your bargain is complete before the vote for Speaker, then yes I am telling you to go back on your agreement with him. If it's not, let me know and we'll work something else out." The whispers around the table returned.

"Look, let's do this," said Daniel stepping in. "Let's take a preliminary vote, just to see where we stand. If you are in favor of this plan, raise your hand."

"We should use a secret ballot," said Michael Kincannon.

"We don't have any," said Daniel. "Ok, so, all in favor raise your hand." Most hands went up in the room. "Ok, those against." Four hands went up: Tayna Allan, Lawrence Mains, Murry Price, and Clint Smith. Michael Kincannon hadn't raised his hand either time. The vote was forty-four in favor, four against, and one not voting. Close, thought Gregory, but not close enough.

Daniel shook his head in frustration. "Ok, let's start with Clint. Why are you against this plan?"

"Well," said Clint. He smoothed his white hair that was barely covering his scalp in a combover. "We just found out about it. I want to think about it a little."

"Ok, you've got," Daniel checked his watch, "a little under an hour before we head up to the chamber. So think about it. Murry, your turn."

Teresa Clothier was making her way up the escalator from Legislative Plaza to the War Memorial building. For the past several weeks she had found it nearly impossible to get out of bed to come to work. She had given this place years of her life; she was one of the few who came in nearly every day on time and stayed until the actual end of the workday. She had never put off a constituent who had called, even the frequent flyers who called every couple of days knowing she would answer. As the legislative assistant to Representative Timmy Pardue, Chairman of the House Commerce Committee, she had taken her duties of note-taking and bill notice filings seriously. Yet lately she had trouble seeing the point, since Rep. Pardue was going to be out as chairman once Joe Humphrey became Speaker. Worse still, she would be out of a job. She was in her mid-forties and had two lines on her resume. Hopefully Rachel Garrison could find her something in another department – she didn't have to work at the legislature, she just wanted to.

Today, however, was different. The first day of session was always the most exciting. Like friends reuniting on the first day of school after spending their summers apart at camp. This was the day for everyone to reunite and be together. Plus, there was the party on the top floor of the AT&T Tower, the so-called 'Batman building', the most recognizable building in Nashville's skyline. The views, the food, the music, the wine; it was one of the few after-work parties Teresa cared for and she didn't want to miss it.

Nor did she want to miss feeling the energy of day one, even if it was one of her last days.

She turned the corner leading into the hallway of War Memorial's ground floor offices. She made her way down the hall lined with pictures and prints of past General Assemblies. She wished she had taken the time to learn some of the stories from the pictures. Surely some of them had experienced something like this. She entered her office suite, which she shared with Maggie Holdsted, the assistant for Vice Chairman Mickey White. Teresa felt bad for Maggie. This was her first job out of college and she had only been here for two years. The poor girl was struggling to find something else. Teresa's new intern, Jacob, was sitting at her computer. It was his second day and if her days weren't numbered, she would've laid into him about fooling around on her machine. It all seemed relatively useless now. Instead she said good morning and the skittish college junior jumped up and hustled to his little cubicle in the corner.

She sat down and looked at Maggie. "Any news?" she asked.

"Dem caucus decided to go in half an hour early, I think they've got something cooked up," said Maggie, not pulling her eyes away from the screen.

"Oh, did our men make it on time?" she asked her officemate.

"Yeah, they got there on the early side, believe it or not." They shared a laugh. "I really think they got something up their sleeves to stop Humphrey."

"Oh, honey," said Teresa, trying to sound nurturing, "you know they don't. Leader Anderson and his crew has done everything to try and beat Humphrey, but nothing worked."

"Yeah, but underdogs do amazing things when their backs are against the wall," said Maggie finally looking at her.

"That's true," Jacob chimed in. "Plus, why go in early if you don't have something serious to talk about?"

"To avoid the press," said Teresa.

"Really?" asked the intern.

"Yep," said Maggie. "Press has to be allowed in unless they change the time or meet accidentally."

"Then," said Jacob thinking. "Then . . . then why wouldn't they want the press there unless they have something planned?"

Teresa knew better. The Plaza had built her hopes up and mowed them down too often before. She said, "Jacob, why don't you straighten your tie and grab your jacket, grab some other interns and go sit in the gallery for session."

"You sure it's ok?" he asked.

"Yeah," she said. "We might not be here in two weeks, but you will. It'll be good for y'all to see how the ball gets rolling. Plus it's been twenty years since the Speaker vote actually mattered. You don't want to miss that."

"Ok, thanks," he said. "I'll have my cell phone, call if you need me."

"Sure thing," said Teresa. She hadn't even bothered to write down his number. Jacob grabbed his coat and walked out.

"Sweet kid," said Maggie after he made his exit.

"He's a goober," said Teresa. "Don't matter to me now, but if I were sticking around I would ask for a different intern. We run a committee here and need an intern that can keep up."

"You really don't think they've got a plan?" asked Maggie.

"I'm afraid I don't believe they do. Humphrey's got it wrapped up." They clicked through their morning websites in silence. A tall, skinny brunette woman, a former Miss. Montgomery County-turned-lobbyist for the Optometrist Association of Tennessee, walked in. At one point in her life, Gaby had been Teresa's intern.

"Good morning, you gloom and doomers," she said as she entered. Gaby commanded attention from any room she walked into, whether she wanted it or not.

"Hey girl!" said Teresa, standing her plump frame up to give Gaby a hug. "Come, sit down, tell me what's new."

"Wish I could," she said. "I was just hoping I could stash my bag here."

"Obviously you can," said Teresa.

As she sat her bag in its usual spot behind Teresa's fake tree she said, in a voice far too cheerful, "Maggie, how's it going?"

"Oh, you know. Looking for new work," Maggie said.

"I honestly think something big is going to happen and y'all will be fine," said Gaby.

"Me too," Maggie said, excited that someone finally agreed with her.

"I don't," said Teresa.

"Why not?" asked Gaby.

"I've been here too long to believe in miracles." Teresa could already feel the need for the morning's first cigarette.

"I happen to agree with you, Gabs," said Maggie. "I really think there's a plot afoot."

"Well, y'all should come up to the second-floor conference room when the bell rings," said Gaby, referring to the session bell that rings ten minutes before the Speakers opens a session of the House.

"What's going on up there?" asked Teresa.

"Debra up there, she put a TV in the conference room, and it gets the live feed from the floor. A bunch of us are going to watch session up there."

"That's cool," said Maggie. "Kind of like C-SPAN."

"Yeah, but get this," said Gaby moving towards the door. "No shit, they call it T-SPAN."

"Nooo," said Maggie laughing.

"I'm serious," said Gaby.

"I'll take a rain check," said Teresa. "I'm not one for public hangings."

"Don't be such a downer, boss," said Gaby. She turned to Maggie, with a face asking for an answer.

"We'll be there," said the young woman.

"Great! See you in about thirty minutes. Bring some coffee if you can," said Gaby as she left.

Teresa stood up with her pack of light cigarettes. "I'm going outside to smoke."

"It's so cold out, though," said Maggie.

"True, guess I'll go down to the lower level garage."

"Or you could quit."

"If I lose my job, I'll quit. There's your silver lining."

"You just said 'if', maybe all hope isn't lost."

"Slip of the tongue," said Teresa with a smile. "You better go on and make that coffee."

"Of course, the queen needs her coffee," replied Maggie with a wink.

"I'll be back when the bell rings, we'll walk up together," said Teresa as she walked out.

"Sounds like a plan," said Maggie, standing up to retrieve an empty carafe.

Tom and Charlie were studying the mural in the Governor's office suite. They were looking at the image of Andrew Jackson and his slave at the Hermitage.

"It's racist," said Tom.

"No," said Charlie dismissively. "It's a product of its time. No harm intended."

"Racism doesn't have to be intended to be racist," said Tom. The door to the Governor's Conference Room opened, and in an unorganized fashion the members of the caucus filed out. Once the line quit flowing, Tom and Charlie went in. Xavier, Daniel, and Gregory were still standing in the far end of the room.

"Well," said Charlie in desperate tones.

"The Speaker withdrew," said Xavier.

"And . . ." said Tom.

"We have forty six of the forty-nine votes," said Gregory.

"Fuck," said Tom.

"Who don't we got?" asked Charlie.

"Kincannon won't tell us one way or the other," said Daniel.

"That fucking prick, he's always pulling this shit. We just have to kiss his ass to make it work," said Tom.

"Price doesn't trust Keith," said Gregory. "I'm not worried about him though. If we can get everyone who votes ahead of him to vote for Keith, he'll fall in line."

"We can have Duncan call the roll alphabetically for the Speaker's vote. Lots of letters before P," suggested Charlie.

"Can we do that?" asked Daniel.

"Yeah, the rules only say roll call vote, they don't say how to call the roll," said Tom.

"I'll tell the Speaker to do it alphabetically. Doubt the Republicans will notice the change," said Gregory.

"Ok, who's number three?" asked Tom.

"Tayna," Daniel and Xavier said in unison.

"Damn, not a lot of letters before A," said Charlie.

"None actually," said Gregory. "She would vote first, and if she sticks with Joe we're screwed before anyone else gets a chance to vote." The group stayed silent.

"Ok, ok, ok," began Tom. "We don't have to tell Keith anything until after the last recess or until we have the votes. Right?" The others nodded in agreement. "We've got ten minutes before the bell, then about an hour before the actual vote. That's plenty of time."

"To do what?" asked Gregory.

"Convince her that voting for Keith after the Republicans vote for her is the ultimate power mover," said Charlie.

"That's right," agreed Tom.

"I don't know," said Xavier. "Playing up to her ego might backfire. The other two will either fall in line or we can scare them into it. Not her."

"Alright," said Gregory. "Let's do it. And let's pray none of our dimwits spill the fucking beans before it happens."

8:40 AM

Across the hall, the Republican Caucus was wrapping up their caucus meeting in the Old Supreme Court Chambers on the first floor of the Capitol. The spacious limestone walled room had actually been home to the state's Supreme Court until they received a building of their own on the western side of Capitol Hill in 1937. After that, their old chambers were divided up into offices and used by a variety of state employees. That was until the Capitol underwent extensive renovations in the 1980s, and the room was restored to its original glory. Once a year, the Supreme Court Justices still meet in the room to hear actual cases. Today wasn't that day. Today the room would be used as a gathering place for politicians to perform for their craft.

Justin Porter was coming to the end of his fiery sermon. It had genuinely moved many members of the Republican Caucus, but had left others, mainly those in leadership, awkwardly pantomiming their way through the service. Ambition had become their God, and while they were more than willing to be seen in a church on Sundays because it was good for votes, any event that might actually bring them face to face with the Holy Spirit was to be avoided if possible. Justin had laid out the blueprint for what he thought was God's plan for the Republican Caucus and the state of Tennessee. Clearly a divine hand had led them to victory in November, and now it was up to them to carry out his will.

"And now, brothers and sisters," Representative Porter said to the packed room full of Caucus members, their families, a few special guests, and some of the more conservative-minded press, wiping the sweat from his forehead he continued. "Let us take this moment to lay our hands on our leaders. Let us pray for them, let us give them the armor of God, so that He might give them the sword of justice to carry it through our land and to our nation. Leaders come forward."

Joe, Mike, Tucker, and the rest of the Republican leaders approached the small stage at the front of the room as the mass followed. Joe could feel hands reaching out and touching his shoulders, his elbows, and fingers interlocking. He could feel an energy coming from them, and he did his best to repel it. This was his day, and he would not share it with anyone else.

"Oh God, my God, our God," said Justin. Shouts of praise came from the crowd. Joe kept his eyes closed and head bowed. "Our maker, the one who breathes life and takes it. Creator of all that is around us and all that is in us. We lift up our servants. We give them over to you. These are no longer our leaders, but they are now your followers, your soldiers, and our generals in your fight for grace in this land you have given us. We ask you to be with them. To know them. To give them the fire to bring righteousness to our state. To end sodomy. To end the murder of babies. To bring your word to earth so we may prosper. We ask you keep them humble. We ask you keep them safe . . ."

The prayer continued until the sound of a bell began to ring. Knowing what that meant, Representative Porter wrapped up quickly. Joe spent the next few minutes shaking hands and shaking off the feeling of being small in the world.

Alyssa walked over to him, fixed the parting in his hair and kissed him on the cheek. "Next time I see you, you'll be the most powerful Republican in state government."

Joe smiled, then whispered, "I already am." He walked her halfway down the aisle, stopping when he saw several pieces of yellow legal pad paper folded together fall out of Keith Zachary's suit jacket as he was putting it on. The paper stayed folded as it hit the ground.

"Hey, Keith!" he said as he bent over to pick the papers up. Keith jumped and turned around. Joe noticed the man was sweating profusely. "You dropped this," Joe said handing the papers back.

"Oh, thank you," said Keith in a meek voice. "I'd lose my head if it wasn't . . . shoot, how's it go?"

"Screwed on tight?" smiled Joe.

"That's it," said Keith, taking the papers and putting them back in his jacket pocket. He turned to walk away.

"By the way, Keith," Joe called after him. Keith turned around. Joe stuck out his hand, Keith shook it. "I just want you to know, one northeast Tennessee boy to another, I'm going to do great things for our neck of the woods."

Keith smiled and nodded his head, "We're all very excited to have one of our own as Speaker. Our area deserves it."

"Thank you, that means a lot," said Joe trying his best to portray humility.

"Don't mention it," said Keith releasing Joe's hand. He turned and walked away quickly.

"Hey, Joe, we need to talk," hollered Mike from the other side of the room, "we have an idea."

Joe looked at Alyssa. She sighed and said, "This is my life now. Go on, duty calls." He kissed her on the cheek, she held him close and whispered in his ear. "Congrats, babe. You've earned this, now enjoy it for today. I love you and I'm so very, very proud of you."

CHAPTER 17

Tuesday, January 13, 2009

The Tennessee House of Representatives convenes in a long, narrow room. It's ornately decorated, with gold and green checkered carpet, intricately designed ceilings surrounding massive chandeliers. The massive room is complete with limestone columns and gold inlays. It has the tendency to take away the breath of first time on-lookers. Viewed from the galleries placed high above either side of the long portions of the chamber, the chaos of politicians, staffers, and family members can leave the viewer disoriented and with the belief that no order is actually being maintained. From the floor, the enormous walls, high ceiling, and seated spectators leave those tasked with actually working in the room feeling as if they are in a cage match fighting for cheering spectators thirsty for blood.

The mahogany desks on the floor reserved for members are paired together, six desks across in two rows of seven in the middle, two rows of nine on the either of the outer edges. At the front and back of the chamber, just below the galleries, voting boards used to help spectators and those on the floor view the names and votes of each member. At the front of the room is the well, a long table with a lectern in the middle for members to stand behind and defend their bills, or to address the House. Behind that is the Clerk's desk, situated on a platform, a three-quarters wall hiding whatever work is being done by the hands of the Clerk and his staff. Behind the Clerk, on a much taller platform is the Speaker's desk. Seated high enough so that they can see the faces of every member at their desk, the Speaker is framed by a grey limestone arc surround by pink limestone, and high above their desk a bronze eagle is perched, peering down upon the members.

The seating arrangements on the floor are entirely up to the Speaker. A member's seat on the floor can indicate a healthy dislike or disrespect from the Speaker. If the member is seated towards the back, or in a blind spot for the Speaker, that member would have very few opportunities to address the entire body, and the Speaker has an easy excuse for ignoring the member. Tradition dictates, but does not require, that the leadership for each caucus be seated in the middle rows. Republicans to the Speaker's left, Democrats to the right. The Party Leader and the Caucus Chair occupy the first row of desks, followed by their assistants, then Floor Leaders and Whips, each on their respective sides. Beyond that, Republicans and Democrats are mixed together. The closer one sits to the Speaker, the more likely their seat will be segregated based on party; the further back in the chamber, the more common it is to see both parties sharing a desk.

The organizational session following an election typically sees incumbents sitting in their seats from the previous year, and new members sitting in the seats of their vanquished foe. It is not unusual for the new members from one party to trade seats with new members from the other party during the first week in order to be closer to their own party. During the two-week recess the Speaker will assign the seats on the floor for the next two years.

The members were roaming around the floor of the House, showing their families the room's decoration and making small talk. Speaker Caputo went up the steps to take his place. Tom and Charlie were standing just to side of the well in an area typically reserved for staffers of a certain rank, and the media were shielded from the members by soundproof glass. Tom elbowed Charlie and pointed up to the gallery. Along one side sat a small platoon of young eager white faces, finely dressed in business attire.

"Those are the replacements," said Tom. Charlie nodded and pointed to a man sitting on a bench along the back wall on the House floor.

"That dipshit back there, he's the Chairman of the RNC, Lawrence or Anthony or some shit like that," said Charlie.

"This is a big deal for them," said Tom.

"Yeah, just look at all the cameras in here. I hope we get to spoil their party," laughed Charlie.

The second bell rang, 9:00 AM on the dot, indicating it was time for session to start. Speaker Caputo picked up the gavel and stared at it. He had it custom made ten years ago from a pine tree at his grandparents' home in Italy. Someone else would get to use it today, and then he would take it home, put it on his mantel and never touch it again. He banged the gavel twice and then spoke with authority into the microphone.

"Mr. Sergeant at Arms! Please invite the members of the General Assembly, and their families, into the chamber and close the doors," he said, hitting the gavel again. He waited a moment; all the members and their families were already in the chamber. Once he saw the three doors leading into the chamber had been shut, he continued. "Pursuant to Article two, sections three and eight of the Constitution of the State of Tennessee, and the authority vested in me as Speaker of the House of Representatives of one-oh-five General Assembly, I hereby declare the organizational session of the House of Representatives of the one hundred and sixth General Assembly of the State of Tennessee, now in session." He picked up the gavel and hit it again. He had the script memorized, and wondered what would take its spot in his brain now that he would never have to say these words again. He had a brief vision of himself in a nursing home, unable to remember the names of his kids, but able to recite these lines.

Xavier left his seat and ran forward, grabbing Tom by the arm. He spoke with urgency. "Listen, I need you to do something. Go into Duncan's office and print off the names of every person that voted in Kincannon's last primary. Should be a spreadsheet you can get from the Secretary of State. You got it?"

"Yeah, give me a minute, I'll do it," said Tom rushing off. Charlie knew what was up Xavier's sleeve and smiled. Xavier winked and gave Charlie the pistol point before slowly strutting back to his seat.

Caputo's voice came over the sound system wired through the chamber: "Will the Representatives-elect, and their guest, and the guests in the galleries, please stand, and remain standing through the Pledge of Allegiance. Representative Mark Cullen, of Rutherford County, is recognized in the well to introduce the Chaplin of the Day." Speaker Caputo waited for Rep. Cullen to reach the well; he watched the small man in a fine suit make hurried steps to the lectern at the front of the room as a tall bald man in a dark suit stood in the clerk's spot behind Cullen. "Representative Cullen, you are recognized."

"Thank you Mr. Speaker, it is my great honor to recognize Thomas Weiner of Mount Horeb Evangelist Church, here in Nashville, as the Chaplin of the Day. With a congregation numbering in the thousands, Reverend Weiner has spread the gospel throughout Nashville. And with a nationally syndicated television program, author of over twenty books, and mission trips around the world, Reverend Weiner has taken the redemptive message of the love and forgiveness found in our Lord and Savior across the world. Mr. Speaker," Rep. Cullen closed the notebook in front of him and turned to the Speaker.

"Reverend Weiner," said Speaker Caputo, indicating the time to proceed.

"Thank you Mr. Speaker," said the preacher in a velvet baritone voice. "It is a humbling honor to be here. Please pray with me," the preacher closed his eyes and lifted his hands. The room went silent. "Dear precious God, we come to you to ask for forgiveness for our many sins. Greed, lust, and our selfish tendencies. I ask that you guide these men and women you have been ordained as the leaders of our state, so that they may carry us into a new decade of peace and prosperity. I ask that you bless them with wisdom, knowledge, and the courage to do what is right. For it is in your Son's holy name that we come to you and pray,

Amen." Amens echoed by hundreds of voices throughout the chamber.

"Representative Cullen," said the Speaker into the microphone, "please lead us in the Pledge of Allegiance." Mark Cullen placed a hand over his heart and turned to face the flag at the front of the room.

Tom was in Duncan Blane's office behind one of the doors one the side of the chamber. He had found the list Xavier had requested and was now waiting for the two hundred pages to finish printing. He felt as if he were running out of time, but he guessed he had at least twenty minutes until the first recess.

"Please return to your seats," said the Speaker. He waited for the room to sit down. "Mr. Clerk, please call the roll by district of the members who have been duly elected and certified by the Secretary of State to serve in this chamber."

Duncan turned to the first page in his ledger book, and began to read off the names, "David Jones, Sullivan County," he said into the microphone.

"Here," called a voice from the back of the room. Duncan put a small check next to the name.

"Joe Humphrey, Sullivan County," said Duncan. There was an outbreak of applause. The Speaker hit the gavel twice.

Joe stood up and simply said, "Here," and returned to his seat. Duncan continued down the list.

Somewhere around district eighty, Tom walked back on to the floor and wordlessly handed Xavier the list. Xavier nodded and found a highlighter in his drawer; he made his way through the list until he found the name he wanted and highlighted it.

Fearing the yellow marking wasn't enough, he found a permanent marker and circled it.

"Xavier Jarvis, Shelby County," said Duncan into the microphone. Xavier didn't hear it, too busy deciding if the marker made the impact he wanted.

"Xavier. Jarvis. Of Shelby County," said Duncan again. Shawn Maddox gave Xavier a quick nudge of the elbow. Xavier snapped back to reality and was aware of what was happening.

He stood quickly and said, "Here." There were some laughs in the room.

Duncan checked the name and then said, "Charles Beckett, Shelby County." He heard a faint 'here' from somewhere unknown and checked the name. "Mr. Speaker, all elected members are here and accounted for."

"I now call on Justice Sheldon Austin to administer the oath of office to the members-elect," said Speaker Caputo.

A small man in a black robe made his way to the well. He adjusted the microphone, "Please raise your right hand and repeat after me . . ."

In the conference room attached to Gregory's office, twelve of the assistants for Democratic Representatives had gathered to watch the events unfold.

"I wish they'd hurry up," said Hillary Thompson.

"Lord, honey, you know they've got to draw this out," said Alice, fixing herself another cup of coffee.

"I don't see why they have to draw it out like this," said Christina Hicks. "Just do the deed and let us go, I feel like I'm waiting on a spanking from my dad when he gets home from work."

"But they have to be fancy and formal about it," replied Dianna Torrey.

With the oath administered and the papers certifying the oaths signed, the temporary rules carried over from the previous General Assembly were adopted by voice vote. "Next order, Mr. Clerk," said the Speaker.

In a voice that sounded like a cliché umpire from a low-budget baseball movie, Duncan said: "Nominations for Constitutional Officers and the Invitation to the Governor to address a joint session of the General Assembly, the Joint Resolutions are spread on the members desks."

"Representative Holcomb, you are recognized, at your desk," said Caputo.

Tracy stood up and picked up her microphone. "Thank you, Mr. Speaker," she said, finding the piece of paper with a number one in the corner, before she began to speak. "Mr. Speaker, I move HJR 1 and HJR 2 be placed on final reading and the rules suspended on the issue."

"That is a proper motion, is there a second," said the Speaker. Several members called out 'second.' "Without object, the rules are suspended and HJR 1 and HJR 2 are placed on final reading." The Speaker hit the gavel.

"Point of order!" called a voice from the middle of the room. It was Matthew Roy. "Representative Roy, for what purpose?"

Representative Roy stood from his seat and grabbed his microphone. "Parliamentary inquiry, Mr. Speaker."

"Proceed," said Caputo.

"Mr. Speaker, is it too late to object to one of the names on the list?" Matthew reached down and squeezed the shoulder of his deskmate, Larry Pickard. The room laughed and Matthew returned the microphone back to its hole in his desk.

It took Speaker Caputo a beat to get the joke, then he laughed and said, "All people nominated for Constitutional offices are highly qualified and deserving of their post, and some will be missed more than others." There was another, much louder laugh. Spontaneous applause erupted for Larry who stood up and waved; he shook a few hands near him. The Speaker allowed this to go on for a moment before banging the gavel. "Next order, Mr. Clerk."

Returning to his performance voice, Duncan said "Election for lower officers for the Tennessee House of Representatives, Speaker Pro Tempore and Deputy Speaker." Speaker Caputo looked at Gregory, Gregory made a circle in the air with his finger indicating there would be no recess at this point. The Speaker nodded.

"Representative Frank, you are recognized," said the Speaker.

"Thank you Mr. Speaker." Rochelle Frank stood up at her desk and read from a note card. "Mr. Speaker it is my honor to nominate for Speaker Pro Tempore the longest-serving member in the House of Representatives. A retired teacher, a woman who marched with Dr. Martin Luther King, Jr., through the streets of Memphis. A woman who has fought for the poor and forgotten. A woman who has weathered impossible storms to emerge stronger than ever. Mr. Speaker, I nominate Mrs. Tayna Allan for Speaker Pro for the one oh six General Assembly." There was a small amount of applause. Joe Humphrey raised his hand.

"Representative Humphrey," said the Speaker. "You are recognized."

"Thank you, Mr. Speaker. It is my honor to second the nomination," he said returning the microphone to the desk. Mike Hayes raised his hand.

"Chairman Hayes, you are recognized," said Caputo.

"Thank you, I move to close the nominations for Speaker Pro Tempore," said Mike thus confirming their end of a bargain.

"Seeing as how there is only one nominee," said the Speaker. "We will do this by voice vote. All those in favor of Representative Allan serving as Speaker Pro say 'aye.'" The Speaker picked up his gavel as shouts of "aye" filled the room. "All those opposed?" He went to hit the gavel when, to the surprise of many, four distinct voices from the Speaker's left called out 'no.' Tayna stood up to see who had said it, but could not make out the faces. Joe remained seated and tried to hide his smile. "The 'ayes' have it, the motion to reconsidered is tabled," said the Speaker, hitting the gavel as a small amount of polite applause came out. "With the power vested in me as Speaker of the House, I declare the election closed. Representative Allan has been duly elected to serve as Speaker Pro Tempore for the one hundred and sixth General Assembly. Next order Mr. Clerk."

As the nominations for Deputy Speaker were underway, Xavier rose from his seat and walked back to Michael Kincannon. Xavier knelt down so he was ear level. "Listen, Mike."

"Don't call me Mike. It's either Michael or Representative Kincannon," said Michael, agitated. The older black man kept his eyes forward, not looking at Xavier.

"OK, Michael," continued Xavier in a whisper. "You don't have to vote with us. But if you chose to vote the other way, it will be one of your last."

Michael keeping his eyes on the Chief Clerk. "Shit, you think they're going to run a Republican in the blackest district in the state? No, they'll owe me."

"You won't have to worry about them."

"Oh, what are you going to do big man? I'm the most popular politician in my district, and so was my daddy. You going to primary me? That could cost you your seat," said Michael with a smug grin. Xavier took the list Tom had given him and put it on Michael's desk. Xavier put one finger on it.

"This," said Xavier, "is a list of all twenty-five hundred people that voted in your primary last year. You break ranks now, every single one of them is going to know you got kicked out of the Democratic Party."

Michael waved him away, "So what? You can't kick me out of the party. You don't control the ballot. Kick me out of the caucus maybe, but not the party."

"Look around, chief. This caucus is the party." Xavier stared at the side of Michael's face. Michael refused to make eye contact. "You know, there's a young man, his daddy is the top black lawyer in Memphis. His granddaddy was the first black city council member." Xavier began to turn the pages of the list on the desk. "This young man has been talking to me about running for office, I've about got him talked into a run at his grandpa's old city council seat. But he happens to live in a House District with an incumbent who is going to kicked out of our caucus very, very soon because he's a fool who thinks he's found a better deal. This means he might as well not be in our party – a member who voted for a Republican Speaker who wants to hand our schools over to his corporate cronies." Xavier stopped turning pages: there was the name George West highlighted and circled. Michael's eyes went wide; he finally turned to look at Xavier. "I'm thinking maybe he should run for State House. What do you think?"

"Michael Kincannon, Shelby County," called Duncan.

"Green!" shouted Michael, before returning to meet Xavier's eyes. "I think we need a recess," said Michael.

"I think you're right," said Xavier.

"Xavier Jarvis, Shelby County," called Duncan.

"I'll let Leader Anderson know we need a break," whispered Xavier.

"Jarvis! Shelby County!" Duncan said again, annoyed.

"Green!" said Xavier, making his way to Gregory's desk as the room laughed at his expense yet again.

"Mr. Clerk," said Speaker Caputo. "Please read the results."

"Final vote, forty-nine votes for Jon Green, fifty votes for Al Grindstaff," said Duncan.

"With the power vested in me as Speaker of the House, I declare the election closed. Representative Grindstaff has been duly elected to serve as Deputy Speaker for the one hundred and sixth General Assembly." He hit the gavel and let the applause for Deputy Speaker Grindstaff play out. He looked at Gregory who was holding up a fist, indicating he wanted a recess. The Speaker hit the gavel, "Leader Anderson, you are recognized."

"Thank you, Mr. Speaker," said Gregory from his desk. "I move we take a thirty-minute recess at this point before we nominate and vote for Speaker." There was a second to the motion by Daniel Burns, but there were also loud cries of objection.

"Proper motion, properly seconded, and objected," said the Speaker. "Rep. Hayes, you are recognized at your desk for your objection."

"Thank you, Mr. Speaker." Mike stood up and adjusted his tie, and moved his reading glasses to the top of his head. "Mr. Speaker, we've had over two months to get ready for this vote. Just because the other side hasn't done their homework is no reason to punish our side with this delay."

"Leader Anderson," said the Speaker.

"Mr. Speaker," said Gregory looking around the room. "We have upwards of one hundred guests here and we need to clear the floor a bit. Some of our guests need to get back to work, and some want to take pictures here on the floor. Now is traditionally the time to do this. That way the Speaker-elect can enjoy the moment after their election." Gregory looked over at Joe Humphrey. Joe crossed his arms and bobbed his head.

"Withdraw it, fuck it," Joe whispered to Mike.

Mike picked up his microphone. "I withdraw my objection."

"Without objection, we are in a thirty-minute recess," said the Speaker, hitting the gavel.

"Democrats, we will caucus in the legislative library, down the hall," Gregory said into the microphone.

Joe laughed and yelled over to Gregory with a smile. "Enjoy that!"

The second-floor conference room of the War Memorial Building was packed. So full, in fact, that many of the staffers who had arrived to watch session there had gone back to watch in their own office by themselves.

The lobbyist for the Tennessee Cable Providers, Eric Smith, said "God, they're never going to get to it."

"I'm telling y'all," said Maggie, "the Democrats have something planned."

"No way," said Allen Van Dyke another legislative assistant. "I heard Holt and Jane talking this morning; the caucus is worried about people voting for Humphrey. That's all they're trying to stop."

"What's it matter if a Dem or two votes for Joe?" asked the IBEW lobbyist Gordon Powell.

"It's a pride thing," said Allen. "They know it's going to be Humphrey, but they don't want the embarrassment of some Dems breaking ranks." The majority in the room seemed to agree.

"Well," said Maggie, "I guess we'll find out in thirty minutes."

The Legislative Library had an impressive spread of finger foods laid out under a banner that read, "Congrats Speaker Humphrey." Daniel rolled his eyes when he saw it; Gregory thought it would only help drive the point home that this was a real possibility. Slowly, begrudgingly, the other Democrats made their way into the legislative library. Some of the members decided to pick their way through the spread on the table. They were quickly scolded by Rochelle Frank.

"Y'all get your hands off those goodies, you know better, they aren't for you," she said.

"The fuck does it matter?" asked Bill Peters. No one rushed to his defense.

"We might end up with Humphrey as our Speaker, but that doesn't mean we have to act like we don't have manners," said Rochelle.

Gregory saw the Speaker walk in and ran over to him. "Did you talk to Duncan?" he asked.

"What about?" asked the Speaker.

"The Speaker's vote, we need it done alphabetically."

"He knows," said the Speaker.

"Then why is he going in order of district?" pleaded Gregory.

"I don't know," said the Speaker with genuine concern. "He's supposed to be doing it by the alphabet, I haven't noticed."

"Well, he hasn't," said Gregory. Tom, who had been listening in, walked over to the duo.

"I'll make sure he does this next time," said the Speaker.

Tom jumped in. "You can't do that. You've already instructed him to do the other elections by district, to change now would be out of order and put all the elections at risk."

"Listen here," said the Speaker, annoyed that a lowly staffer would challenge his handle on the rules of order, "them boys are going to be thrown for a loop, they'll be so busy trying to figure out why we nominated this bozo that they won't notice if I smudge the rules a little bit. If they want to take it to court the case will take at least two years, by then all this shit will be behind us."

Tom thought for a moment, digesting what the Speaker had said. "Ok," was the only response he could think of.

"I'll talk to Duncan beforehand, make sure he knows," said the Speaker who left for the other side of the room and began to help himself to the food.

Daniel, standing to the side of the room, clapped his hands to get everybody's attention. "Is there anyone in here who isn't a member of the caucus?" Daniel looked around the room as a hum of conversation began to spread. "Press, family, friends, staff, anybody like that?" Tom and Charlie slipped out one of the doors, closing it behind them. Daniel spoke up to regain the group's attention. "Listen, we're down to about fifteen or twenty minutes, we have to get this sorted out. Let me see a show of hands, again, who is on board?" Hands went up; Daniel quickly realized it would be easier to count the hands that weren't raised. Murry Price and Tayna Allan. He quickly looked and was pleasantly surprised to see Michael Kincannon's hand was raised.

"Murry," said Gregory. "What do we have to do to get you on board?"

"I'm not sure," said Representative Price. "I guess I just don't want to vote for a Republican. Never have and never will."

Gregory rolled his eyes. "Look around. Do you want to be the guy who stops this from happening? Be the one who goes up against all this?" Murry shrugged. "Listen, he won't be a Republican after this, they'll kick him out. He won't be a Democrat either because we don't get elected up there. Do this, just this once, and you might just save our party. Don't forget, the person we are about to elect as Speaker gets to draw the lines for redistricting. Wouldn't you rather have the guy who does that on your side?"

Murry nodded and scratched his chin. "Ok," he said. "But only if everyone who votes before me votes for him. If even one person votes for Humphrey I'm gonna vote 'present.'"

"That's fair," said Gregory.

Xavier cleared his throat. "Tayna, what's your hold up on this?"

"I'll be honest," said Tayna. "I don't trust Joe Humphrey, but I also don't trust him," she pointed at Gregory, "him," she pointed at Daniel, "or him," she pointed at Caputo. "Joe Humphrey already held up his end of my deal, I'm not inclined to go back on mine now."

Gregory thought about what he could say to her. The district argument that seemed to work on Murry Price would have no effect on Tayna; her district was going to be safe no matter how they drew it. Being in the General Assembly as long as she had, no amount of threats would move her. He couldn't offer her a position she wanted because she had that. He could offer her Speaker but then they would lose Keith's vote. He could try flattery but she already declared her lack of trust in him, so anything he could say would come up hollow. Did she know about his attempt to trade her office for a vote?

Hannah Vick spoke up. "Tayna, I get it. I don't trust these white boys either, but what I do know is that every single one of them would stab us in the back if they had the chance. That includes Joe Humphrey." Hannah began to walk towards Tayna in the space between the Speaker Pro Term and Gregory. "Let me put it this way, though. If you vote for Joe, he's going to push you to the side and ignore you at best. More likely he'll double cross you. Then what are you going to do? Do you think your vote is going to matter to him once he's got that hammer? Then in two years he won't even need your vote, and he's going to put someone else in at Speaker Pro, you can bet on it." She was standing directly in front of Tayna now. "But, you vote for this other boy. You'll not only be sticking it to every white man who tried to peek up your skirt while you moved out of their way on a sidewalk, but you'll be sticking with the devil you know, because any of these mother fuckers," she pointed behind her at Gregory and Daniel, "mess with you then you got power to get them out of this room. You won't have that with Joe Humphrey."

Tayna stood there, arms folded, tapping the toe of her red heels. The room was tense and quiet. Finally she said, "I don't appreciate your language."

"Ok, everybody listen," said Gregory in a bit of shock at the dialogue that had just taken place. "We're going back in there. This vote will be alphabetical, not by district. So, Tayna, you have about ten minutes, maybe less, to make up your mind. You'll be the first name called." He looked at Tayna. "Vote your district, vote your party, but most importantly vote your conscience. Let's get back in there." It was a cliché. He hated clichés, but since all of politics is a cliché he decided to play it up.

Gregory walked out of the room. Tom and Charlie were waiting for him in the hall. They flanked either side of him.

"Well, what are we doing?" asked Charlie.

"Everyone is onboard except Tayna," the two staffers groaned. "We have no idea where she stands."

"What should we tell Keith?" whispered Tom.

Gregory thought for a second, then said, "Give him the signal that we're good to go."

"But what if Tayna doesn't stick with us?" asked Charlie.

"Then he's fucked with the rest of us," said Gregory, with a small rage burning inside him. "I want to put her on the fucking spot."

Tom walked back into the House chambers and scanned the room. It appeared as though the Republicans hadn't left the room during the break; they were all standing about the floor in small groups discussing whatever was on their minds. He saw Keith standing in one of the alleyways between the desks on the right side of the room, facing the doors in the back. Tom began to walk down the center aisle. He glanced over his shoulder and saw Charlie several steps behind. Tom turned to his right and made his way through the rows of desks heading to the side of the room where Duncan's office sat. He passed by Keith; Tom felt his heart stop beating. He went through the open door into Duncan's office and turned around at the precise moment Charlie passed behind Keith. Charlie smiled and used his fist to give Keith two quick taps in the middle of the older man's back.

"Keithster," said Charlie.

"Exciting stuff," replied Keith.

Charlie laughed, and trying to sound sarcastic he said: "Sure is." This drew a laugh from the small group of Republicans with Keith. Charlie walked into the office.

"What was that?" Tom asked him.

"The signal, I had to make it look unassuming," said Charlie defensively.

"That was the wrong sign," said Tom with concern.

"No it wasn't," Charlie cut back.

"It's a shoulder squeeze if we're doing it, two taps if we aren't."

"You sure?"

"Fucking, positive." Tom's face was stone.

"Oh shit, are you sure?" Charlie began to sweat. His eyes darted back out to Keith. He could feel sudden waves of heat take over his body. Charlie began to wonder how he could get back out there and squeeze Keith's shoulders without it looking weird. Tom laughed. Charlie stared at him, and then suddenly understood his friend was playing a trick on him. "Fuck you, you know it? Fuck you. That wasn't funny."

"Sorry man, couldn't help it," said Tom still smiling.

"Boys, watch your language," said Duncan standing by the window holding a folder; he was writing something inside. His assistant, Margie, was seated at the desk – neither Tom nor Charlie had noticed them.

"Duncan, make sure you call this next vote in alphabetical order," said Charlie.

"I'm aware," said Duncan, lowering his voice. "The Speaker just filled me in. Is it going to work?"

"We think so," said Tom.

Speaker popped his head into the office, "The hour is nigh, my brethren. Ring the bell." Caputo walked away.

Duncan turned looked at his assistant. "Hit it, Margie."

The old woman stepped on the pedal under her desk without saying a word. The bell outside the chamber door echoed through the halls of the Capitol and throughout the Plaza. She counted to twenty and then let go. Duncan walked past Tom and Charlie on his way to his spot behind the well. Tom and Charlie followed, closing the door behind them.

The Speaker hit the gavel several times. "Mr. Sergeant at Arms! Please invite the members of the General Assembly and their distinguished guests into the Chambers and close the doors!" Caputo waited until all the doors in the back of the chamber were closed and the Sergeant at Arms was seated in his chair. He then quickly scanned all the desks to make sure each was occupied. Once satisfied he continued. "Next order, Mr. Clerk!"

"Nominations for Speaker of the House for the one oh sixth General Assembly of the state of Tennessee," said Duncan in his performance voice. Caputo looked down at his notes; he hadn't written down the name of the person who would be nominating Humphrey. He looked at Duncan who mouthed the name to him.

"Representative Wallace, you are recognized!" said the Speaker.

"Thank you, Mr. Speaker," said the old man seated a few rows behind Humphrey, in a voice that had lived through enough Wall Street cigarette smoke to last three lifetimes. Tom Wallace was reading his nominating speech off a piece of paper lying on his desk, hunched over and holding the microphone against his lips in such a way that no one could see his face, but they could hear every breath the man struggled to take. "I rise today to make an historic nomination that will forever change the course of our state. I nominate this man because I have seen the dedication he has given to our state, and the faith he lives out in his life. A sixth generation Tennessean, whose family's roots go back in this state to the time before we were a state. A man of integrity, wisdom, bold vision, with a servant's heart, and a true leader. Mr. Speaker, it is my true and sincere honor to nominate Joe Humphrey," applause began to ring out, and Tom Wallace had to raise the volume of his voice, "for the position of Speaker of the House for the one oh six General Assembly." The cheers and clapping continued for several seconds, ignoring the calls for silence made by Speaker Caputo's gavel.

The room finally quiet, Speaker Caputo checked the notes Duncan had hastily written down for him and spoke into his microphone, "Representative . . . Ellington you are recognized."

Lynn Ellington stood up at her desk and flipped her curly hair over her shoulder; she held a note card and spoke into her microphone, "Mr. Speaker, it is my great honor to address this body for the first time as a member in order to second the nomination of Joe Humphrey for Speaker of the House." There was a sudden mix of hot energy filling the limestone box. A jubilant and eager feeling came over half the room. The Speaker hit the gavel twice, Representative Ellington continued. "I ran for office to shrink the size of government, and to protect the unborn children who are too often denied the right to life, liberty, and the pursuit of happiness. Joe Humphrey shares these goals and has proven himself to be the honorable leader we, the people, deserve from this body." She smiled as cheers began to ring out and returned the microphone to the hole in her desk.

Gregory stood up, holding his nominating speech. He waved at Duncan to be recognized, Duncan pointed and nodded at him.

Joe smacked Mike Hayes on the arm several times. Mike stood up, grabbing his microphone, and desperately waved at the Speaker hoping to be recognized.

The Speaker saw Mike out of the corner of his eye. He pointed at him and said: "Representative Hayes, for what purpose?"

Mike spoke quickly into his microphone, "Mr. Speaker, I move to close the nominations for Speaker of the House." There was a sudden wave of voices and cheering. Loud cries of objection and seconds swept through the room. The Speaker looked down at Duncan; the Clerk could only shrug, it was a legal motion.

"Hold on, everybody," said Speaker Caputo lifting his hand. "Now everybody just hold on." He looked around the room as the volume came back down. "First thing first, there was a lot of noise in here, was there a second?" Several voices in unison called out 'second.' "I thought I heard about forty-nine people say it, ok." There were laughs throughout the chamber. Caputo, himself, smiled and noted that this would probably be the last time he was able to make a joke from the Speaker's chair. "Ok, I also clearly heard objections. So, Leader Anderson you are recognized for your objection."

Gregory felt his anger begin to boil; had he been alone rather than in a room full of egotistical narcissists, of which he most certainly considered himself to be, he would have cried with anger. He checked his emotions, "Mr. Speaker, I object because I have a nomination to make. Look, I know the other side is lusting to finally have some power in this chamber but that's no reason to not follow the tradition of decency we have here at the Capitol." Laughs and boos at Gregory's expense could be heard.

Speaker Caputo turned his microphone off and leaned over his desk to talk to Duncan. "What can I do?"

"Nothing," said Duncan. "It's a legal motion, properly seconded, and objected. We vote on the objection; a simple majority overrules the objection and the motion stands." The Speaker stood up and nodded his head. Duncan waved at him, telling him to lean back down. "You could just say it was an improper motion. It would take two-thirds to overrule you."

"I like that," said Caputo. He straightened up again, turning on his microphone, "Ok folks, here's what going to happen. I knew that Leader Anderson was going to nominate someone, and he was next on my list. I saw Chairman Hayes raise his hand and thought he was going to add his own words to Leader Humphrey's nomination. I considered it a point of personal privilege. So, I'm going to say the motion by Chairman Hayes was out of order." There were groans and boos. The Speaker stood there waiting for them to go away. Joe Humphrey stood up and raised his hand. "Yes, Leader Humphrey."

Joe picked up his microphone in one hand and held the other out like a preacher in the middle of a sermon. "I am sorry to do this. Mr. Speaker, I challenge the ruling of the chair." Joe dropped the microphone on his desk, he put his hands on his hips and gave Speaker Caputo the coldest look he could. The Republicans on the floor and in the gallery erupted; they were gushing over the tough guy act put on by their next Speaker. Duncan motioned for Humphrey to come to the well.

"Would the two leaders approach the well? The Clerk wants to talk," said Caputo. Gregory and Joe walked forward.

"Listen," Duncan said to both of them. "It takes a two-thirds majority for a challenge to a chair to stand. Are you sure you want to do this?"

"You don't have two-thirds, Joe. Come on," said Gregory. "My guy deserves to be nominated; he's earned it." Joe could only look at Gregory with pity. "Be decent right now and you can punish us all later."

"Fine," said Joe. "But make it quick. I withdraw my motion."

"Thank you," said Gregory. He walked to the well and waited.

Joe walked back over to his desk, he looked at Mike and shrugged. He said, loud enough for everyone on his side to hear, "Takes two-thirds, we're going to withdraw the motion. Let them send the bastard off with a nice little speech." He took his seat as the people around him laughed and applauded.

"Mr. Clerk, the motion to close nominations has been withdrawn," said Caputo in the microphone. "Leader Anderson, you are recognized in the well."

Gregory approached the lectern at the front and center of the room. He suddenly felt the eyes of the entire state on him. He wished, in that moment, he had worn a blue suit instead of black. He briefly stopped to consider what he was about to do – nominate a member of the opposing party to one of the highest offices in the state. He liked Keith Zachary, he trusted him, but deep down Gregory knew Keith wasn't up to the task of being Speaker. It was going to be two years of chaos if it worked. Two years of a nice guy in a strongman's job. Keith was going to get pushed out of his party just by being nominated and there was no guarantee that all the Democrats were going to vote for the man. Keith might be on the cusp of the greatest achievement in his political career, but he was absolutely on the cusp of the end of that very same career. Gregory smoothed out the paper in front of him. Could he actually put this man through it? Gregory thought about nominating Caputo one last time; he could wing the nomination speech, and the old man deserved it. He looked up and made eye contact with Keith, who smiled. Gregory took a deep breath, and began.

"Mr. Speaker, I rise today, to also make history. The office of Speaker of the House is one that should be approached with great humility and awe. The holder of the gavel should be frightened by the responsibility that comes with such an awesome office. That is why I arise to nominate a man who is selfless and has always put people over politics . . ." There were sudden cries of laughter.

Tom was standing next to Charlie in the press box to the Speaker's right. He leaned over and asked Charlie, "Why are they laughing?"

"The dicks think Gregory is talking about Caputo," said Charlie turning to face Tom. "They're about to stop laughing really fucking quick."

Gregory ignored the laughter and continued, "and a man who will approach this position with the humble touch it demands. I know this because this man comes from humble roots. I am making history in that, to my knowledge, this is the first time a member of my party has nominated a member of the opposing party for this position." The room got deathly quiet. Gregory paused, bit struck by the sudden lack of noise. Soon there were whispers throughout the floor and gallery.

Joe leaned over to Mike, "What the fuck did he just say?"

Mike responded, "Exactly what you heard. Who the fuck is it?"

"I don't know," said Joe. He felt his face turned blood red.

Gregory pressed on, "It is also historic for another reason. As far back as I could find, this is the first time in our state's long history that one Elizabethton native has nominated another for Speaker of the House."

Mike looked at Joe and said, "Elizabethton? Could be Zachary, or Flagler, or even Arnold, they're all Elizabethton natives aren't they?" Joe could not speak; he was too consumed by rage.

Gregory looked up to take in the shocked faces of the crowd. He continued. "As a small business owner and a farmer, this man knows both commerce and agriculture, our state motto. Ladies and Gentlemen, it is my highest honor to nominate, for Speaker of the House, Keith Zachary, of Carter County." There were gasps on the floor, in the gallery, and throughout the Plaza. The electric energy that had so recently consumed the room to the point of combustion now engulfed the House chamber in confusion and rage.

Charlie focused on Joe Humphrey. Joe had been so red in the face Charlie had been concerned the man might pass out. Now Charlie watched as the blood slowly drained from Joe's body, turning him ghostly white. The change in color started on his forehead and worked its way down, like an ink pen whose ball point had fallen out. Charlie smiled.

Maggie, watching the events unfold on a tv screen in the second-floor conference room looked at Allen Van Dyke. She smiled.

"It's not over yet," said Allen. "Joe has a couple of Dems on his side."

The viewing party in Gregory's office was ecstatic. Tears were being shed and no emotion was being held back. They all knew this might mean they were safe, but they also knew if it didn't work they were screwed. Alice sat in her chair stunned, not at what was happening but by the fact that she hadn't known about it until this moment.

Mike grabbed Joe's arm, "We're gonna fucking bury that son of a bitch for this." Mike stood up and joined the chorus of Republicans pointing and shouting at Keith. "YOU JUDAS SON OF A BITCH!" Mike yelled and shook his fist. A short woman as wide as a tractor was standing beside Keith, daring anyone to make the first move.

Joe tried to stand up. As chaos was beginning to take form all around him, he was paralyzed. The feeling in his arms and legs was gone. Out of all the scenarios, this had never been discussed. Joe had never considered that Caputo would willingly step aside to let a Republican be nominated by his party. Moreover, no one in Republican Caucus had thought one of their own would have the guts to join with the Democrats to run against Joe. He finally found some strength to stand up. Tucker Pyle came over and put his arm around Joe.

"We still have Tayna, and J.A., and a couple of their blacks, you're good," Tucker said, patting Joe on the chest. Joe turned to look at Tayna across the room. They made eye contact; Joe nodded. Tayna smiled at him. He suddenly felt better, and he chuckled a little bit.

The Speaker watched his House turn into a shouting match. He knew he should stop it and move things along, but this was the first time in decades that he hadn't heard his name called as a nominee for Speaker of the House. He didn't know what to do. He looked at Duncan.

Over the noise, Duncan cupped his hands over his mouth shouted up to the Speaker, "Recognize Xavier Jarvis! Jarvis! Then, Michaels!"

The Speaker snapped back to reality and banged the gavel four times, he lifted his left hand in a call of silence. He hit the gavel a bit harder three more times and silence finally came. "Representative Jarvis, you are recognized."

Xavier stood up at his desk and bent over, barely picking up the microphone, "I don't have much to say, I second the nomination, Mr. Speaker." This caused another outcry by the Republicans.

"Representative Michaels, you're recognized," Speaker Caputo said quickly, not even waiting for Xavier to put his microphone away.

Holt Michaels stood up, "Mr. Speaker, I move we close nominations for Speaker of the House." There were shouts of second. The Republicans could have objected and tried to stall for time but they were all too busy fuming with anger and bewilderment to realize what was happening.

"I hereby declare the nominations closed," said the Speaker. The noise was again too loud for many members to hear him, but he decided not to hit the gavel just yet. "We will vote by roll call. Mr. Clerk, please call the roll alphabetically, with the Democratic names first, followed by the Republicans." Calls for hushed silence went across the floor. The Speaker had just changed the voting pattern, not only by calling for the roll in alphabetical order but also by party. This was a major violation; Duncan looked up at the Speaker unsure if he heard the order correctly. Caputo, well aware of what he had just said, and knowing Duncan had those exact lists in his ledger, nodded to the Clerk. Duncan knew this was a violation of the rules of order, but with no objections he was powerless to stop it. He also had no desire to stop it.

Duncan flipped a few pages in his ledger book to where he kept the names divided by party, in alphabetical order. He looked at his young male assistant clerk controlling the board. "Red for Humphrey, blue for Zachary. Got it?" The fresh-faced recent college graduate made a note on a piece of paper nearby, he looked at Duncan and nodded.

Duncan cleared his throat and took a sip of water. The chamber got quiet.

"Representative Allan," said Duncan.

Tayna stood up. Joe walked to the middle of the floor and looked at her smiling. She could end this spectacle right now. Tayna starred at Joe with a small grin. She felt an immense pressure on her chest; in Joe's face she saw every white man who had ever promised her and her people the world, only to back out. She suddenly recalled the house, in Collierville, that her parents had scraped together enough money to buy only to have a white realtor refuse to sell it to them. She saw the faces of the white boys screaming at her with hateful pubescent rage as she marched for equal justice. She saw the white professors at her college who had refused to give her the grades she deserved because a black woman could not be the top performing student. She saw all of them in Joe Humphrey's smug, smiling face. She widened her grin.

"Zachary!" she said with more force than anything she had ever said. Joe's face began to shake, he quickly turned around and pointed at Keith with two fingers. He slowly started making his way back to Keith's desk.

"Allan votes, Zachary," said Duncan. He made a note in his ledger. The name 'Allan' switched from white to blue on the voting screens.

"Representative Anderson," called Duncan.

"Zachary!" said Gregory, who was still standing at the front of the room. After casting his vote, he walked back to his seat and sat down. He wanted to enjoy the show more than anyone else.

"Anderson votes, Zachary," said Duncan. 'Anderson' switched from white to blue.

"Representative Burns."

"Zachary!"

"Representative Burns votes, Zachary. Representative Byrd."

"Zachary!"

"Representative Byrd votes, Zachary. Representative Caputo."

The Speaker could barely get the name out, when it finally came it was barely above a whisper. "Zachary," he said and he sat down in his chair, holding the gavel in his right hand and lightly smacking his left palm.

"Representative Caputo votes, Zachary. Representative Carter."

"Zachary!"

"Carter votes, Zachary. Representative Cole."

"Zachary!"

"Cole votes, Zachary. Representative Cross."

"Zachary!"

"Cross votes, Zachary. Representative Daniels."

"Zachary!"

Joe's slow march to Keith's desk ended when he was five feet away; the short woman stood between him and Keith. Keith remained seated, leaned back in his chair, legs crossed, and slowly stroked his mustache. He was staring at the buttons on his desk not looking up.

"Daniels votes, Zachary. Representative Dobbins." Joe waited to hear how Dobbins would vote.

"Zachary!" called J.A.'s voice from somewhere behind Joe. Joe was starting to lose whatever hope he had left.

"Dobbins votes, Zachary. Representative Dunne."

Joe looked at Keith. "What do you want? Huh?" He tried to keep his voice calm; he didn't want to be another one of the angry mob after Keith. He wanted to plead with him.

"Zachary!"

"Dunne votes, Zachary. Representative Frank."

Keith was refusing to look at Joe. The woman between them spoke up. "I think he wants to be the motherfucking Speaker of the House! What do you think he wants?"

"Zachary!"

"Frank votes, Zachary. Representative Green."

He looked around the woman, directly at Keith. "Name it Keith, it's yours!"

"Zachary!"

"Green votes, Zachary. Representative Griffin."

"Seriously, do you want to keep your assistant? Done! Be party chair? Done! You want to run for Governor? DONE!"

"Zachary!"

"Griffin votes, Zachary. Representative Hampton."

"Fucking name it, Keith! Please! PLEASE! LOOK AT ME!"

"Zachary!"

"Hampton votes, Zachary. Representative Hawkins."

"Zachary!"

"You won't even look at me?" Joe asked as he felt his contained anger reach its limit. Keith stared straight ahead.

"Hawkins votes, Zachary. Representative Herron."

"You're a real piece of shit, Keith! Fuck you," said Joe, the redness returning to his face.

"Zachary!"

"Herron votes, Zachary. Representative Hyde."

Keith kept looking at his desk. "What I really want," he said, without looking up.

"Zachary!"

"Hyde votes, Zachary. Representative Jarnigan."

"What I really want," Keith continued in a calm voice, "is to be Speaker of the House and for you to go back to your seat."

"Zachary!"

"Jarnigan votes, Zachary. Representative Jarvis."

"You fucking heard him, get the fuck out of here." The woman moved as if she was going to push Joe. Joe flinched.

"Zachary!"

"Jarvis votes, Zachary. Representative Jones, of Davidson."

Joe turned and slowly began to walk back to his seat. The sound of the room faded to a muddled stream of blurry voices. He looked up at the board and watched as the names Jones, Kelly, and Kincannon switched to blue. With Kincannon's name

Joe knew it was done. He got back to his seat as the names King, Landry, Macellan turned blue. He realized how cocky he had been. To assume that once Larry Pickard was out, the gavel would be his. He sat there in silence. Maddox, Mains, Michaels, Miller, and Murphy all went blue. Joe looked up and saw the number thirty-one in blue. It was almost over. He stayed seated.

"Murphy votes, Zachary, Representative Murray."

"Zachary!"

"Murray votes, Zachary. Representative Nolan."

"Zachary!"

"Nolan votes, Zachary. Representative O'Sullivan."

"Zachary!"

Gregory was in his seat, eyes glued to the board. It's going to work, he thought. He saw Parcell, Pardue, Parker all turn blue. He thought about election night; it was a humiliating defeat, then Joe danced on his grave by literally measuring the Speaker's before moving in. That son of a bitch deserves this, he thought. Parks, Patton, Peters, and Price went blue. He couldn't help but feel pride at the moment. The national party had counted out the entire state, the State Party had written off the House, the Senate Dems were running scared. Yet he, and his staff, had salvaged a small victory out of this debacle. Reid, Sanders, Smith, Smith, Vick all turned blue. He wondered at the sight of all the blue names. Even the ones he didn't think they were going to get had stepped up and voted with little hesitation. Walsh turned blue. Gregory decided to really listen and take in the next two names.

"Walsh votes, Zachary. Representative White."

"Zachary!"

"White votes, Zachary. Representative Wright."

"Zachary!"

"Wright votes, Zachary." Duncan stopped, he wrote the number forty-nine at the bottom of the page. Gregory felt tears begin to build in his eyes. Joe felt tears too, but for a different reason. The voting boards on either side of the room were blazoned with blue forty-nines.

Duncan turned to the next page in the ledger. The chamber was so quiet the movement of the paper could be heard in the galleries high above. He began to call the names, "Representative Arnold."

"Humphrey," called a meek voice from the middle of the room.

"Arnold votes, Humphrey," Duncan said, making a note in his ledger. On the voting board the name Arnold switch from white to red. "Representative Beckett."

"Humphrey!"

"Beckett votes, Humphrey. Representative Brown." The name Beckett turned red. Joe and Gregory both looked at the boards.

"Humphrey!"

"Brown votes, Humphrey. Representative Cartwright." the board now had a red number three.

"Humphrey!"

"Cartwright votes, Humphrey. Representative Cullen."

"Humphrey!"

"Cullen votes, Humphrey. Representative Edmunds."

"Humphrey!" Joe could feel the conclusion running at him full steam.

"Edmunds votes, Humphrey. Representative Ellington."

"Humphrey!"

"Ellington votes, Humphrey. Representative Evans."

"Humphrey!"

"Evans votes, Humphrey. Representative Flagler."

"Humphrey!"

"Flagler votes, Humphrey. Representative Grindstaff."

"Humphrey!"

"Grindstaff votes, Humphrey. Representative Guess."

Mary Ellen stayed in her seat; she was at a loss for words. She could feel herself somewhere between surprise and anger. She knew Keith had betrayed her, the caucus, and the state. She was worried about her own ambition and plans; this could mean the end of those. Yet part of her admired Keith Zachary, he had seen his chance, and took it. She took note, and would seize her next opportunity. "Humphrey!" she shouted from her seat.

"Guess votes, Humphrey. Representative Hayes."

Mike was standing, leaning over with his fists on his desk. "Humphrey!" he shouted. There had to be something they could do to stop this, he thought. Joe had already promised Keith everything he could want and had been turned down. Mike was waiting for this to be over – an emergency caucus meeting was necessary. Keith Zachary might go to sleep that night as Speaker but he would not go to sleep a Republican.

"Hayes votes, Humphrey. Representative Hill."

"Humphrey!"

"Hill votes, Humphrey. Representative Hockett."

"Humphrey!"

"Hockett votes, Humphrey. Representative Holcomb."

"Humphrey!"

"Holcomb votes, Humphrey. Representative Holly."

"Humphrey!"

"Holly votes, Humphrey. Representative Hope."

"Humphrey!"

"Hope votes, Humphrey. Representative Humphrey." The few noises that had started to build back up stopped; the room was quiet again.

Joe was stuck in his own mind. He heard his name, but he was wishing Grindstaff, or Cullen, or Brown had struck a deal with the Democrats instead of Zachary. The waiting for the inevitable was killing him. "Humphrey," he said from his seat, feeling people patting his back with condolences. He had expected this to be Caputo's political funeral, but it was his.

"Humphrey votes, Humphrey. Representative Jason."

"Humphrey!"

"Jason votes, Humphrey. Representative Jones, of Sullivan."

"Humphrey!"

"Jones, of Sullivan, votes Humphrey. Representative Krammer."

"Humphrey!"

"Krammer votes, Humphrey. Representative Liston."

"Humphrey!"

"Liston votes, Humphrey. Representative Mackey."

"Humphrey!"

"Mackey votes, Humphrey. Representative Mansfield."

"Humphrey!"

"Mansfield votes, Humphrey. Representative McCray."

"Humphrey!"

"McCray votes, Humphrey. Representative Minor."

"Humphrey!"

"Minor votes, Humphrey. Representative Moseby."

"Humphrey!"

The conference room on the second floor of War Memorial had gone quiet along with the rest of Legislative Plaza. Maggie was holding her head up by her hair. Halfway through the list, and they had to wait for the end to know their fate.

"Moseby votes, Humphrey. Representative Newman."

"Humphrey!"

"Newman votes, Humphrey. Representative Noel."

"Humphrey!"

"Noel votes, Humphrey. Representative Pickard."

Larry weighed his options. This was his chance to stop Joe, and he knew it. He liked Keith, but was unsure the man was up to the task of being Speaker. It was too late for the General Assembly to nominate someone else for Secretary of State without having to recall his nomination, which would take a simple majority, and he knew the Democrats would surely not vote to recall. Yet Secretary of State was a job he could keep for years; voting for Keith would mean he'd be out as Secretary in 2011. He wanted to vote for Keith, but he couldn't. He stood up, "Humphrey," he said.

"Pickard votes, Humphrey. Representative Pope."

"Humphrey!"

"Pope votes, Humphrey. Representative Porter."

"Humphrey!"

"Porter votes, Humphrey. Representative Pyle."

Tucker was full of anger, and blinded by it. He wanted to make a statement with his vote. He picked up the microphone from his desk and stood up. "I vote for the only real Republican nominee, Joe Humphrey!" This brought some applause to the lifeless Republicans that went away as quickly as it came.

Duncan made a mark in the ledger, ignoring the dramatic improvisation. In his clerk cadence he said: "Pyle votes, Humphrey. Representative Reynolds, of Knox."

"Humphrey!"

"Reynolds, of Knox, votes Humphrey. Representative Reynolds, of Bradley."

"Humphrey!"

"Reynolds, of Bradley, votes Humphrey. Representative Richardson."

"Humphrey!"

"Richardson votes, Humphrey. Representative Roy."

"Humphrey!"

"Roy votes, Humphrey. Representative Sells."

Christina Hicks was sitting with the small crowd in Gregory's office eyes glued to the TV. She was fidgety. "Y'all I need a smoke, how many more names do they got?"

"Well there's fifty Republicans and they just got to S, so they're about done," said Rose.

"Lord I hope so," said Christina with a sigh. "I can't remember the last time I needed a smoke so bad."

"Humphrey." Harry Sells' voice was dejected. He suddenly wished he had sided with Larry during the caucus race. Perhaps that would have avoided this entire debacle.

"Sells votes, Humphrey. Representative Slater."

"Humphrey!"

"Slater votes, Humphrey. Representative Stricland."

"Humphrey!"

"Stricland votes, Humphrey. Representative Tanner."

"Humphrey!"

"Tanner votes, Humphrey. Representative Thornsburry."

"Humphrey!"

"Thornsburry votes, Humphrey. Representative Van Dyke." Joe stood up and buttoned his jacket. He walked halfway down the aisle and stopped. He glared at Keith who hadn't changed his position since their earlier exchange. Joe wanted to watch Keith sign his own death warrant.

"Humphrey!"

"Van Dyke votes, Humphrey. Representative Wagner."

"Humphrey!"

"Wagner votes, Humphrey. Representative Wallace."

"Humphrey!"

"Wallace votes, Humphrey. Representative Weber." Gregory turned his chair to face the back corner. His legs were shaking and would not allow him to stand, but he wanted to hear Keith's voice.

"Humphrey!"

"Weber votes, Humphrey. Representative Williams."

"Humphrey!" Representative Williams proclaimed proudly. The chamber was so quiet that his voice echoed.

"Williams votes, Humphrey. Representative Wolf."

"Humphrey!"

"Wolf votes, Humphrey. Representative Zachary." The world stopped turning. Duncan looked up for the first time to see Keith in the back of the Chamber.

Keith reached up and placed a hand on his sister's shoulder for support as he stood. When he first thought of this plan he had played out several scenarios for this moment. One had been him getting eighty votes and his final vote resulting in cheers. He had planned to say 'With God's Help, I vote Zachary.' But he realized there was a lump of nervous expectation stuck in his throat. He looked down the aisle as he buttoned his jacket. He made brief eye contact with Joe Humphrey. Keith felt an icy chill run over his body. He could see Mike Hayes, standing with his arms crossed, unable to look in Keith's direction. His sister patted his hand. This was his moment: not Joe's, not Mike's, but his. He looked up at the board, every name in red or blue, except his, still in white. The tally was forty-nine to forty-nine; he was his own tie breaker.

He said, in the strongest voice he could force from his body, "Zachary!"

It was over. The House erupted. There were boos coming from the Republicans in the chamber. These were quickly countered with a standing ovation from the Democrats seated on the floor, led by Gregory who shot out of his chair before Keith had finished saying his own name. Joe walked back to his desk, red in the face with rage, and sat down. Charlie put his arms around Tom and shook him. "We fucking did it," he said. Tom could only laugh.

There were cheers throughout the Plaza. Marcy, who was sitting alone at her desk watching session from her computer, even caught herself feeling relieved and grasping her hands together with a smile. She felt tears beginning to creep out from her eyes; they were mostly for her friends who were safe now, but a few were for her boss.

Maggie looked at Allen in the conference room – it was packed with hugging bodies and exclaiming voices. She pointed at Allen. "I fucking told you, you prick."

Christina wrapped her arms around Rose who was crying; she gave her friend a quick kiss on the cheek. They were safe.

Alice held a hand over her mouth. "They did it," she whispered to herself.

Governor Welch was standing in his shirtsleeves, arms crossed, behind Katy Dill. They had watched the entire vote in stunned silence. The Governor felt a sudden rush of adrenaline; he could get even more done now, perhaps enough to find his way on to the new President's Cabinet.

Simon and the rest of the camera crew turned to each other; they turned off their cameras and found an empty bench on the floor to take in the rest of session as spectators.

Speaker Caputo hit his gavel three times in a plea for order. Once the volume was lowered to an acceptable level, he said, "Mr. Clerk, please read the vote."

"Mr. Speaker, final vote is forty-nine for Humphrey, fifty for Zachary," said Duncan.

Bob Caputo quickly moved to the next line in the script. "Honorable Representative Keith Zachary, having received the majority of the votes cast––"

"Fucking Judas!"

"You piece of trash!"

"Hillbilly motherfucker!" These cries were coming from unknown Republicans who felt betrayed by Keith, both on the Chamber floor and in the gallery above. The Democrats, unable to contain their own excitement, began to cheer.

Caputo hit the gavel again, calling for order. "Ladies and gentlemen!" he exclaimed to no avail. He continued to hit the gavel harder each time. "Ladies and gentlemen! Please!" The noise came to an abrupt halt. Caputo hit the gavel again. "Ladies and gentlemen! Mr. Sergeant at Arms, any more outbursts and I want you to remove them from the House Chamber, got it?" Caputo straightened the notes on his desk. "Now," he found his spot and started over, reading much faster this time, "Honorable Representative Keith Zachary, having received the majority of the votes cast, I hereby declare, the Honorable Keith Zachary of Carter County, duly, legally––"

"He's not honorable!" came a voice from the floor. Caputo picked up the gavel but did not hit it; he held up his hand as a warning.

Caputo continued, "and constitutionally elected the Speaker of the House of Representatives for the one hundred and sixth General Assembly of the Great State of Tennessee. Without objection, the motion to reconsider goes to the table!" Caputo hit the gavel again, and small cheers rang out. "I now call on the honorable Justice Sheldon Austin of the Supreme Court of Tennessee, to administer the oath of office. Speaker-elect Zachary, please come forward."

Justice Austin took a pen out of his pocket; he marked out the name Joe Humphrey on his script and quickly scribbled Keith Zachary.

Keith, following closely behind his sister, slowly made his way to the front of the room. He stopped to get handshakes with the few nearby Democrats while avoiding the gaze of his fellow Republicans.

Keith's sister took the Bible from Justice Austin and held it. Keith placed his left hand on it and raised his right hand. Gregory looked at the event like a proud parent watching a child graduate.

"Justice Austin," said Caputo.

"Repeat after me . . ." said the Justice.

Duncan looked up at Caputo. The man was stoic; Duncan could not tell if he was satisfied or depressed. He handed Caputo a folder.

Caputo leaned over. "what's this?" he whispered.

"It's the script, for the new Speaker," Duncan whispered back. "I'm assuming he doesn't know what to do. It would probably be best if you stayed up there beside him so we can keep things moving." Caputo nodded.

"So help me God . . ." said the Justice.

"So help me God," repeated Keith.

"Congratulations," said Justice Austin, extending his hand to Keith. There was another wave of mixed emotions from the chamber.

Gregory walked over to Keith, shook his hand. Keith brought Gregory in for a hug.

"How do you feel, Mr. Speaker?" asked Gregory with a smile.

"I feel great," said the Speaker. His smile unending.

Caputo hit the gavel a few more times. "Mr. Speaker," he said. He choked a little on the words; he prayed no one had notice. "Now is the time to address the chamber."

The Speaker turned to face the body at the lectern in the well. He pulled out of his breast pocket some folded yellow legal paper. Joe, who had been sitting lifeless at his desk, recognized the paper immediately. He felt his stomach turn, he was going to be sick. He leaned over to Mike and whispered, "I want the motherfucker out of the caucus as soon as we are done here." Mike could only nod in agreement.

"Thank you, Speaker Caputo," said Keith, his voice shaking as the microphone broadcasted it across the state. "Let's not forget, once Speaker, always Speaker. Thank you for your service to this state. Ladies and Gentlemen, I am humbled by this election." A chorus of boos broke out, one voice could be heard crying out fuck you; Keith's sister looked in the direction of the voice but she could not place it. Caputo hit the gavel and the boos continued. "That's alright," said Keith.

"Ladies and Gentlemen," said Caputo, hitting the gavel. "This is your final warning. Give our new Speaker the respect his office deserves or you will be escorted out." Tucker Pyle briefly considered leaving the chamber in protest, but decided to stay to watch the madness unfold.

"That's alright, really it is," said the Speaker. "I've been booed my whole life. Those calling me 'Judas,' you should know I was raised in church. I've been preached at my whole life – right now I need prayers not preaching." He waited as some applause drifted through the House. He returned to the speech he had written. "I intend to be a fair and reasonable Speaker. I believe in small government, even within government. That's why each member of this House will get to run their office how, and with who, they see fit." Cheers could be heard outside the chamber after this line. Legislative Plaza was flooded in relief. "We have an even split in this House. There are forty-nine Democrats and fifty Republicans, although I bet there will only be forty-nine Republicans by supper." This line brought laughs from members. "We are a divided chamber, in a divided state. I intend to unite our chamber, and our state, by setting the House Committees up fairly with an even split between the parties. I ask, again, for your prayers and your help. Thank you," Keith finished. He was again met by boos and cheers.

Tom leaned over to Charlie and said, "he's not the most eloquent choice."

"Yeah, that's true," said Charlie. "But he speaks like the rest of the state."

The Speaker made his way up to his new desk. He and Bob posed for a picture, a ceremonious passing of the gavel. Duncan and Caputo quickly ran through the rest of the agenda with the new Speaker during the swearing in of the other two officers, coaching him on his next lines. The rest of that session should have only lasted twenty minutes, but the Speaker mumbled and fumbled his way through the script. He was stopped every few words by Caputo or Duncan, who fed him the lines verbatim. As they finally approached the motion to adjourn, Mike Hayes raised his hand.

"Point of order," he said. Caputo and Duncan pointed at Mike, altering the Speaker to recognize the member.

"Yes," said the Speaker. "What is it?"

Mike grabbed his microphone. "Quick announcement," he said making sure to leave off the obligatory 'Thank you, Mr. Speaker.' "After we adjourn, the Republican Caucus will be meeting in the Legislative Library––" Joe, who had been catatonic through the session after the vote, suddenly sprang to life. He grabbed Mike by the arm, with fear and dread in his eyes he shook his head and whispered.

"No, no, not there."

Mike, remembering the banner and the now-cancelled party, quickly changed the location. "Scratch that," he said. "We will be meeting as a caucus right here, at my desk. Should only take a minute." Mike put the microphone away and sat down; he was smiling with a mouth on the verge of watering.

"Looking forward to it," said the Speaker getting laughs. Caputo pointed to the next line on the paper. The Speaker read the line, "With no other business . . . before us, I now decry, excuse me, declare the House of Representatives of Tennessee, of the great State of Tennessee, adjourned until tomorrow, Wednesday, January the fourteenth, at nine o'clock in the morning. We are adjourned. Hit gavel. Oh wait." The Speaker picked up the gavel and quickly hit it against the block. Caputo patted the Speaker on the back. People started to file out of the chambers, and the Republicans began to congregate around Mike's desk.

"Don't worry," Caputo said. "You'll get the hang of it."

"I doubt I'll have the time," said the Speaker.

"By the way, you'll have a different gavel tomorrow, this one here is a custom one for me," said Caputo. "We have some standard gavels down in my, sorry, your office."

"That's quite alright," said the Speaker. He looked down at his caucus. All eyes were looking back up at him. "Guess I should probably go do this now. Looks like I won't be leaving the room with a party."

"You will be leaving it as Speaker," said Caputo with a smile. "A bunch of us are gonna wait outside the door for you, we'll walk you down. I'll show you around your new office." He and the Speaker shook hands.

Keith took a deep breath and descended the stairs to the floor level. The caucus parted the water so that he could walk up to the desk Mike shared with Joe. The Speaker made eye contact with Humphrey. Joe was still seated, his eyes bloodshot.

"Let's make this quick," said Darren Hope.

"You got it," said Mike. He raised his voice so anyone near the chamber could hear. "Voice vote! All those in favor of removing Keith Zach--"

"SPEAKER Zachary," said Keith. He lowered his brow to look Mike in the eyes.

"Not here, you aren't," said Joe in a broken voice.

Mike continued. "All those in favor of removing Zachary from the caucus say 'aye'!"

In unison, nearly every voice said: "AYE!" Larry Pickard stood at the back of the huddle; he kept his mouth shut.

"Now wait just a minute," said Keith. "I am pro-life, I'm pro-family, I want to shrink government, I want to lower taxes!" His voice was raised to the point of screeching. "What makes me not a Republican?" He stared at Mike.

Mike held the eye contact. "All opposed, say 'no'," he said calmly. He looked around, daring anyone to speak up.

"No," said Keith.

"Vote's closed," said Mike. He pointed at the Speaker. "You're out," he said. "Enjoy these next two years. After that, we'll set things right."

Keith said nothing. He straightened his tie and checked his cufflinks, then made his way out of the chamber. He was greeted by the entire Democratic Caucus, waiting for him. They rode the elevator down from the Capitol to the legislative tunnel, a limestone structure that stretched two hundred feet. With its buffed walls and bright lights it looked as though it was ripped from the set of a high-budget science fiction movie. At the end of the tunnel were escalators running underground to Legislative Plaza. As they descended, they heard cheering. The entirety of the Legislative Plaza staff had lined the hall, even those who worked for Senators and Republicans were there, forming two lines cheering and screaming as the victors made their way down the corridor. Keith stopped to shake hands and pose for pictures. Bob Caputo put his arm around the Speaker's shoulder and led him into his new office.

CHAPTER 18

Tuesday, January 13, 2009

The sun had set hours ago and the party in the AT&T Tower was beginning to wind down. The time between the adjournment of session and the party had been a chaotic storm of media requests, phone calls, and planning. The organizers of the party, Tennessee Telecommunication Cooperative, had worried that the events in the House would have dampened their soiree, perhaps even keeping people away.

Quite the opposite. The legislative staffers, thrilled to still have jobs, decided to turn the party into a celebration. The Democratic House Caucus turned the party into their victory lane, swapping stories with staffers and lobbyists. By the end of the night twenty different people had laid claim to the idea of making Keith Zachary the Speaker of the House. The House Republican Caucus, eager to move on with their lives, had shown up to drown whatever lingering sorrows they may have had. With their emotions mostly recovered, most in attendance had found that the first few hours under the Zachary Speakership wasn't too far off from the way things had always been.

The members of the State Senate, who had been in their own chambers conducting their organizational session, hadn't learned about the events in the House until they had adjourned. They came to the party to hear first-hand stories from their House colleagues, and to watch the awkwardness unfold between the respective House Caucuses. They were sadly disappointed when by 8:30 PM things were essentially back to normal.

Joe Humphrey had decided to skip the party. He could not bear the thought of rubbing elbows with Democrats, or be given condolences by people outside the situation. He was in bed by seven thirty, sad, embarrassed, and lonely. He fell asleep with his wife's arms wrapped around him, telling himself it wasn't over yet. He was too upset to begin planning his vengeance.

While Joe was unwilling to attend, Mike was at the party with his wife acting as if the events of the day were not a surprise. Telling people they knew the Dems were planning something like this, but they ran out of time to sniff it out. He shook hands, he smiled, he joked, he drank, and he ended up leaving at half past nine with the lobbyist for the Belltronics. His wife had left the party at half past seven.

The Speaker made a brief appearance, mostly out of a new-found sense of obligation to be seen. He stayed a total of twenty minutes; Duncan Blaine had given him three binders worth of material to study and a script to memorize before the next day. He left, telling everyone "Duty calls," as he walked out the door.

Bob Caputo had also made a brief appearance. He thought the wine was too sweet, the chicken was overcooked, and the company wasn't as enjoyable as it had been in the past. He left after thirty minutes to return to his downtown apartment to drink alone.

Larry Pickard made his way to the observation room on the far end of the floor. A room which typically only held board meetings, it offered wide views of the Nashville skyline, construction cranes, and the Broadway bars far below. He sipped his whiskey and coke. The lights were off in the room, illuminated only by the lights of the street below and the moon. This is where Mary Ellen found him. She looked around the room to make sure they were alone and closed the door behind her. Larry peeked over his shoulder and saw it was her. She walked over to him, put her arms around him, careful not to spill her white Zinfandel. She laid her head on his chest, feeling the softness of his muscles.

"Hell of a day," he said, putting an arm around her and rubbing her shoulder with his thumb.

"Hmmm," she said, void of emotion.

"I mean, Keith Zachary? I never saw that coming," Larry said taking a sip of his drink.

"No one did." She closed her eyes. "Well, no except Gregory, I guess."

They stood in their embrace, in silence, enjoying each other's scent. Then Larry asked, "Are you going to kick him out of the party?"

She sighed. "No, I don't think I can. We don't have party registration in Tennessee so technically I can't keep him out. We'll disavow him, we won't let him run as a Tennessee Republican, he won't get money from the State Party, but he can still call himself a Republican."

"Who the hell is going to work for him?"

She opened her eyes to take in the sights of the city. "Well, I've already made some calls. I may not like what he did, but he is a conservative, and the Speaker. I felt obligated to make sure he doesn't run the House into a ditch. We've got a communications intern at the party; she'll be his press secretary. I think the RNC is going to send him some other low-level staff from other states, mostly from the group of kids Joe was going to hire, trying to give them some experience. That's the thing about what we do, there's always someone who is desperate enough to take a job they know won't lead anywhere else as long as it looks good on a resume."

Larry shook his head. "I can't imagine saying you worked for Keith Zachary would look good on a resume."

"It wouldn't, but working for the Speaker of the House of any state does."

"Hadn't thought of it like that," said Larry returning to his drink. There was a pop behind them. Mary Ellen quickly let go of him and drank some wine. "It's just this tall building in the wind."

"Well, Mr. Secretary, how are you feeling?" she asked.

Larry laughed and shook his head. "You know," he said before stopping himself. He thought for a moment and then started over. "You know, effective at ten tomorrow morning I will officially be resigned from the House of Representatives. I'll be leaving all this behind."

"I know, you'll be so relieved, lucky you," she said with a laugh.

"Mary Ellen," he said, turning to look her in the eyes. "I mean all of this." He made a circle in the air with his finger.

"I know what you mean, Larry," she said. "I'm an adult, I know what you mean. Y'all will have to move here, to Nashville. We'll be too close for comfort. I know what you're going to say, so just leave it be. I understand."

"We still got tonight," he said.

"We still have until ten tomorrow morning," she corrected him. He bent down and pressed his lips to hers; he ran his hand over her cold cheek, while she put her fingers in his hair. Then she took a step back. "Save some for later." He smiled and watched her take a long drink of wine. "Who's your replacement going to be?"

"I don't know," said Larry. "I think there's a county commissioner back home that's going to step in to finish my term. He'll be sworn in when y'all get back from the two-week break."

Mary Ellen laughed. "So we'll only have forty-eight members until then."

"Yeah, I guess you will," said Larry doing the math. He waited a moment and then took her by the hand and asked: "What's your next move?"

"You'll see," she said flirtatiously.

"No," he said, "I mean in politics. Joe isn't Speaker, it'll be open in two years. You going to run against him? I think you should."

"Oh, I'm going to run for Speaker in two years," her voice was confident. Larry knew in that moment she was going to win. "But, Joe's not. He couldn't keep the caucus together, not to mention he gave up his leadership role when he decided to go for

Speaker. No way he tries again. It'll be me, Mike, maybe Tucker, and probably some old fuck who doesn't stand a chance, like Grindstaff."

"You really think Joe's done?"

"I know he is; I can tell by looking at him. Sure, he may stick around for another term or two, but deep down he wants out. He'll make a good lobbyist." She finished her wine. "Four years there's a Governor's race; a Secretary of State running for it would look good to voters."

"No," said Larry quickly.

"Why?" she asked. "We've got a racist masquerading as Lieutenant Governor, two dopes who are Congressmen, and a couple of mayors. That's our statewide Republican field. You would have a shot."

"No," he said again. "I could be Secretary of State for a decade, why would I risk it?"

"There's also a Senate seat up in two years, I heard Helman is retiring," she said enticingly.

Larry shrugged, "Hadn't heard that. That's interesting."

"Just think about it," she said. "I'm sure the State Party Chairman would be supportive of your run." They laughed. She slowly, gently, pulled her hand away. "I've got to get back out there. I'll be at your place around 11:30 tonight, ok?"

"Ok," he said. He admired her as she left the room. He turned back to the windows and sipped his drink some more. The US Senate wasn't on the cards, but he knew the party needed someone to run. It was interesting. He would have to talk to his wife about it.

Gregory, Tom, and Charlie had found a table in the corner of the main room. They spent their afternoon drinking in Gregory's office, telling anyone who came by the story of how it all came together. They left out the parts about accepting the fate of Joe Humphrey as Speaker. A few of the more trusted members of the press had come by the office for a quote, but were instead handed a drink and told the entire drama, glossing over the stress and anger. They had gotten to the party forty-five minutes after it started and were treated as the main attractions. Not once had any of them gone to the bar, yet they always had drinks. Now they were sitting down, eating for the first time that day, and not speaking. They were enjoying each other's presence.

Xavier walked over, grabbing a chair from another table and sat down between Charlie and Gregory. Charlie handed him a plate of shrimp; Xavier perked up and began to eat. Xavier had spent the day being told by several members of the Black Caucus that in two years he was out as their Chairmen. He was ok with that. Charlie heard the rumor that Hannah Vick was eyeing a run at Xavier for his position as Chairman, but deep-down Charlie wished she would run against Gregory. He knew it was time for the Black Caucus to take over, and he was praying it would happen. Xavier lifted his beer in the air. Without saying a word Gregory, Tom, and Charlie lift theirs. Then they all drank.

"Hell of a run boys," said Xavier.

"Yeah," sighed Gregory. "Tomorrow it's back to work, I reckon."

"Reckon?" Tom looked at Gregory. "You hear this dude? He nominates one guy from east Tennessee and suddenly regains his native tongue."

"That's how he speaks when he's drunk," said Charlie with a laugh.

"Reckon, I do," said Gregory. The party was ending, but they all wanted to stay in the moment.

CHAPTER 19

Wednesday, January 14, 2009

Secretary Pickard was standing in the lobby just outside the House chambers, wearing a brand new dark blue suit and red tie, staring at a bust of Cordell Hull. He could not help but feel a small connection to the Nobel Prize winner. They had both been members of the Tennessee House of Representatives, and now they had both been Secretaries of State. Of course, Cordell Hull had helped lead this country through World War II, as Secretary of State for the United States, and Larry had just been sworn in an hour ago in the Old Supreme Court Chamber. He had been meeting with Darrell Clarkson every day since he had agreed to be nominated for the job, and he felt confident he was ready to start. He was waiting with other cabinet members to be introduced by the Sergeant at Arms to the Joint Session in the House chambers, but the House was behind schedule.

Inside the chamber, the Speaker was struggling. He had performed admirably during the morning session. He had stuck to the script, and when moments popped up that weren't on the paper, the Speaker had followed the commands of Duncan. Duncan couldn't remember a time when he had to work this much.

Yet the afternoon session had not gone according to plan. The galleries, packed with visitors in attendance for the Governor's State of the State address, had seen the new Speaker crack under the pressure of being in the spotlight. At one point he had picked up the gavel to order the House on to the next agenda item, but his hands were so sweaty that the small wooden hammer slipped from his grip and flew backwards. The proper words had escaped him, he forget to ask for objections to motions, he had ruled a motion proper before it was seconded. At one point he tried to provide his own opinion on a rule that was being debated as if he were a regular member. Luckily, Duncan cut his microphone before the Speaker got too deep into his take on the matter.

Joe Humphrey was in attendance, sitting in his caucus leader's desk; it was his until the Speaker made floor assignments. Joe was confident the new Speaker would move him to the back of the room, so he was enjoying his time upfront while he could. He had gotten up early in the morning and started making calls. He may have been out of leadership, but he had every intention on being Speaker of the House in 2011; he still had his war chest, but he needed to let the powers that be know he wasn't going anywhere. Over breakfast Alyssa had convinced him that all his plans were still on the table. Speaker for two years was plenty of time to build on his already statewide reputation; he could still be Governor if he wanted, and he could most certainly be Speaker. First step would be to increase the Republican majority, second was to become Speaker, and third was to wait for the right moment to jump in the Governor's race. Easy-peasy. In his mind, he was only forty-five months away from being Governor.

Gregory did not enjoy watching the Speaker struggle, wincing with every awkward pause and misspoken word, but he was powerless to help. Every time he looked up, he could see Tom and Charlie holding back their laughter. Gregory felt responsible. He decided he would do everything he could to help train the Speaker during the upcoming two-week recess.

Bob Caputo was sitting in Speaker Zachary's old desk. It had been a long time since he had sat at a member's desk, much less one this far back. He could not see anything. Every time the Speaker was too slow or incorrect, Bob would silently mutter to himself what the Speaker should be saying.

"Next order," said the Speaker. Duncan rolled his eyes and turned to Zachary with an imploring look. "Sorry. Next order, Mr. Clerk."

"That completes the House calendar," said Duncan in his clerk's cadence. There was some sarcastic applause by House members, thankful to finally be done.

The Speaker used one finger to track the words on the paper and read, "We now stand adjourned and will await the entrance of our extinguished, excuse me, distinguished colleagues for our joint session. The-House-stand-adjourned-until Thursday, January 15th, 2009, at nine o'clock in the morning." He stopped and looked around, but no one moved. Daniel Burns made a motion like he was hammering a nail, the Speaker realized the signal. He picked up his gavel and lightly hit it against the block. He sat down in his seat, exhausted.

One by one the State Senators began to slowly find their way into the House chambers. Keith stayed seated as they entered. Folding chairs had been brought in and placed near the well for the State Senate, Supreme Court, and cabinet officials. Duncan had told the Speaker that he did not have to do anything during the Joint Session. The Lieutenant Governor, being in the higher-ranked office, would serve as the Speaker for the session. Keith was upset when he first heard the news, but now he was thankful to be the lower-ranked official and free of responsibility.

As the members of the two chambers mixed and mingled with small talk and gossip, an older gentleman, tall and thick with white hair slicked straight back, strode into the chamber in his black pinstripe suit. His arrival seemed casual, but his existence in the room demanded attention and respect. People slowly gravitated toward him, offering handshakes and smiles. He spoke loudly to each person he encountered; his voice sounded as if he was always in the middle of a laugh. He made his way to the well, then up the steps to the Speaker's desk.

Speaker Zachary stood up and held out his hand. "Lieutenant Governor Reilly, welcome to the House."

The old man took Speaker Zachary's hand, and in an accent that was a bit too thick to be real, said: "Speaker Zachary, thank you. Congratulations, by the way, I wanted to tell you at the reception last night but you were gone so quick I didn't get the chance."

"Yeah, well, old Duncan down there is trying to get me up to speed," said the Speaker with a laugh.

"Yeah, Duncan will keep you straight. Don't worry, by Valentine's Day you'll be a pro at this," said the Lieutenant Governor with a smile and a pat on the back. "Just so you know, you can call me Jeff when it's just the two of us. Lieutenant Governor Reilly is too long."

"Right-o," said Speaker Zachary. "You can call me Keith."

"Yes sir," said Reilly. "I'm glad we got another east Tennessean up here with me, even if it wasn't the one we expected."

"Yes, Jeff, I think it's good for our region, you and me being up here. You're actually my State Senator."

"How about that? And both Republicans to boot!"

"Well, not so much, they kicked me out."

"Yeah, figured they would. Still, you're a conservative and that's what counts." The Lieutenant Governor gave the Speaker a wink. Richard Giffords, the Chief Clerk of the State Senate, walked into the well carrying a massive mahogany gavel with a brass band around the top. He handed it up to the Lieutenant Governor.

"Shew, buddy," said the Speaker. "Where did you get that?"

"Oh, I got a guy back home in Piney Flats. I'll set you up with him," he said with another wink.

It was another twenty minutes, nearly forty-five minutes late, before the Lieutenant Governor hit the gavel and instructed the Sergeant at Arms to invite in the first guest.

"Mr. Speaker!" the Sergeant at Arms cried out. "The Supreme Court of Tennessee." Four white men, and one white woman, dressed in black robes entered the chamber to polite applause. They quickly made their way down the center aisle, not stopping to shake hands or speak to any members on the floor. They reached the front and stood in front of their seats.

The Lieutenant Governor hit the gavel, calling for silence. "Mr. Sergeant at Arms! Please invite the next group of guests into the chambers to take their seats!"

"Mr. Speaker! The Cabinet Members of Tennessee!"

The twelve cabinet members walked in, two by two. Secretary Pickard was in the fourth row to enter, the applause from the floor picked up as he walked down the aisle. They had been instructed to go straight to their seats and not to shake hands, but Larry couldn't help but reach out to a few friends as he walked by. He looked over at his old desk; it had been draped with a black blanket, a vase of roses sat on top, an honor reserved for members who died while in office. He laughed when he saw the display, as did the other House members who noticed their old friend realizing the prank. The cabinet members filled in the seats behind the Justices of the Supreme Court.

The Lieutenant Governor waited a few extra moments to allow the House to give their former member a bit more applause before he hit the gavel. "Mr. Sergeant at Arms, inform the joint committee of the State of the State we have all the members of the General Assembly, and honorable guests, on the floor and we await the Governor's presences, to deliver to us, his address regarding the state of Tennessee!"

The Sergeant at Arms poked his head out of the door at the back of the chamber. He reemerged and announced, "Mr. Speaker! The Governor of the great state of Tennessee!"

The doors opened. Governor Welch walked into the room greeted by thunderous applause and cheers. Several General Assembly members from both chambers followed close behind him. He took his time walking down the aisle, making sure to shake the hands of every member along the way. He finally made it to the front, only to shake the hand of every Justice of the Supreme Court, each member of the Senate, every cabinet member, and both Chief Clerks. He looked up at the Speaker and Lieutenant Governor, and mimed tipping his hat; the Speaker waved and the Lieutenant Governor bowed. Governor Welch stood at the lectern at the front of the chamber, thanking the crowd and encouraging them to sit down.

Finally he said, "Y'all should really take your seats or we'll all miss our dinner reservations." This brought laughter to the room. As silence finally settled in, he opened the binder on the lectern and put on his reading glasses. He looked out over the faces in the room and began. "Lieutenant Governor, Mr. Speaker, Members of the General Assembly, and distinguished guests, thank you for being here. Our country is facing a horrendous economic crisis, threats from abroad, and division deeper than we have seen in a generation. Our state is not immune from this. The makeup of our General Assembly reflects our own divide here in Tennessee. We are not immune from the economic woes of our country, but together we have been able to slow the progress of the recession in our state. I am thrilled to report to all of you, the state of our great state is once again strong and getting stronger." There was applause throughout the chamber. Though a Democrat, the Republicans in the room saw his dominating performance on election night. Governor Welch was by far and away the most popular politician in Tennessee, and so they knew better than not to applaud.

"I want to take a moment and congratulate all of you, members of the General Assembly, for your victories in November.

I know as well as anyone how hard it is to win an election, and you should all be proud. To the members of the State Senate, every incumbent up for reelection was victorious. This speaks volumes to your hard work and dedication to your constituents and I congratulate you. To the members of the House, new and . . . not so new," he paused for laughter, "I congratulate you on making it here and taking on the awesome task of being leaders in your communities. I also want to thank you for allowing one of your own, Larry Pickard, to leave your body and take on the role of Secretary of State for Tennessee." He waited while applause for Secretary Pickard reached its peak. Larry stood up and waved bashfully. Once the applause started to fade, Governor Welch continued.

"Your respect for him and his love for this state are both self-evident. I also want to congratulate new House Speaker Keith Zachary on his miraculous rise to the Speakership." The Democratic Caucuses of both the House and Senate suddenly stood up to cheer. Both Republican Caucuses remained in their seats. Joe Humphrey turned red, he could feel his heart pound and his hands began to shake. The Lieutenant Governor leaned over and shook the Speaker's hand. Governor Welch motioned for his party members to calm down. "I know the job before you is daunting, Mr. Speaker, but with faith in God and a trusted team around you, you can't go wrong.

"And last," the Governor said smiling, looking for and finding Gregory Anderson. The two men made eye contact. "I want to congratulate, my dear friend, fellow Nashvillian, and my State Representative, Democratic Leader Gregory Anderson. Who, by a strange quirk of events, and despite leading a caucus with only forty-nine members, finds himself, for at least two more weeks, as the Majority Leader in the Tennessee House of Representatives." The chamber broke out in applause by the Democrats and laughter by all. Even the Republicans could appreciate the joke.

CHAPTER 20

Thursday, March 11, 2010

"Next order, Mr. Clerk," said the Speaker, hitting his gavel. It had taken nearly a full year and two training conferences, but Keith Zachary had finally gotten the hang of being Speaker of the House. He was praying next year someone, anyone, would nominate him to serve again, but he knew this was futile because he would never find a second. The writing was on the wall; he only had a few short months left as Speaker. Then it was on to a primary fight between some young hotshot lawyer backed by the establishment Republicans in the state, a former school-teacher backed by the local Elizabethton Tea Party, and himself. He knew he should worry about his seat in the House, but he had really grown to love being Speaker so keeping the gavel occupied his mind.

"Personal orders!" announced Duncan.

"Personal orders . . ." said the Speaker looking around the room. He saw Joe Humphrey raise his hand in the back of the chamber. "Representative Humphrey, you are recognized." Joe walked forward and pointed to the lectern in the front of the room. "You are recognized in the well."

Joe made his way to the podium and sat a single piece of paper in front of him. He adjusted the microphone, buttoned his seersucker jacket, and felt the knot on his tie.

"Thank you, Mr. Speaker," he began. "I come before this body a humbler man than ever before. It was fourteen months ago that I lost an election for the first time in my life, and I lost to you, Mr. Speaker. It was a tough pill to swallow, and I tried to find God's plan at work, but I did not see what it was at the time. Well, I found out His plan last week, last Thursday to be exact. That's the day my wife, Alyssa, and I got the phone call; we are going to be parents to a beautiful baby boy," he stopped. His voice was breaking, and he bit his lip to fight back tears as the House showered him with applause. He held up his hand and nodded, showing his gratitude. "We will be flying to Philadelphia this weekend to pick up our baby, Andrew James Humphrey, and we can't wait to meet him." His voice broke again, and a few tears came out. The members of the House gave the former future Speaker a standing ovation.

He regained his composure and continued, as the applause slowly faded away. "Finding out I'm going to be a father has changed my perspective on things. Had I become Speaker, I would be working around the clock to make this chamber, and this state, the best in the country. But I lost, and I have to admit, I have been surprised by the results that followed. We are a chamber that is evenly split, often divided by a single vote. Our Speaker has set up our committees in such a way that each caucus has had an equal voice and an equal say in all things. Because of you, Speaker Zachary, this House is actually functioning in a bipartisan way, unlike the partisan overreach we see from Washington every day." There was applause for the Speaker, who stood up and gave a few quick bows. Though no Republican, and most Democrats, were willing to vote for him again, they all stood up to show their appreciation.

"God has a way," Joe continued, "of giving us the leaders we need at the time we need them, even if we don't know it. My loss to Speaker Zachary was part of God's plan for both of us. Now, I'm going to be a father, and I have decided . . ." He clutched the sides of the lectern and exhaled. He began to break down. He sniffed, trying to fight the tears, but he couldn't. Mike Hayes, who knew what was coming, stood up and put an arm around his friend and mentor. Comforting him. "I have decided," Joe went on in a broken voice, "to dedicate my life to my little boy. All my time, energy, everything, will now be his. And so, I'm announcing today I will not seek reelection. I will miss all of you, even you Democrats." Joe pointed at Gregory as the chamber gave polite laughter. "Thank you all for your trust in me, for allowing me to serve, and for serving this state we all love. Thank you, and God bless you, and God bless the magnificent state of Tennessee." The House gave Joe Humphrey another standing ovation. Members from both parties came forward to shake his hand, to hug him, and to congratulate him on being a new father.

Tom and Charlie were joining in on the applause from the press box on the Speaker's right-hand side. Charlie felt particularly moved by the speech. He leaned over to Tom and said,

"That man has really come a long way. I'm surprisingly happy for him."

Tom responded, "That man just got a six-figure offer to be a part time lobbyist. He gets to do that and keep his business back east. The dude is swimming in cash now."

Charlie stopped clapping. "Damn it to hell. I can't trust anyone these days."

"You always got me, buddy," said Tom with a smile.

The Speaker hit the gavel. "Next order, Mr. Clerk!"

THE END